Physics

Peter Gale • Penny Johnson • Carol Tear

with Brian Turner and Rob Wensley

www.pearsonschoolsandfe.co.uk
✓ Free online support
✓ Useful weblinks
✓ 24 hour online ordering

0845 630 33 33

Series editor
Nigel English

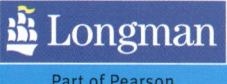

Longman
Part of Pearson

Longman is an imprint of Pearson Education Limited, Edinburgh Gate, Harlow, Essex, CM20 2JE.

www.pearsonschoolsandfecolleges.co.uk

Text © Pearson Education Limited 2011
Edited by Stephen Nicholls
Typeset by Tech-Set Ltd, Gateshead
Original illustrations © Pearson Education Ltd 2011
Illustrated by Tech-Set Ltd, Geoff Ward, Tek-Art
Cover design by Wooden Ark
Cover photo: Artist's impression of a spiral galaxy seen face-on. The blue spiral arms contain hot, young stars, and the yellow central core contains a dense population of older stars. © Corbis: Mark Garlick Words & Pictures Ltd / Science Photo Library.

The rights of Peter Gale, Penny Johnson and Carol Tear to be identified as authors of this work have been asserted by them in accordance with the Copyright, Designs and Patents Act 1988.

First published 2011

15 14 13 12 11
10 9 8 7 6 5 4 3 2 1

British Library Cataloguing in Publication Data
A catalogue record for this book is available from the British Library

ISBN 978 1 408253 83 0

Advisory Board

Simon Hunt
Manchester Grammar School

Linda Carlsson
St Mary's School Ascot

Miles Smith
Colyton Grammar School

Carol Chapman
Science Education Consultant

Frank Sochacki
Kent College Canterbury

Dr Nick Cox
Colchester High School for Girls

John Taylor
Rugby School

Richard Grime
Ripon Grammar School

Anna Wicking
Manchester Grammar School

Copyright notice

All rights reserved. No part of this publication may be reproduced in any form or by any means (including photocopying or storing it in any medium by electronic means and whether or not transiently or incidentally to some other use of this publication) without the written permission of the copyright owner, except in accordance with the provisions of the Copyright, Designs and Patents Act 1988 or under the terms of a licence issued by the Copyright Licensing Agency, Saffron House, 6–10 Kirby Street, London EC1N 8TS (www.cla.co.uk). Applications for the copyright owner's written permission should be addressed to the publisher.

Printed in Italy by Rotolito Lombarda.

Acknowledgements

The authors and publisher would like to thank the following individuals and organisations for their kind permission to reproduce photographs:

(Key: b - bottom; c - centre; l - left; r - right; t - top)

viii Science Photo Library Ltd: TRL Ltd. **2–3** Science Photo Library Ltd: NASA. **4** iStockphoto: Antony Veale (r). Shutterstock.com: Morgan Lane Photography (bl); Matthew Cole (t). **5** Pearson Education Ltd: Gareth Boden (t). Shutterstock.com: Bill McKelvie (b). **7** Shutterstock.com: Falk Kienas. **8** PhotoDisc: Cole Publishing Group / Michael Lamotte. **9** iStockphoto: zoomstudio (tc); Izabela Habur (bc). Pearson Education Ltd: Guillaume Dargaud (br). Photos.com (tr). Science Photo Library Ltd: NREL / US Department of Energy (l). **11** Shutterstock.com: yampi. **12** Shutterstock.com: JackF. **13** Shutterstock.com: JG Photo (t); Christian Musat (b). **16** Pearson Education Ltd: Trevor Clifford. **18** Alamy Images: Stock Image / Pixland (t); Shenval (b). **19** Alamy Images: Image Source. **26** Pearson Education Ltd: Rob Judges (cr). Shutterstock.com: Monkey Business Images (cl); Jackiso (l); Chad McDermott (r). **28** Pearson Education Ltd: Trevor Clifford. **29** Peter Gould (t). Shutterstock.com: LeahKat (b). **30** Food Features (tr). Sally Farndon (tl). Shutterstock.com: Stephen Coburn (b). **31** Pearson Education Ltd: David Sanderson (r). www.imagesource.com: Nick White (l). **32** Photos.com: Jupiterimages. **34** Shutterstock.com: Ivars Linards Zolnerovics. **35** Science Photo Library Ltd: Ria Novosti. **36** iStockphoto: TT (b). Nature Picture Library: Laurie Campbell (t). **37** Shutterstock.com: I. Quintanilla. **38** Shutterstock.com: Zoia Kostina (t); Terry Davis (br); RazvanZinica (bl). **41** Pearson Education Ltd: Ikat Design / Ann Cromack (t). Shutterstock.com: Brendan Howard (b). **43** iStockphoto: Alexey Dudoladov. **44** Elena Wright (r); (l). **50–51** PhotoDisc: StockTrek. **52** PhotoDisc: Photolink. **53** iStockphoto: jamesbenet. **59** Shutterstock.com: Maxim Tupikov. **60** Philip Parkhouse. **61** PhotoDisc: Russell Illig. **62** PhotoDisc (r). Photos.com: Jupiterimages (tl). www.imagesource.com: Nigel Riches (bl). **65** Shutterstock.com: foray. **66** iStockphoto: kshishtof (b). Shutterstock.com: Sean Prior (t). **67** Alamy Images: Bobo (c). PhotoDisc (l). Science Photo Library Ltd: Ted Kinsman (tr). **68** Alamy Images (t). Peter Gould (b). **69** Shutterstock.com: roseburn3Dstudio. **72** Shutterstock.com: Ashley Pickering. **74** PhotoDisc: StockTrek. **76** Corbis: Roger Ressmeyer (t). Science Photo Library Ltd: NASA / WMAP Science Team (b). **88–89** PhotoDisc: Karl Weatherly. **90** PhotoDisc: StockTrek (b). **92** Science Photo Library Ltd: Prof. Harold Edgerton (t). Shutterstock.com: Philip Date (b). **95** PhotoDisc: Photolink. **96** PhotoDisc: Photolink. **100** Pearson Education Ltd: Jules Selmes (l). Science Photo Library Ltd: Takeshi Takahara (r). **101** Shutterstock.com: Kondratenkov Vadim. **103** Alamy Images: Paul Bernhardt. **105** Shutterstock.com: Craig Jewell. **107** Shutterstock.com: Selena. **112** Shutterstock.com: daseaford. **113** Science Photo Library Ltd: TRL Ltd.. **120–121** PhotoDisc: StockTrek. **127** Shutterstock.com: Feng Yu. **136** Pearson Education Ltd: Gareth Boden. **137** Pearson Education Ltd: Trevor Clifford (r). Shutterstock.com: StudioSmart (l). **141** Pearson Education Ltd: Trevor Clifford. **144** Pearson Education Ltd: Trevor Clifford. **148** PhotoDisc: StockTrek. **154** Science Photo Library Ltd: Ria Novosti. **158** image courtesy of NASA Earth Observatory. **160** PhotoDisc: StockTrek. **162** PhotoDisc: StockTrek. **164** Alamy Images: Paul Bernhardt. **171** Shutterstock.com: StudioSmart (r); stopwarnow (l). **174–175** Corbis: Roger Ressmeyer. **176** Science Photo Library Ltd. **177** Science Photo Library Ltd: Science Source (tr); Alexander Tsiaras (br). www.imagesource.com (l). **179** Science Photo Library Ltd: Paul Rapson. **180** Corbis: Ocean. **181** Alamy Images: Jupiter Images / Brand X (t). PhotoDisc. **182** iStockphoto: Mark Kostich (b). Pearson Education Ltd: Richard Smith (t). **183** Getty Images: Sami Sarkis (tr). PhotoDisc: Photolink (b). Shutterstock.com: jovannig (tl). **184** Guillaume Dargaud. **186** Pearson Education Ltd: Jules Selmes. **187** Alamy Images: David R. Frazier Photolibrary, Inc.. **188** Science Photo Library Ltd: Manuel Presti. **190** Alamy Images: Momentum Creative Group. **191** Shutterstock.com: Armin Rose. **192** Photos.com. **193** Getty Images: SSPL via. **194** Alamy Images: sciencephotos. **195** Shutterstock.com: Monkey Business Images (b); Macs Peter (t). **199** PhotoDisc. **202–203** Shutterstock.com: Racheal Grazias. **205** iStockphoto: Darren Baker (b). Photolibrary.com (t). Shutterstock.com: George Filyagin (c). **206** Alamy Images: Radius Images (b). Shutterstock.com: David Woolfenden (t). **207** Pearson Education Ltd: Gareth Boden (l). Shutterstock.com: picamaniac (r). **208** Alamy Images: Blackout Concepts. **209** Elena Wright. **211** Pearson Education Ltd: Trevor Clifford (tr). Shutterstock.com: Tan Kian Khoon (tl); Jan Kaliciak (b). **212** PhotoDisc: C Squared Studios (t). Shutterstock.com: oriontrail (b). **213** Shutterstock.com: ARENA Creative. **214** Shutterstock.com: Carlos E. Santa Maria (b). Getty Images: LatinContent (t). **217** PhotoDisc: Photolink (l). Shutterstock.com: Chee-Onn Leong (r). **221** Alamy Images: Steve Lindridge (l). Shutterstock.com: knotsmaster (r). **222** Shutterstock.com: ID1974. **223** Alamy Images: David J. Green - tools. **224** Shutterstock.com: Yury Kosourov. **225** Pearson Education Ltd: Trevor Clifford (l). Shutterstock.com: terekhov igor (r). **233** Shutterstock.com: Phil MacDonald Photography. **238** Shutterstock.com: Tim Arbaev.

All other images © Pearson Education

Every effort has been made to contact copyright holders of material reproduced in this book. Any omissions will be rectified in subsequent printings if notice is given to the publishers.

Introduction

This student book has been written by experienced examiners and teachers who have focused on making learning science interesting and challenging. It has been written to incorporate higher-order thinking skills to motivate high achievers and to give you the level of knowledge and exam practice you will need to ensure you get the highest grade possible.

The book follows the AQA 2011 GCSE Physics specification, the first examinations for which are in November 2011. It is divided into three units, P1, P2 and P3. Within each unit there are two sections, each with its own section opener page. Each section is divided into chapters, which follow the organisation of the AQA specification.

There are lots of opportunities to test your knowledge and skills throughout the book: there are questions on each double-page spread, ISA-style questions, questions to assess your progress and exam-style questions. There is also plenty of practice in the new style of exam question that requires longer answers.

There are several different types of page to help you learn and understand the skills and knowledge you will need for your exam:

- Section openers with learning objectives and a check of prior learning.
- 'Content' pages with lots of challenging questions, Examiner feedback, Science skills, Route to A*, Science in action and Taking it further boxes.
- 'GradeStudio' pages with examiner commentary to help you understand how to move up the grade scale to achieve an A*.
- 'ISA practice' pages to give you practice with the types of questions you will be asked in your controlled investigative skills assessment.
- Assess yourself question pages to help you check what you have learnt.
- Examination-style questions to provide thorough exam preparation.

This book is supported by other resources produced by Longman:

- an ActiveTeach (electronic copy of the book) with BBC video clips, games, animations, and interactive activities
- an Active Learn online student package for independent study, which takes you through exam practice tutorials focusing on the new exam questions requiring longer answers, difficult science concepts and questions requiring some maths to answer them.

In addition there are Teacher Books, Teacher and Technician Packs and Activity Packs, containing activity sheets, skills sheets and checklists.

The next two pages explain the special features that we have included in this book to help you learn and understand the science and to do the very best in your exams. At the back of the book you will also find an index and a glossary.

Contents

Introduction	iii
Contents	iv
How to use this book	vi
Research, planning and carrying out an investigation	viii
Presenting, analysing and evaluating results	x

P1

Energy — 2

1 Heat
P1 1.1 Infrared radiation	4
P1 1.2 Kinetic theory	6
P1 1.3 Conduction	8
P1 1.4 Convection	10
P1 1.5 How fast can energy be transferred by heating?	12
P1 1.6 Heating buildings	14
P1 1.7 Specific heat capacities	16

2 Energy and efficiency
P1 2.1 Energy transfers	18
P1 2.2 Efficiency and Sankey diagrams	20
P1 2.3 Reducing energy consumption	22
Assess yourself questions	24

3 Electrical devices
P1 3.1 Electrical energy	26
P1 3.2 Paying for electricity	28
P1 3.3 Using different devices	30

4 Generating electricity
P1 4.1 Power stations	32
P1 4.2 Comparing power stations	34
P1 4.3 Electricity from renewable resources	36
P1 4.4 Renewables and the environment	38
P1 4.5 Electricity distribution and voltage	40
P1 4.6 Meeting the demand	42
ISA practice: keeping drinks hot	44
Assess yourself questions	46
GradeStudio	48

Waves and the Universe — 50

5 Waves
P1 5.1 What is a wave?	52
P1 5.2 Measuring waves	54
P1 5.3 Wave behaviour	56
P1 5.4 Electromagnetic waves	58
P1 5.5 Radio waves and microwaves	60
P1 5.6 Mobile phones	62
P1 5.7 Making light work	64
P1 5.8 Light and infrared	66
P1 5.9 Sound	68
Assess yourself questions	70

6 Red shift
P1 6.1 The Doppler effect	72
P1 6.2 The expanding Universe	74
P1 6.3 The Big Bang theory	76
ISA practice: modelling optical fibres	78
Assess yourself questions	80
GradeStudio	82
Examination-style questions	84

P2

Forces and motion — 88

1 Forces and motion
P2 1.1 Introduction to forces	90
P2 1.2 Forces that change shapes	92
P2 1.3 Distance, speed and velocity	94
P2 1.4 Acceleration	96
P2 1.5 Slowing down and stopping	98
P2 1.6 Terminal velocity	100

2 Forces and kinetic energy
P2 2.1 Force and energy	102
P2 2.2 Power	104
P2 2.3 Potential and kinetic energy	106
P2 2.4 Momentum	108
P2 2.5 The law of conservation of momentum	110
P2 2.6 Car safety	112
ISA practice: materials for crumple zones	114
Assess yourself questions	116
GradeStudio	118

Electricity, radiation, atoms and the stars — 120

3 Electrical circuits
P2 3.1 Static electricity	122
P2 3.2 Current, potential difference and resistance	124
P2 3.3 Non-ohmic conductors	126
P2 3.4 Potential difference in series circuits	128
P2 3.5 Parallel circuits	130

4 Electrical safety
P2 4.1 Electricity at home	132
P2 4.2 Mains plugs	134
P2 4.3 Fuses, earth and circuit breakers	136
P2 4.4 Current, charge and power	138
Assess yourself questions	140

5 Atoms and radiation

P2 5.1 What is an atom like?	142
P2 5.2 Nuclear radiation	144
P2 5.3 Ionising power	146
P2 5.4 Alpha particles	148
P2 5.5 Beta particles and gamma rays	150
P2 5.6 Half-life	152
P3 5.7 Hazards and safety in the radioactive environment	154

6 Nuclear fission and nuclear fusion

P2 6.1 Nuclear fission	156
P2 6.2 Nuclear fusion	158
P2 6.3 The lives of stars	160
P2 6.4 Where stars come from	162
ISA practice: speed and braking distance	164
Assess yourself questions	166
GradeStudio	168
Examination-style questions	170

P3

Medical applications of physics 174

1 Medical applications of physics

P3 1.1 X-rays	176
P3 1.2 Ultrasound	178
P3 1.3 Medical uses of waves	180
P3 1.4 Advantages and disadvantages of ultrasound, X-rays and CT scanning	182

2 Lenses and light

P3 2.1 Refraction	184
P3 2.2 Magnifying glasses	186
P3 2.3 Images and ray diagrams	188
P3 2.4 The eye	190
P3 2.5 Correcting vision	192
P3 2.6 Total internal reflection and lasers	194
ISA practice: ultrasound for density detection	196
Assess yourself questions	198
GradeStudio	200

Making things work 202

3 Making things work

P3 3.1 Moments	204
P3 3.2 Levers	206
P3 3.3 Centre of mass	208
P3 3.4 Why things topple over	210
P3 3.5 Hydraulics	212
P3 3.6 Pendulums	214
P3 3.7 Circular motion	216

4 Keeping things moving

P3 4.1 Magnetic fields	218
P3 4.2 Electric motors	220
P3 4.3 Transformers	222
P3 4.4 Transformers and power	224
ISA practice: power loss in transformers	226
Assess yourself questions	228
GradeStudio	230
Revision questions	232
Examination-style questions	234
Glossary	*238*
Index	*246*

How to use this book

These two pages illustrate the main types of pages in the student book and the special features in each of them. (Not shown are the end-of-topic Assess yourself question pages and the Examination-style question pages.)

Section opener pages – an introduction to each section

An introductory paragraph to help put what you will be learning into context. There are two section openers for each unit.

Test yourself on what you should have learned previously that will help with your understanding of this section.

A list of the learning objectives you will have achieved by the end of the section.

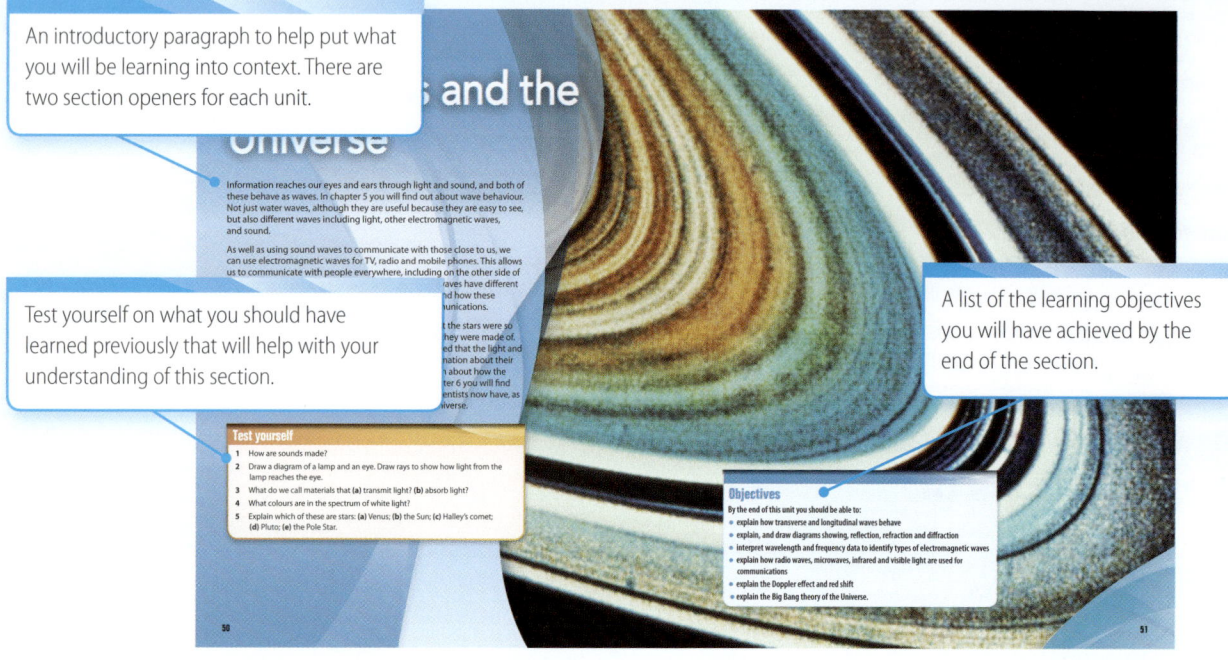

Content pages – covering the AQA specification

A list of objectives for the spread; you can use these to check your progress.

Clear, detailed artwork helps to explain the science.

Keywords are in bold and are listed with their meanings in the glossary at the back of the book to help with revision.

Science in action boxes highlight new, exciting applications of science.

These boxes will help you with your controlled assessment and focus on investigative skills.

Examiner feedback helps you do better in your exams.

Lots of questions at the end of each spread in order of increasing difficulty. The last question on each spread requires a longer answer and is worth six marks.

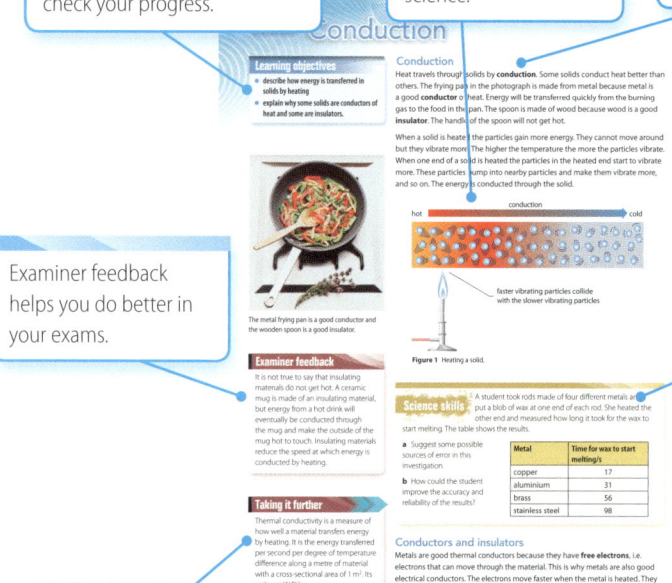

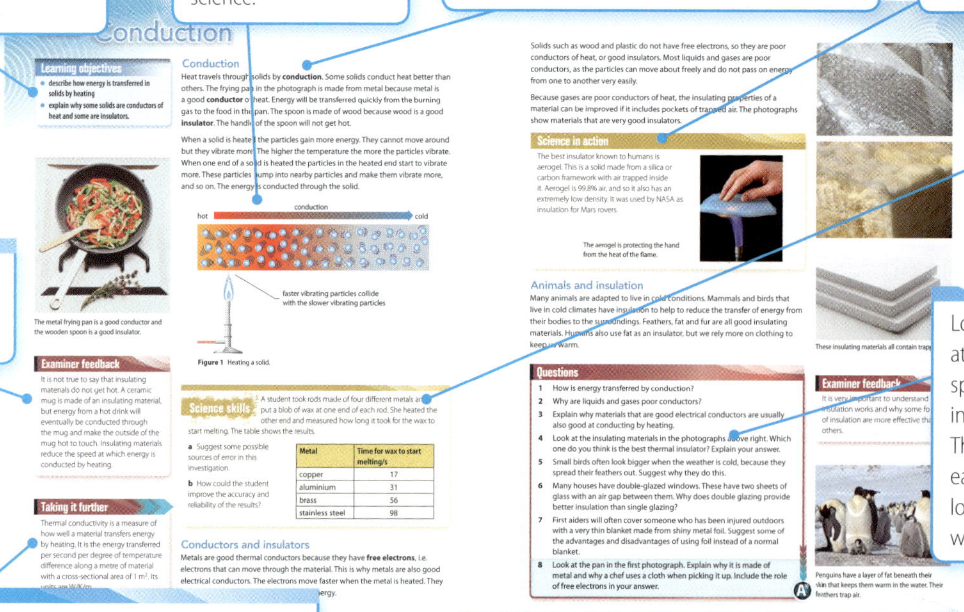

Taking it further boxes cover content that extends from GCSE to A level. You will not be examined on this content but it will provide helpful background.

Route to A* boxes (not shown) highlight specific content or ways to answer questions that will help you get an A* grade.

vi

ISA practice pages – to help you with your controlled assessment

The questions are similar to the ones you will be asked in your controlled assessment papers.

Section 1 deals with planning, prediction and risk assessment.

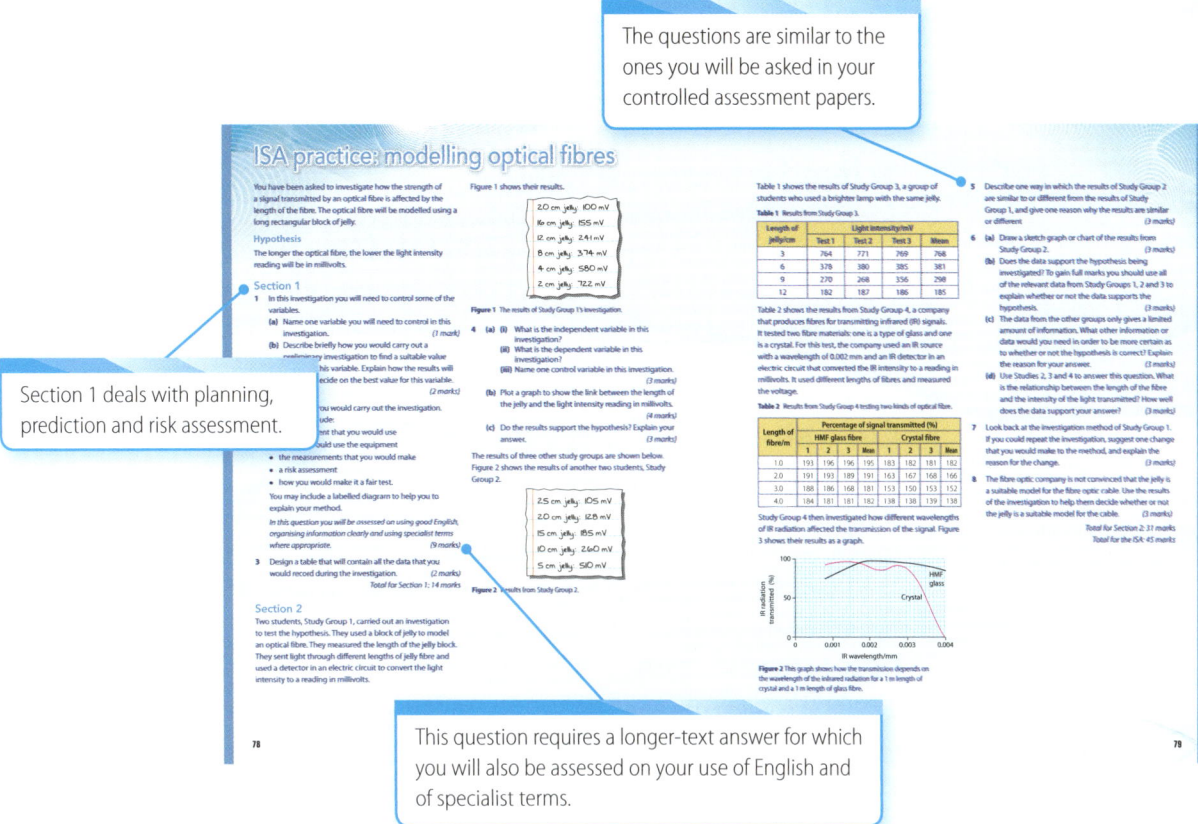

This question requires a longer-text answer for which you will also be assessed on your use of English and of specialist terms.

GradeStudio pages – helping you achieve an A*

'GradeStudio' questions focus on the new exam questions, which require a longer answer.

Three student answers are given at three different grades, B, A and A*, so you can see how they improve.

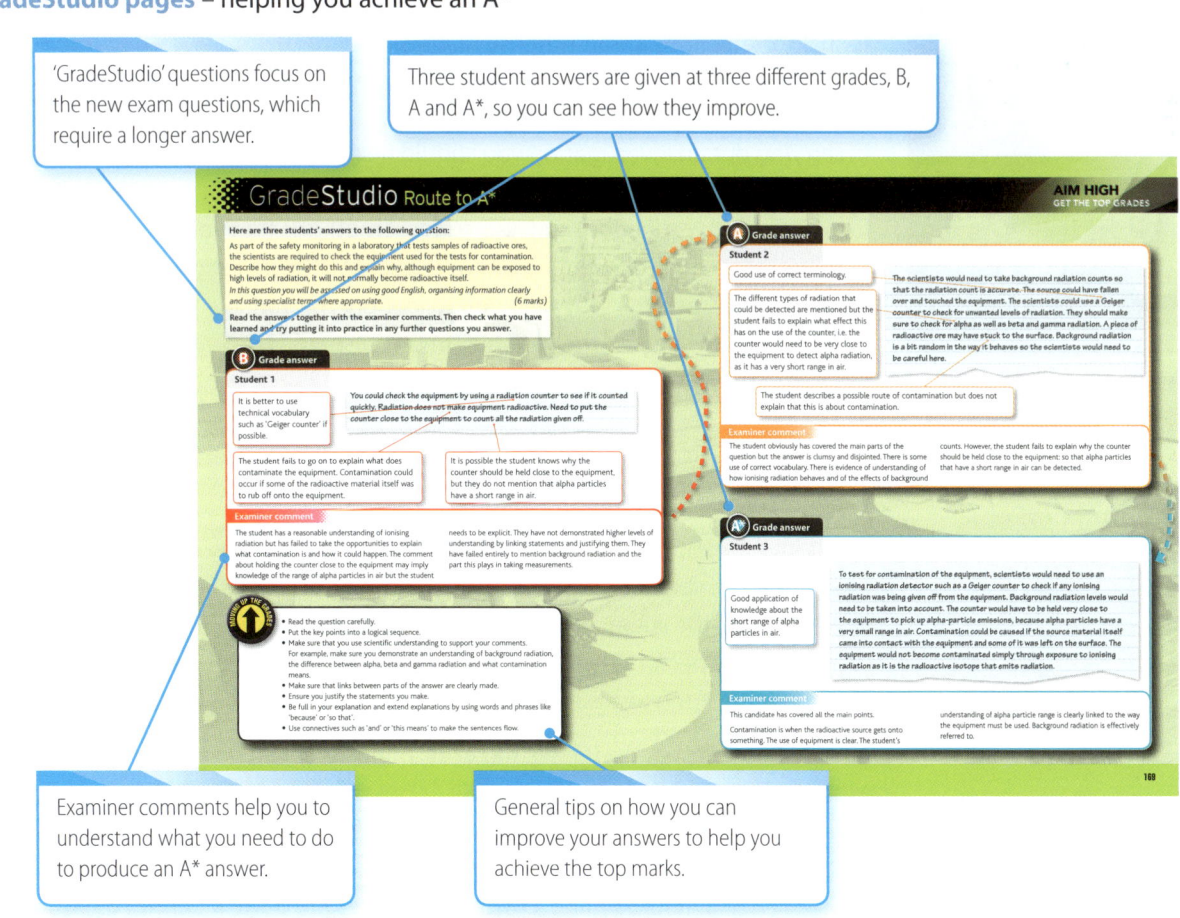

Examiner comments help you to understand what you need to do to produce an A* answer.

General tips on how you can improve your answers to help you achieve the top marks.

vii

Researching, planning and carrying out an investigation

Learning objectives

- research and analyse scientific problems, suggest hypotheses, and make predictions about these problems
- research and describe practical ways to test predictions fairly
- describe how variables can be controlled
- describe different types of variables and how to measure them
- describe how preliminary work helps make sure the investigation produces meaningful results
- explain the risks present in an experimental procedure and how to minimise them
- understand the terms repeatability, reproducibility and resolution.

In road safety tests, dummies are often used to assess the damage caused to pedestrians in a collision.

Examiner feedback

When writing a plan for an investigation, make sure you write the plan in a logical order, so someone else can follow your instructions. You need to say how you will change the independent variable, what the **range** of it will be, how you will measure the dependent variable, and how you will make sure other variables are kept constant.

Scientific understanding

Science is all about understanding how things work, and making decisions on that basis. This understanding must be based on evidence, and ideas and explanations must relate to that evidence. Scientists also consider the quality of the evidence, and whether other possible explanations might fit it. They ask: What might make my explanation wrong?

Case study: traffic accidents

Every year around 2500 people die in road accidents, and ten times this number are seriously injured. Doctors and the police noticed that injuries were less severe, and there were fewer deaths, when pedestrians were hit by slow-moving cars than in high-speed collisions. They used their **observations** to make a **hypothesis**: a good idea that explains the observations. The hypothesis was: 'The faster a car moves, the greater the force when it collides with a pedestrian. The greater the force, the more damage is caused to the pedestrian's body, and too much damage causes death'.

They then made a **prediction** about the speed needed to kill someone. Predictions provide a way to test a hypothesis – if the prediction is wrong, the hypothesis is likely to be false. After several investigations in which the prediction is proved to be right, then the hypothesis may become a **theory**, and can be used to make predictions about other similar events.

Testing the prediction

In carrying out an investigation you should first research what other scientists have already done. This is helpful as the research can suggest possible methods for your own investigation, and also suggest methods that you shouldn't use as they are too time-consuming or not relevant to the investigation you are planning. Your research may help you to identify the variable that could affect the results. Here are some of the variables in this case:

- speed of car
- mass of car
- make of car
- height of person hit by car.

In this investigation, the **independent variable**, the one you change or select to examine, is the speed of the car. The **dependent variable**, the one that changes as you change the speed of the car, and which you measure, is the amount of damage to the person. The other variables are **control variables** and need to be kept the same if the test is to be fair.

All scientific investigations have **hazards**, things that can go wrong with the experiment and cause injury to people or objects. The biggest hazard in this investigation is the death of someone taking part. The history of science is full of scientists who died as a result of their own experiments. To minimise the **risk**, or the chance of it happening, **control measures** are used. A control measure is something that reduces the hazard to a level of risk that is acceptable. The control measure in this case would be to replace a living person with a dummy, and then to assess the amount of damage to the dummy. Alternatively, the investigator could research data from real accidents to find out how speed affects pedestrians hit by cars.

Making measurements

However you carry out your investigation, you need to make some measurements or collect data.

You need to decide on the **range** of your independent variable – the slowest and fastest speeds you plan to investigate. Within this range the values should be evenly spaced, using at least six different values if possible, and the range should be wide enough to ensure any trend can be identified.

When making measurements you need to consider the **resolution** of the measuring instrument. This is the smallest change in value that your instrument can detect. Most car speedometers have a resolution of 2 mph, that is, the smallest division on the scale represents 2 mph. Digital speedometers have a higher resolution, measuring to 1 mph.

Your measurements should be **repeatable**. This means that when you repeat the measurement you get nearly the same value each time. The closer the measurements are to each other and the mean of the results, the greater the **precision** of the results. This does not mean that your results are **accurate**. For your results to be accurate they must be close to the true value.

If you change the method or use different equipment, or if someone else does the investigation, and the results are still similar, then we say that the results are **reproducible**.

Validity

It is important that you check the **validity** of your investigation: has it actually investigated the hypothesis and the prediction you made? Have you controlled all the variables that should be controlled? If not, then the findings may not be valid. You can also check validity by looking for similar evidence in data provided for you. Make sure, though, that the data you use are relevant, and not just similar to the hypothesis.

Questions

1. List six variables that could affect an investigation into speed and road fatalities. State if each is a continuous or categoric variable.
2. Explain the difference between a hypothesis and a prediction.
3. Describe the difference between a hazard, a risk and a control measure.
4. Many councils introduced speed cameras in an attempt to slow drivers down and reduce the severity of accidents. One council has stopped using speed cameras. A spokesman for the council said: 'Since the introduction of speed cameras there has been no reduction in road injuries and fatalities in the borough.' However, a neighbouring council is increasing the number of speed cameras; their spokesman said: 'There has been a significant reduction in accidents at speed camera sites since they were introduced.' Explain why both spokesmen could be right.
5. Suggest a hypothesis to explain the findings in question 4.
6. Plan an investigation to prove your hypothesis.

Science in action

Elizabeth Ascheim worked with her brother-in-law, a medical doctor, on the first X-ray machine in San Francisco. She carried out numerous self-administered experiments into X-rays. She subsequently developed a very aggressive cancer, and died from it.

Jean-François De Rozier was the first recorded victim of an air crash, when the hot air and hydrogen balloon he had designed, built and was testing crashed to the ground from 1500 feet.

Examiner feedback

Calculating a mean value for a series of trials reduces random errors in the data you've collected. It also makes it more likely that the value you get will be close to the true value. When dealing with data provided to you, check that means have been correctly calculated. Look for any anomalous results first. If the mean is wrong be sure to mention this in your answer.

Presenting, analysing and evaluating results

Learning objectives
- describe how to report and process your experimental data
- evaluate the data collected, identifying errors
- understand the term calibration
- analyse the evidence.

Recording and displaying results

It is best to collect your results in a table that you have already prepared. Table 1 shows a table for recording the percentage of damage done to a crash-test dummy by a car travelling at different speeds. The independent variable, that is, the one you change, is usually recorded in the left-hand column. In this case the independent variable is the speed. The right-hand columns are for the dependent variable. Put the units in the heading, to save writing them out each time.

Table 1 Example table for recording results of an investigation.

Speed of car/mph	Damage to the body of the dummy (%)				
	Trial 1	Trial 2	Trial 3	Trial 4	Mean
10					
20					
30	12	16	27	14	
40					
50	52	56	51	54	
60					

Identifying errors in results

All scientists get errors in their results. The different types of errors are:

- **anomalous** results don't fit the pattern at a value of the independent variable, sometimes called 'outliers'.
- **random errors** make the results spread around the true value. Scientists calculate the mean to try to reduce the effect. The more values used to calculate the mean, the nearer it should be to the true value, provided there is no systematic error (see below).
- **systematic errors** occur when something is causing the readings to be spread about another value, rather than the true value. It may be the way the reading is recorded, the instrument being used or something about the environment. Repeating the measurement cannot correct the problem; a change of equipment or method is needed to get fresh results for comparison.
- **zero error** – this is a systematic error in which the instrument used for measurement is not set at zero and either adds or subtracts a set amount whenever a reading is taken. For example, bathroom scales always need to be set to zero before you weigh yourself if you are to get the true weight.

If there are errors in the data, it may be that the measuring instruments are not correctly calibrated. A balance for weighing, for example, is **calibrated** by first setting the balance to zero, then placing a weight of known mass on it and marking the scale with that weight. A scale is then marked between the two points.

Speed cameras have to be calibrated, but even then there is a degree of **uncertainty**. The camera cannot be assumed to give the exact true value. The uncertainty of a speed camera is ±10%, so only if the camera records 33 mph can the police be sure the car is being driven too fast.

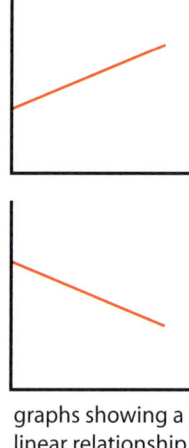

graphs showing a linear relationship

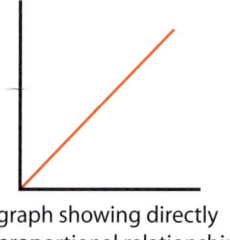

graph showing directly proportional relationship

Figure 1 Examples of line graphs.

Repeatability

To check your results are repeatable you should carry out each measurement several times. Ideally, you should get nearly identical results. If not, you may have errors in your measuring methods.

If the results are numerical you can then calculate the mean for each set of measurements, to get a value close to the true value.

If the results at 30 mph were: 12, 16, 27 and 14, you would discard 27 as it is not close to the rest, then calculate the mean as: $\frac{(12 + 16 + 14)}{3} = 14\%$

Patterns and relationships

Sometimes you can spot a trend or pattern in a set of results from the table, but it is more likely that you will need to see them as a chart or graph.

The speed of the car is measured as a number, and variables which are numerical are **continuous**. A line graph should be used, with a best-fit curve or line drawn to show the trend. If you were investigating the make of the car, this would be a **categoric** variable, and you would draw a bar chart, as there is no trend.

The best-fit line or curve tells you the relationship between the two variables. In Figure 1, the top graph shows a **positive linear** relationship, while the middle graph shows a **negative linear** relationship. If the line goes through the origin, where the axes meet, then the relationship may be **directly proportional**. This is only the case when the origin of the graph is truly zero on both axes. Curved lines indicate a more complex relationship.

Analysing the evidence

Your conclusion must relate to the investigation. The graph in Figure 2 shows that as the speed increases, the amount of damage to the crash-test dummy increases. The data collected give no information about the amount of damage needed to cause death, so you can draw no conclusion about this.

It is important not to go any further than the evidence you have. At the lower end of the graph it looks as though doubling the speed will double the damage, but this relationship cannot be correct at higher speeds. For example, at 45 mph the damage is over 50%, but doubling the speed to 90 mph could not make the damage greater than 100%.

Questions

1. Explain the difference between an anomalous result and a random error.
2. Calculate the mean value for damage to the body at 50 mph. Use the data in Table 1.
3. Explain why a zero error is a type of systematic error.
4. Describe how you could deal with a zero error.
5. A coroner tells you that there is a negative linear relationship between age and minimum speed causing death in pedestrian collisions after age 25. What does she mean?
6. The coroner also tells you that at 40 years of age people can survive accidents that cause 60% body damage, but at 80 years old, no more than 30% body damage is survivable. What conclusions can you draw from this? Use the graph from Figure 2 to help you.

Route to A*

When calculating a mean, make sure you discard anomalous results, and record the mean calculated to the same number of decimal places as the original readings.

Similarly, when you plot a graph, leave anomalous points out of the best-fit line or curve.

If you get an anomalous result, think about it – was it an error in measurement, or do you need to amend your hypothesis or your experimental technique?

Examiner feedback

In science you should only plot your line with the data you have. Unless you have a value for the origin, do not plot it or connect your line to it. Not all graphs meet the axes at the origin. For example, remember that in winter the temperature drops to less than 0°C. This means that 0°C is not zero for a temperature axis. in fact the lowest possible temperature, the true value for zero, is −273.15°C.

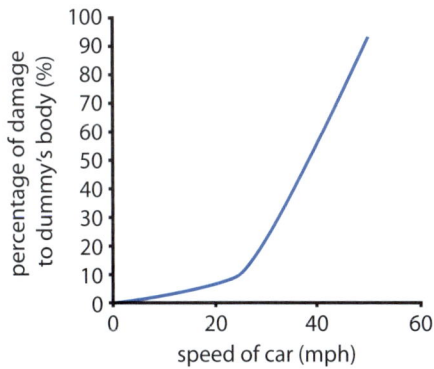

Figure 2 Line graph showing damage to dummy at different speeds.

How science works 1

P1 Energy

The astronaut in the photograph is wearing a spacesuit carefully designed to keep her body at a comfortable temperature while she is working in space. In the first part of this unit you will learn about the different ways in which energy can be transferred by heating, and how objects can be designed to increase or reduce the transfer of energy.

The backpack worn by the astronaut includes a battery to provide power for radios and life support systems. These systems are designed to waste as little energy as possible. In the second part of this section you will learn about different kinds of energy transfers, and how efficiency is calculated.

The astronaut is working on an array of solar cells that produce electricity for the space station. In the third part of this unit you will look at why electricity is such a useful way of transferring energy. The final part looks at different energy resources that can be used to generate electricity, including renewable and non-renewable resources, and their advantages and disadvantages.

Test yourself

1. **a** Describe the different properties solids, liquids and gases.
   b Use the idea that everything is made of particles to explain these differences.
2. List six different forms of energy, and give an example of each.
3. Suggest some ways of reducing the amount of energy we use.
4. **a** Explain the difference between renewable and non-renewable energy resources.
   b Give three examples of each.

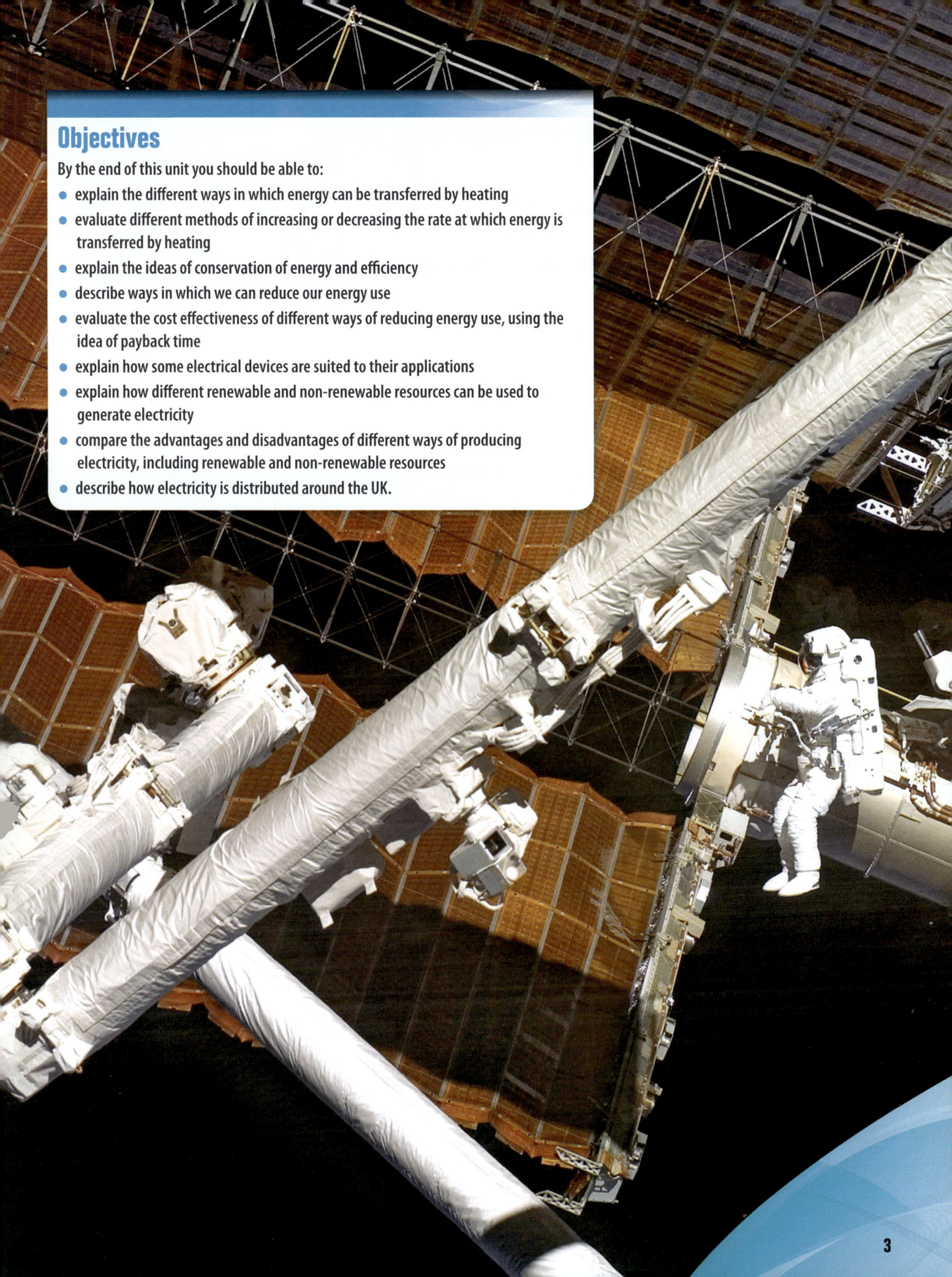

Objectives

By the end of this unit you should be able to:
- explain the different ways in which energy can be transferred by heating
- evaluate different methods of increasing or decreasing the rate at which energy is transferred by heating
- explain the ideas of conservation of energy and efficiency
- describe ways in which we can reduce our energy use
- evaluate the cost effectiveness of different ways of reducing energy use, using the idea of payback time
- explain how some electrical devices are suited to their applications
- explain how different renewable and non-renewable resources can be used to generate electricity
- compare the advantages and disadvantages of different ways of producing electricity, including renewable and non-renewable resources
- describe how electricity is distributed around the UK.

P1 1.1 Infrared radiation

Learning objectives
- explain what infrared radiation is
- describe the factors that affect the amount of infrared radiation emitted or absorbed by an object
- explain how infrared radiation can be used.

Transferring energy
If two objects are at different temperatures, energy will be transferred from the hotter to the cooler object until they are both at the same temperature. This can happen in different ways: infrared radiation, conduction and convection (see lessons P1 1.3 and 1.4).

Infrared radiation
Energy can travel through transparent materials or through a vacuum as **infrared radiation**. Infrared radiation transfers energy by **electromagnetic waves**. Infrared waves are similar to light waves, except that we cannot see them.

Everything **emits** and **absorbs** infrared radiation. The amount of infrared radiation absorbed or emitted by a body depends on its temperature and on the nature of its surface.

If two objects are the same size and shape, with the same type of surface, the hotter one will radiate more energy in a given time than the cooler one.

Emitting and absorbing infrared radiation
A surface will reflect some of the infrared radiation that reaches it, and absorb the rest. Light-coloured, shiny surfaces are good at **reflecting** radiation, so they are poor at absorbing it. Dark, matt surfaces are good at absorbing radiation.

Surfaces that are good at absorbing radiation are also good at emitting it. Dark, matt surfaces are good emitters of radiation, and light, shiny surfaces are poor emitters.

The coffee is hotter than its surroundings. The cola is colder than its surroundings.

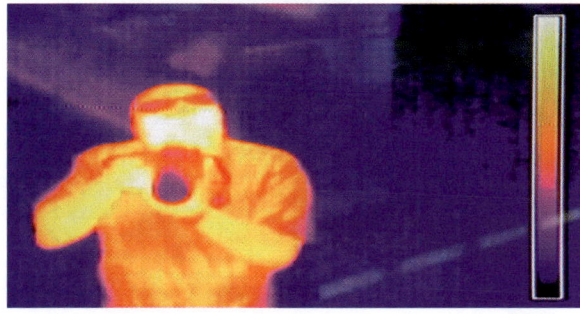

A thermal image of a photographer. The colours show the amount of infrared radiation emitted by different parts of his body and the surroundings. White represents the most radiation, and blue and black represent the least.

Using infrared radiation for heating
Infrared radiation from the Sun is used in many countries to heat water for washing up and bathing. Water in pipes on the roof absorbs infrared radiation from the Sun.

Heaters or lamps that emit infrared radiation can be used for heating buildings. They are also used in hair salons and for physiotherapy.

Sensing using infrared radiation
The image of the photographer was made using a **thermal imaging camera** that detects infrared radiation instead of visible light. The police use thermal

Route to A*

A thermal image of a military airfield can show which aeroplanes have recently been refuelled, and can also show whether some aeroplanes have recently left the airfield. Can you explain how a thermal image can show these things?

Science skills

Figure 1 shows an investigation into how surfaces absorb and emit infrared radiation. Three identical containers with equal volumes of cold water were covered in different materials and allowed to stand in the Sun. The temperature of the water was measured at regular intervals. Graph A shows the results. The same three containers were then filled with equal volumes of hot water and allowed to cool down. Graph B shows the results of this second experiment.

 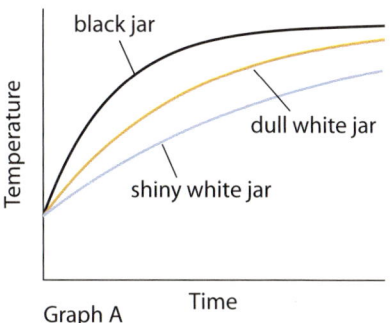 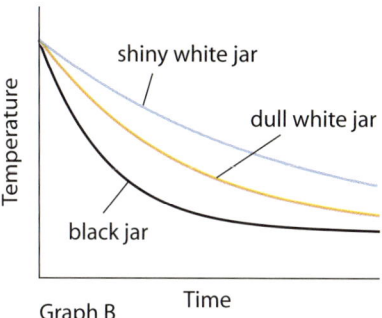

Figure 1 Investigating absorption and emission.

a List all the variables, and say if they are continuous or categoric.
b Which one is the independent variable?
c What is the dependent variable?
d Explain why this is a fair test.

imaging cameras to track criminals at night. The fire service uses thermal imaging cameras to help to find people trapped in collapsed buildings.

Many burglar alarms rely on sensors that detect the infrared radiation emitted by the human body. These are called **passive infrared devices**, or PIRs. The 'passive' part of the name indicates that they only detect radiation; they do not emit it.

Questions

1. Describe two uses for devices that: **(a)** emit infrared radiation; **(b)** detect infrared radiation.
2. Explain what will happen over time to the temperatures of the drinks in the photograph on page 4.
3. Which will emit more infrared radiation, a glass of milk taken from the fridge or a cup of tea? Explain your answer.
4. You can buy insulated mugs to keep hot drinks hot. Explain what would be the best colour for an insulated mug.
5. Cars of many different colours are parked in the sun. Which cars will be the hottest inside? Explain your answer.
6. Which will emit more infrared radiation over a period of 5 minutes, a white mug full of hot tea or a white mug full of lukewarm tea?
7. Look at the experimental results in Figure 1 Graph B. **(a)** Explain why the graph for the black jar becomes horizontal. **(b)** Why are the graphs curved?
8. Look at the second photograph on these pages. Explain how the image was made and how you can use the image to determine whether the person is wearing thick or thin clothing.

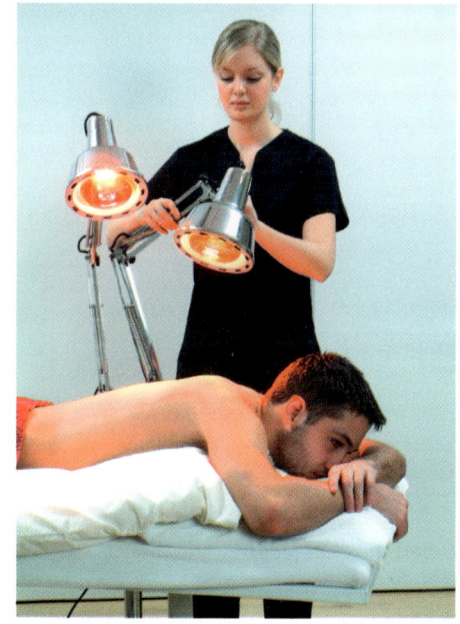

A physiotherapist uses infrared radiation for pain relief after a sports injury.

Passive infrared sensor in a home.

Heat

P1 1.2 Kinetic theory

Learning objectives
- describe the arrangement of particles in solids, liquids and gases
- describe the different amounts of energy that the particles have
- explain how energy is transferred by evaporation and condensation
- describe and explain the factors that affect the rate of evaporation and condensation.

Kinetic theory
The **kinetic theory** states that everything is made of tiny particles, and the arrangement and movement of the particles determines the properties of solids, liquids and gases.

In solids, particles are held closely together by strong bonds (forces). They can vibrate but they cannot move around. This explains why solids keep their shape and usually can't be compressed.

In liquids, the bonds between the particles are not quite as strong and the particles can move past each other. Liquids can flow and take the shape of their container. The particles are still very close together, so liquids usually can't be compressed.

In a gas, the particles are far apart and moving around quickly. Gases are compressible, and expand to fill their container.

Changing state
When a solid melts the particles break away from their fixed positions and move around. They have more **kinetic energy**. A solid takes in energy while it is melting but because this energy is being used to break the bonds between the particles the temperature does not change. Figure 2 shows how the temperature changes as a substance is heated.

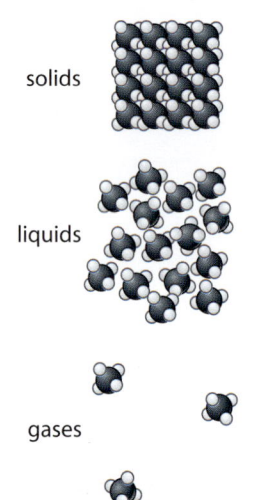

Figure 1 The arrangements of particles in solids, liquids and gases.

Taking it further
As a substance is cooled down the mean kinetic energy of its particles gets less. If it is cooled enough, the particles will eventually stop moving and the substance cannot get any colder. The temperature at which this happens is called absolute zero, and is the same for all substances (−273.15 °C).

The Kelvin temperature scale measures temperatures relative to absolute zero. Zero kelvin (0 K) is absolute zero. One degree on the Kelvin scale measures the same temperature difference as one degree on the Celsius scale. So the melting point of ice is 273.15 K.

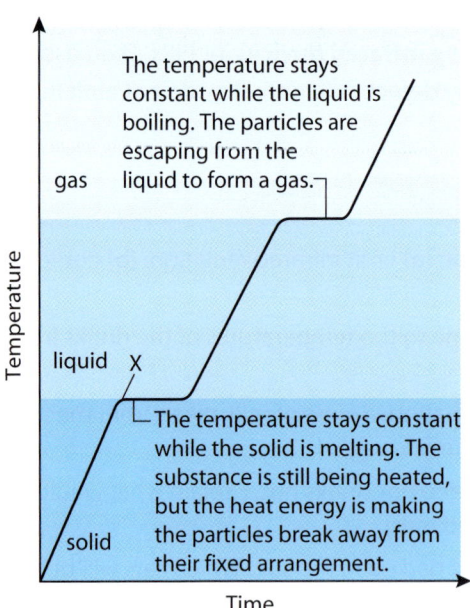

Figure 2 A heating curve.

Cooling by evaporation
The particles in a liquid or gas have a range of different energies. The temperature of a substance is determined by the average kinetic energy of its particles.

Some of the particles in a liquid will have enough energy to escape the liquid and become a gas. When these particles leave the liquid the average energy of the remaining particles is less, so the liquid is colder. Evaporation has transferred energy away from the liquid.

Sweating helps us to cool down. The liquid absorbs energy from the body to evaporate.

Condensation and scalds

When a gas condenses to form a liquid, energy is released as the particles become closer together and form strong bonds. This is why a scald from steam is so painful. The steam is hot, which is painful enough. However, it releases more energy when it condenses on your skin. Energy is also released when a liquid freezes.

Factors affecting evaporation and condensation

Evaporation will happen faster if:
- the temperature is higher
- there is more surface area from which particles can escape
- air is moving over the surface of the liquid – this carries away any evaporated particles so they cannot condense back into the liquid again.

If the air over a liquid is not moving it will eventually become **saturated**, when the number of particles evaporating each second is the same as the number condensing. Evaporation and condensation are still happening but the overall amount of gas in the air does not change.

Condensation happens when a gas cools down. This often happens when it comes into contact with a cold surface, such as a mirror or window in a bathroom or kitchen. Condensation happens faster if the temperature is colder.

> ### Examiner feedback
> Evaporation from a liquid can happen at any temperature. When a liquid boils, evaporation is happening throughout the liquid and bubbles of gas form in the liquid. These are bubbles of the substance that is boiling, *not* bubbles of air.

Science skills

A student recorded the temperature every minute while a liquid substance cooled.

a Draw a graph to show these results.

b Draw a curve of best fit, ignoring any anomalous results.

c Explain the shape of the curve.

d Explain why a line graph is the best way of showing these results.

Time/min	Temperature/°C
0	90.0
1	76.0
2	65.0
3	56.0
4	55.0
5	54.5
6	48.0
7	42.5
8	48.0
9	34.0
10	31.0

Questions

1. Why can gases be compressed, but not solids or liquids?
2. Explain the best weather for hanging washing out to dry.
3. Look at Figure 2. At X the substance is still being heated, but the temperature has stopped rising. Explain what is happening to the energy going into the substance.
4. Explain how sweating helps to keep you cool.
5. Look at the photograph. What effect would water have on their body temperature if the hikers got wet? Explain your answer.
6. Alcohol has a lower boiling point than water. Explain why a drop of alcohol on your skin feels colder than a drop of water.
7. Sketch a graph similar to Figure 2 to show the change in temperature as the same substance is allowed to cool.
8. Explain in detail the shape of the graph you drew for question 7.

These hikers are trying to keep dry.

P1 1.3 Conduction

Learning objectives
- describe how energy is transferred in solids by heating
- explain why some solids are conductors of heat and some are insulators.

Conduction

Heat travels through solids by **conduction**. Some solids conduct heat better than others. The frying pan in the photograph is made from metal because metal is a good **conductor** of heat. Energy will be transferred quickly from the burning gas to the food in the pan. The spoon is made of wood because wood is a good **insulator**. The handle of the spoon will not get hot.

When a solid is heated the particles gain more energy. They cannot move around but they vibrate more. The higher the temperature the more the particles vibrate. When one end of a solid is heated the particles in the heated end start to vibrate more. These particles bump into nearby particles and make them vibrate more, and so on. The energy is conducted through the solid.

The metal frying pan is a good conductor and the wooden spoon is a good insulator.

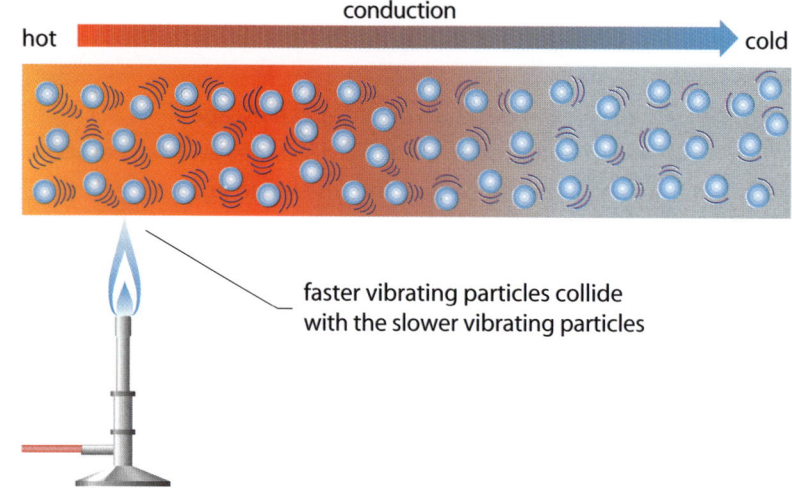

Figure 1 Heating a solid.

Examiner feedback

It is not true to say that insulating materials do not get hot. A ceramic mug is made of an insulating material, but energy from a hot drink will eventually be conducted through the mug and make the outside of the mug hot to touch. Insulating materials reduce the speed at which energy is conducted by heating.

Science skills

A student took rods made of four different metals and put a blob of wax at one end of each rod. She heated the other end and measured how long it took for the wax to start melting. The table shows the results.

a Suggest some possible sources of error in this investigation.

b How could the student improve the accuracy and reliability of the results?

Metal	Time for wax to start melting/s
copper	17
aluminium	31
brass	56
stainless steel	98

Taking it further

Thermal conductivity is a measure of how well a material transfers energy by heating. It is the energy transferred per second per degree of temperature difference along a metre of material with a cross-sectional area of 1 m². Its units are W/K/m.

Conductors and insulators

Metals are good thermal conductors because they have **free electrons**, i.e. electrons that can move through the material. This is why metals are also good electrical conductors. The electrons move faster when the metal is heated. They collide with other particles and transfer energy.

Solids such as wood and plastic do not have free electrons, so they are poor conductors of heat, or good insulators. Most liquids and gases are poor conductors, as the particles can move about freely and do not pass on energy from one to another very easily.

Because gases are poor conductors of heat, the insulating properties of a material can be improved if it includes pockets of trapped air. The photographs show materials that are very good insulators.

Science in action

The best insulator known to humans is aerogel. This is a solid made from a silica or carbon framework with air trapped inside it. Aerogel is 99.8% air, and so it also has an extremely low density. It was used by NASA as insulation for Mars rovers.

The aerogel is protecting the hand from the heat of the flame.

Animals and insulation

Many animals are adapted to live in cold conditions. Mammals and birds that live in cold climates have insulation to help to reduce the transfer of energy from their bodies to the surroundings. Feathers, fat and fur are all good insulating materials. Humans also use fat as an insulator, but we rely more on clothing to keep us warm.

These insulating materials all contain trapped air.

Questions

1. How is energy transferred by conduction?
2. Why are liquids and gases poor conductors?
3. Explain why materials that are good electrical conductors are usually also good at conducting by heating.
4. Look at the insulating materials in the photographs above right. Which one do you think is the best thermal insulator? Explain your answer.
5. Small birds often look bigger when the weather is cold, because they spread their feathers out. Suggest why they do this.
6. Many houses have double-glazed windows. These have two sheets of glass with an air gap between them. Why does double glazing provide better insulation than single glazing?
7. First aiders will often cover someone who has been injured outdoors with a very thin blanket made from shiny metal foil. Suggest some of the advantages and disadvantages of using foil instead of a normal blanket.
8. Look at the pan in the first photograph. Explain why it is made of metal and why a chef uses a cloth when picking it up. Include the role of free electrons in your answer.

Examiner feedback

It is very important to understand why insulation works and why some forms of insulation are more effective than others.

Penguins have a layer of fat beneath their skin that keeps them warm in the water. Their feathers trap air.

P1 1.4 Convection

Learning objectives
- describe how energy is transferred by heating in liquids and gases
- explain an application of convection.

Examiner feedback
Remember that both liquids and gases can be described as fluids.

Convection currents

Fluids (liquids and gases) are poor conductors, which is why insulating materials such as polystyrene foam contain pockets of trapped air. However, air and other fluids can transfer energy if they are free to move. This process is called **convection**.

When a fluid is heated the particles move around faster and take up more space. This makes the fluid less **dense**, so it rises up past the colder fluid around it. This sets up a flow called a convection current. Figure 1 explains how a heater on the side of a fish tank can cause heating of all of the water in the tank.

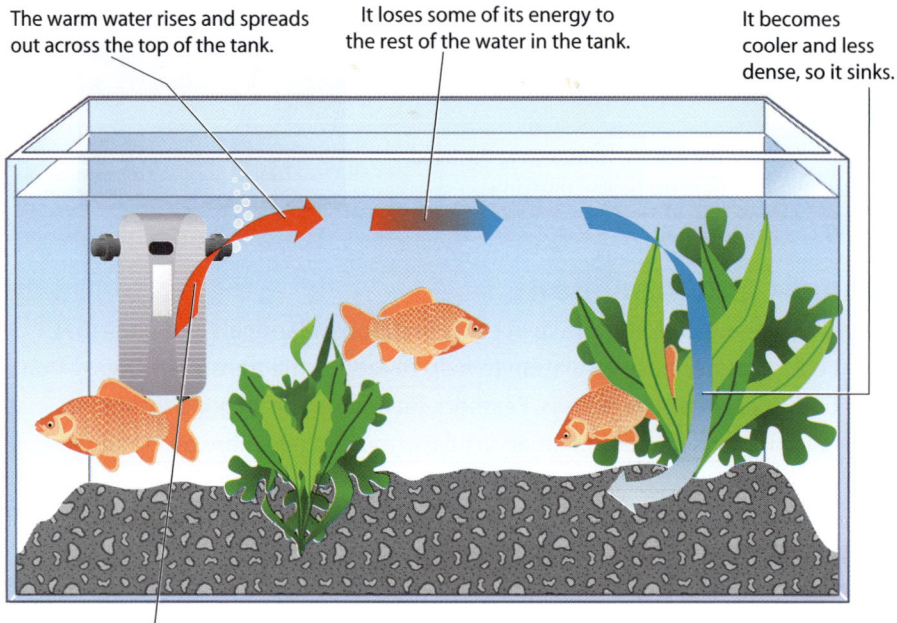

The warm water rises and spreads out across the top of the tank.

It loses some of its energy to the rest of the water in the tank.

It becomes cooler and less dense, so it sinks.

Water near the heater gets warmer and less dense.

Figure 1 Convection in a fluid.

Examiner feedback
People often explain convection by saying that 'hot air rises'. This is not a very accurate statement and will not gain credit in an exam. A fluid rises if it is hotter, and therefore less dense, than the surrounding fluid.

Convection currents can form around any object that is warmer or cooler than its surroundings. For example, energy from a mug of hot tea will be transferred to the air around it, and this air will warm up and rise. Cooler air flows in to take its place, and this makes the tea cool faster. Convection currents can also form around cold objects. Energy is transferred from the air to the cold object so the air cools down. The air becomes more dense and sinks. Warmer air takes the place of the sinking air.

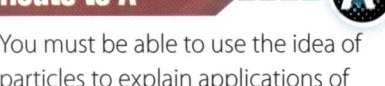

Route to A*

You must be able to use the idea of particles to explain applications of convection.

Using convection

Domestic hot water systems make use of convection, as shown in Figure 2. A boiler heats cold water, which then becomes less dense and rises. Hot water is stored in the hot water tank until it is needed.

Most rooms in homes are heated by radiators or fires, as shown in Figure 3.

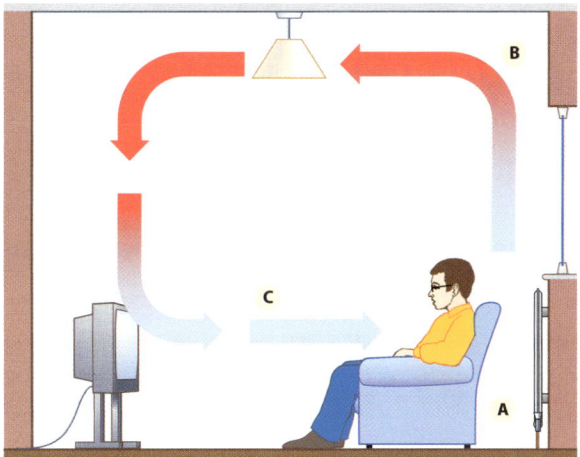

Figure 3 Heating a room using convection.

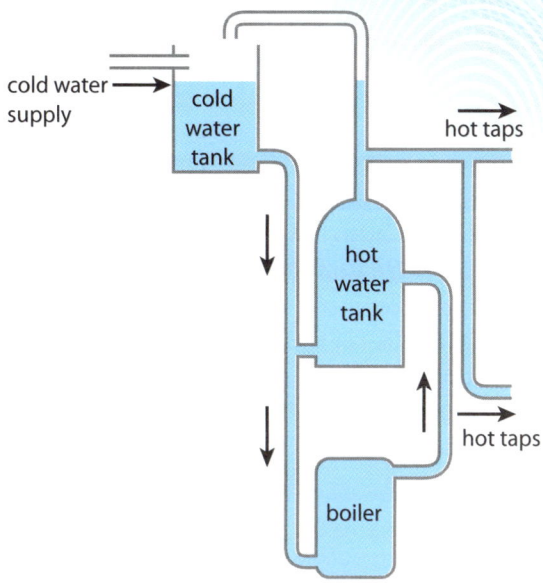

Figure 2 A hot water system.

This conservatory is being cooled by a convection current.

Examiner feedback

In spite of their name, central heating radiators mainly transfer energy to a room by convection, not radiation.

The radiator heats the air near it (A). The particles move faster and so this air becomes less dense and rises. At B it cannot rise any further, and is pushed along the ceiling by more warm air rising beneath it. As the air moves away it gradually transfers heat to the air around it. It descends when it reaches the far wall, and moves across the room to replace the air rising at A.

The photograph shows how a room can be also cooled by a convection current.

Questions

1. What is convection? Explain in as much detail as you can.
2. Why doesn't convection happen in solids?
3. If the heating is turned off on a day in winter, why is the coldest place in a room likely to be under a window?
4. **(a)** Explain why the cooling element in a freezer is usually at the top. **(b)** Explain why the coldest part of a fridge is usually at the bottom.
5. Explain why smoke detectors are usually fitted to ceilings rather than walls.
6. Mercury is a metal that is liquid at room temperature. **(a)** Why might mercury be a good conductor? **(b)** Why might it be difficult to measure the conducting properties of mercury?
7. Look at Figure 2. **(a)** Why does the pipe for the hot water taps come out of the top of the hot water tank, not the bottom? **(b)** The hot water tank also has an electric immersion heater. Explain where this should be positioned in the tank.
8. Look at the photograph of the conservatory. Write a paragraph for a marketing brochure to explain how opening a roof vent near the top can help to cool the whole space. Use ideas from lessons P1 1.1 and P1 1.3 in your answer.

P1 1.5 How fast can energy be transferred by heating?

Learning objectives
- describe the factors that affect the rate at which energy is transferred by heating
- explain the design of devices to increase or decrease the rate of energy transfer by heating.

Science in action
Polythene is normally a very good insulator. In 2010 scientists working in the USA stretched polythene into very thin fibres only tens of nanometres thick. These fibres are better conductors than iron, because stretching the polythene gives the molecules a more ordered structure. The new material could be used to make lighter radiators for cars.

Examiner feedback
It will be useful to remember that 1 nanometre is 1×10^{-9} m or one millionth of a millimetre.

Factors affecting energy transfer by heating
Energy is transferred from hotter objects to cooler ones. The greater the temperature difference, the greater the rate at which energy is transferred.

A thick metal bar will conduct energy along its length more quickly than a thin wire, because there are more particles to pass on vibrations. The material from which the bar is made also affects the rate of transfer. Some materials are better conductors than others.

There are other factors that affect the rate at which an object transfers energy to its surroundings. The motorbike engine in the photograph has metal fins on the outside. These help to cool the engine by providing a large surface area of hot metal in contact with the cooler surrounding air.

The surrounding material also makes a difference. If the motorbike has its engine running while it is not moving, the air near the engine will heat up very quickly. This will reduce the temperature difference between the fins and the air, and the rate of energy transfer will go down. If the motorbike is moving, or if there is a breeze, the temperature difference will remain high.

Fins on a motorbike engine help to transfer heat to the surroundings.

It takes more energy to heat up water by 1 °C than it takes to heat up air by 1 °C (you will learn more about this in lesson P1 1.7). If a hot object is put into water, it can transfer more energy to the water before the temperature difference gets less and reduces the rate of energy transfer.

Evaluating designs
A vacuum flask is designed to keep hot drinks hot, or to keep cold drinks cold. It has several features that are designed to reduce the transfer of energy between the contents of the flask and its surroundings.

Vacuum flasks are designed to reduce all energy transfers as much as possible. However, the solar panel shown in Figure 2 is designed to reduce energy transfers in some places and increase it in others.

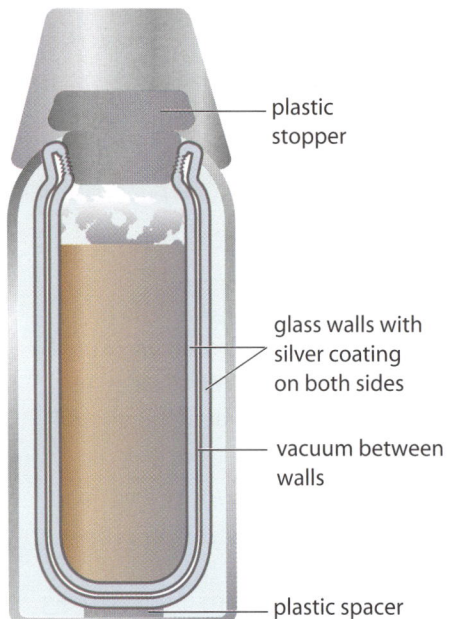

Figure 1 How does this vacuum flask reduce energy transfers?

- plastic stopper
- glass walls with silver coating on both sides
- vacuum between walls
- plastic spacer

Science skills Solar hot water panels are a technological development that can help us to reduce our energy bills.
  a Suggest what scientific knowledge was used by the engineers designing the panel.
b What factors would a householder consider before installing a solar panel?

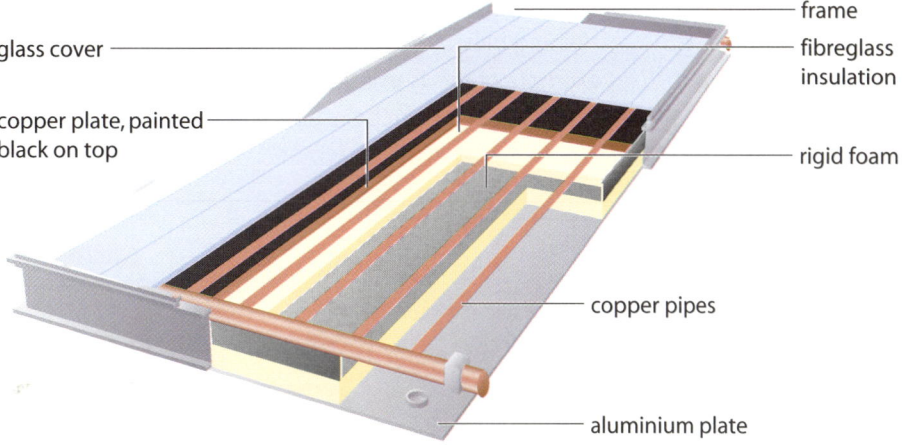

Figure 2 A solar panel for heating water.

Animal adaptations

Animals that are adapted to live in hot or cold climates often have adaptations to their body shape or size. The photographs show an Arctic fox and a fennec, or desert fox. The large ears of the desert fox help it to keep cool.

Animals that live in cold climates are often larger than related species that live in warmer areas. Their large size means they have a smaller surface area in comparison to their total volume and thus transfer less energy to their surroundings than animals in hot climates.

The Arctic fox (top) is adapted to live in cold climates. The desert fox (bottom) is adapted to live in hot conditions.

Questions

1. Look at Figure 1. Explain which features of the flask reduce energy transfer by: **(a)** radiation; **(b)** conduction; **(c)** convection.
2. Many vacuum flasks have steel walls instead of glass.
   (a) How would this affect how fast hot coffee in the flask cools? Explain your answer. **(b)** Why do you think steel is used instead of glass?
3. Would the flask keep a cold drink cold on a hot day? Explain your answer.
4. Look at Figure 2. Explain the design of the parts of the solar panel that are intended to: **(a)** let infrared radiation go through; **(b)** absorb infrared radiation; **(c)** reflect infrared radiation.
5. Explain why the desert fox's large ears help to keep it cool.
6. Describe two adaptations the Arctic fox has for living in a cold climate.
7. Explain why air moving over an object can increase its rate of cooling.
8. Explain how and why parts of the solar panel are designed to reduce heat transfer by convection, conduction and radiation.

Heat

P1 1.6 Heating buildings

Learning objectives
- explain how solar panels can be used to heat buildings or water
- use the idea of payback time
- explain what U-values measure
- evaluate the effectiveness of materials used for insulation
- evaluate building designs.

Examiner feedback
Don't get solar panels and **solar cells** mixed up. Solar panels are used for heating water, and solar cells are used to produce electricity using energy from the Sun.

Reducing heating bills

The cost of heating a house can be up to £1000 per year. Some of this money is wasted if energy escapes from the house. The amount of energy lost can be reduced by insulating the house.

Heating bills can also be reduced by installing alternative sources of energy. One example of this is using solar panels to heat water. This water can be used to heat the building, or can be used to provide hot water for washing and bathing.

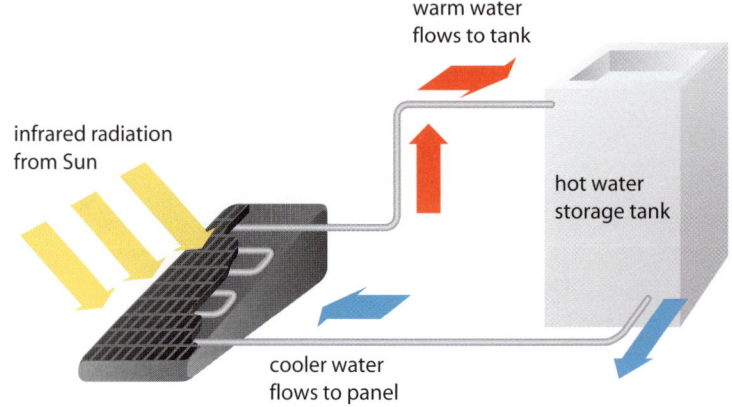

Figure 1 Heating water using infrared radiation from the Sun.

Table 1 Various methods of reducing energy bills.

Energy-saving measure	Typical cost / £	Savings per year / £
solar panels	3500	70
loft insulation	150	150
double glazing	3500	200
cavity wall insulation	350	100
insulating the hot water tank	60	15
draught-proofing doors and windows	50	15

However, it costs money to install extra insulation or solar panels, and so a homeowner would need to look at the **payback time** for different insulation methods before choosing which to use. The payback time is the length of time it takes to save the amount of money that the improvement cost. For example, if it costs £60 to insulate a hot water tank and this saves £15 per year in energy bills, the payback time is four years. The shorter the payback time, the more **cost effective** the insulation method.

Energy from the Sun can also be used to heat houses directly. The house shown in Figure 3 is heated by the Sun as the conservatory along the front allows radiated energy in and traps it. Conservatories used for heating have to be carefully designed as part of the house; a conservatory added later is not likely to contribute much to heating the house.

Designing better houses

There are many government building regulations that specify how buildings should be designed and the materials that can be used. These are intended to make sure homes are safe to live in and do not waste too much energy.

Part of the regulations defines the **U-values** for roofs, walls and floors. The U-value shows how good a material or a building component is as an insulator. The lower the U-value, the less energy the material transfers. Table 2 shows some typical U-values.

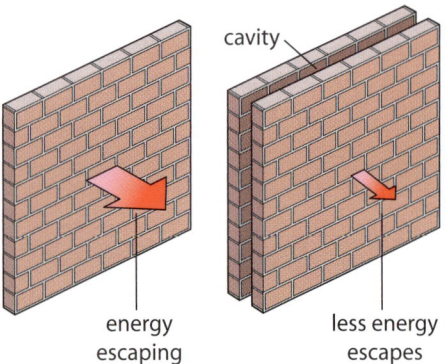

Figure 2 A solid brick wall and a cavity wall.

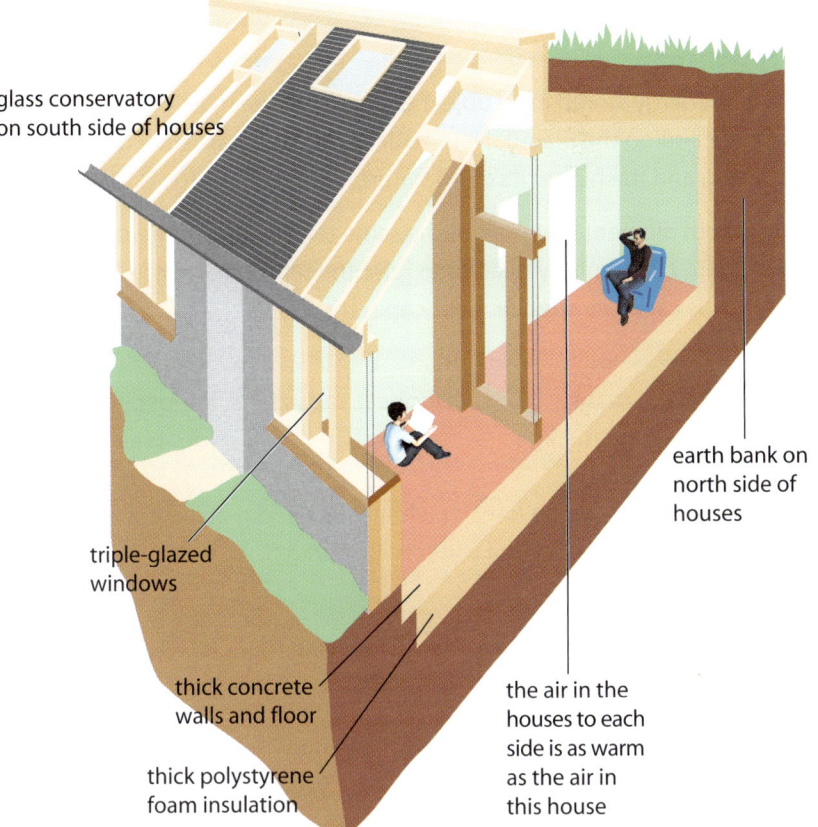

glass conservatory on south side of houses

triple-glazed windows

thick concrete walls and floor

thick polystyrene foam insulation

earth bank on north side of houses

the air in the houses to each side is as warm as the air in this house

Figure 3 An energy-efficient house.

The design of the home can make a big difference, as well as the materials from which it is made. Figure 3 shows the structure of a row of low-energy houses at the Hockerton Housing Project, near Nottingham.

Questions

1. How can solar panels help to reduce heating bills?
2. Look at Table 1. Which method will save the most energy? Explain your answer.
3. How can someone work out which type of insulation would be the most cost effective?
4. **(a)** Work out the payback times for all the energy-saving methods shown in Table 1. **(b)** Which method has the shortest payback time?
5. Why might someone decide to insulate their hot-water tank first, even though it does not have the shortest payback time?
6. Modern houses usually have cavity walls. Explain why they are now built with a layer of insulation between the two parts of the wall.
7. **(a)** In Table 2, which type of window transfers the least thermal energy? Explain how you worked out your answer. **(b)** Explain why this type of window transfers the least energy.
8. Explain why the house shown in Figure 3 uses hardly any energy for heating.

Examiner feedback

You do not need to remember the values in Table 1 or Table 2.

Table 2 U-values of some building materials and components.

Component	U-value W/m² °C
solid brick wall	2.2
cavity brick wall, no insulation	1.0
cavity brick wall with insulation	0.6
single-glazed window, metal frame	5.8
single-glazed window, wood or uPVC (plastic) frame	5.0
double-glazed window, wood or uPVC (plastic) frame	2.9

Science skills

Different building materials are tested in laboratories using standard procedures. Standard procedures are set ways of testing things, and allow different laboratories to get the same results if they are testing the same materials. Results that are the same when measured by different people are said to be reproducible.

a Why do building materials need to be tested?

b Why do testing laboratories follow standard procedures?

c How could a laboratory make sure its results are reliable?

d How could the laboratory use the range of its results to determine how accurate they are?

Heat 15

P1 1.7 Specific heat capacities

Learning objectives
- explain what specific heat capacity is
- use the equation for specific heat capacity
- evaluate the use of materials according to their specific heat capacities.

Storing energy

The amount of energy stored in an object depends on the mass of the object, its temperature and on the material it is made from. For a particular object, the greater its mass, and the higher its temperature, the more energy is stored.

The same mass of different materials at the same temperature store different amounts of energy. The energy needed to raise the temperature of 1 kg of a material by 1 °C is called its **specific heat capacity**.

$$E = m \times c \times \theta$$

heat transferred = mass × specific heat capacity × temperature change
(joules, J)   (kilograms, kg)   (J/kg °C)   (degrees Celsius, °C)

Example 1
How much energy does a kettle transfer when it heats 1 kg of water from 10 °C to 100 °C? The specific heat capacity of water is 4200 J/kg °C.

$$E = m \times c \times \theta$$

heat transferred = mass × specific heat capacity × temperature change
= 1 kg × 4200 J/kg °C × 90 °C
= 378 000 J, or 378 kJ

Example 2
It takes 4500 J of energy to heat a 1 kg block of iron by 10 °C. What is the specific heat capacity of iron?

$$\text{specific heat capacity} = \frac{\text{heat transferred}}{\text{mass} \times \text{temperature change}}$$

$$= \frac{4500 \text{ J}}{1 \text{ kg} \times 10 \text{ °C}}$$

$$= 450 \text{ J/kg °C}$$

How much energy does a kettle transfer?

Examiner feedback
In an exam you will be expected to be able to re-arrange equations to put the quantity you need to calculate on the left.

Science skills
Figure 1 shows apparatus used to find the specific heat capacity of a metal. The energy supplied by the electric immersion heater can be measured accurately.

a Explain why the results using this method might show a systematic error.

b What effect will this have on the value of specific heat capacity worked out from the results?

c Suggest how the size of this systematic error could be reduced or eliminated.

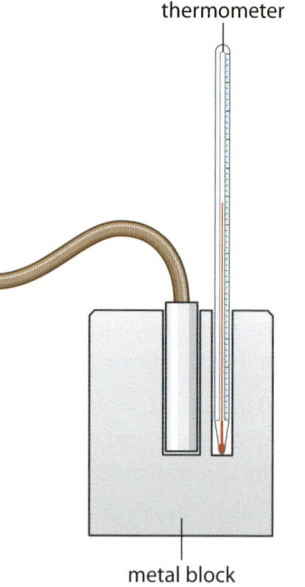

Figure 1 Apparatus for measuring specific heat capacity.

Heat sinks

The components inside computers are cooled using a block of metal, called a **heat sink**, attached to the component. The large mass of the heat sink compared with the component means that a lot of energy can be transferred to it without raising its temperature much. The heat sink then transfers the energy to the surrounding air.

Radiators and storage heaters

Central heating systems use water to transfer heat energy from a boiler to the radiators around the home. Water has a very high specific heat capacity, and so it can store a lot of energy. The energy is transferred to the rooms in the home as the hot water passes through radiators.

Some homes use electricity for heating. Storage heaters heat up using cheaper electricity available at night (you will learn more about this in lesson P1 4.6). Figure 3 shows how storage heaters work. Concrete has quite a high specific heat capacity, and the mass of concrete used in each heater is large, so each storage heater can store a lot of energy. This heat is released gradually during the day to keep the home warm.

Oil-filled radiators are portable electric heaters. Once the oil inside them is hot the electricity can be switched off. They will continue to heat the room for some time after the electricity is switched off.

Table 1 The specific heat capacities of some materials.

Material	Specific heat capacity J/kg °C
air	100
aluminium	899
concrete	900
copper	390
iron	450
lead	130
oil	540
water	4200

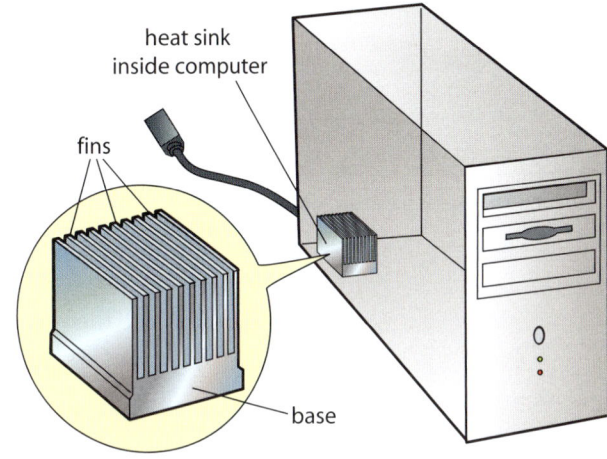

Figure 2 A heat sink in a computer.

Questions

1. A student heats a 1 kg block of aluminium and a 1 kg block of copper to 50 °C. Explain which block will be storing the most energy.
2. Why does it take longer to boil a kettle full of water than one only half full?
3. Explain why stand-alone radiators are filled with oil, instead of being filled with air.
4. How much energy does it take to heat up 500 g of lead by 30 °C?
5. A washing machine heats 10 kg of water for each wash cycle. How much energy is saved by washing clothes at 30 °C instead of 50 °C?
6. A storage heater contains 100 kg of concrete. 1800 kJ of energy is transferred to it. What is the temperature change of the concrete?
7. A student heats up a 500 g block of iron from 18 °C to 46 °C, using 6280 J of energy. **(a)** Calculate the specific heat capacity of iron using these results. **(b)** Suggest why your answer is different to the value in Table 1.
8. Explain why the heat sink in Figure 2 has fins, and why the metal used to make it should have a high specific heat capacity and be a very good thermal conductor.

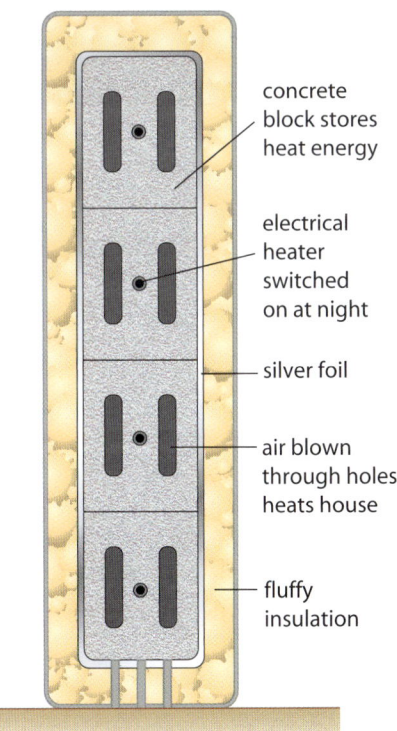

Figure 3 How a storage heater works.

P1 2.1 Energy transfers

Learning objectives
- describe the energy transfers in a range of devices
- identify where energy is wasted
- explain why wasted energy is difficult to use.

Forms of energy

Energy is needed to keep us working, and to operate all the machines around us. Different forms of energy include light, sound, electrical, potential and **kinetic energy**.

Energy can also be stored. **Nuclear energy** is stored inside atoms. Food, fuels and electrical batteries are all stores of **chemical energy**. Anything that is squashed, stretched or twisted stores **elastic potential energy**. It takes energy to move an object upwards against the force of gravity. Any object in a high position stores this energy as **gravitational potential energy**.

Energy transfers

Machines transfer energy between different forms. For example, an mp3 player transfers stored chemical energy into electrical energy and then sound.

Sometimes more than one energy transfer is involved. The engine in a car transfers chemical energy in the petrol into kinetic energy, which is useful. However, some of the energy is transferred by heating and sound. These forms of energy are not useful, so we call them wasted energy.

Sometimes one form of energy can be both useful and wasted. A boiler uses the chemical energy stored in gas or oil to heat water. The energy that is transferred to the water being heated is useful energy. However, the boiler itself will also get hot and this energy is wasted energy.

The bent bow is storing elastic potential energy.

Taking it further

You may have read about 'thermal energy'. The term 'thermal energy' includes the kinetic energy of particles moving around, as well as energy stored by rotating or spinning molecules, electrons and nuclei. 'Internal energy' includes these energies, and also energy stored in bonds between atoms and between subatomic particles.

The rollercoaster carriages are transferring gravitational potential energy into kinetic energy as they fall. The kinetic energy will be transferred back into gravitational potential energy as the carriages go up the next rise. The next rise cannot be as high, as friction will cause some of the energy to be wasted in frictional heating.

Conservation of energy

Energy cannot be created or destroyed; it can only be transferred usefully, stored or dissipated (wasted). The total amount of energy does not change. This is called the **principle of conservation of energy**.

If you could measure the total energy stored in the petrol used by a car, it would be exactly the same as the total energy produced by the engine.

Spreading out

If you look at an energy transfer it can often seem as if some energy has 'disappeared'. A cup on the table has gravitational potential energy, but what eventually happens to this if you knock the cup to the floor? The falling cup transfers gravitational potential energy to kinetic energy, and when it hits the floor this is transferred to sound energy and to increased energy in some of the particles in the floor. All of this energy ends up spreading out – dissipating – into the surroundings, which become warmer.

A car uses chemical energy stored in its fuel. The fuel stores a lot of energy in a small space. This chemical energy is eventually transferred by heating into the surroundings, which become warmer. This dissipated energy is very difficult to use for further energy transfers.

The light bulb transfers energy by heating and light. In this case the energy transferred by heating is wasted energy, but for a heater, it would be the useful form of energy.

Examiner feedback

Apart from machines designed to heat something, energy is wasted or dissipated in nearly every energy transfer. In many cases, *all* the original energy ends up heating the surroundings.

Science skills

The idea that energy is conserved was originally a hypothesis that was tested by gathering experimental data.

a Suggest some of the difficulties in confirming this hypothesis using a rollercoaster and explain why more precise results could be obtained under laboratory conditions.

Questions

1. What are the energy transfers in a torch?
2. You are running a race. What forms of energy are you transferring that are: **(a)** useful? **(b)** wasted?
3. A car uses a litre of petrol when it is driven to the shops and back. What happens to the chemical energy that was stored in the petrol?
4. What are the forms of wasted energy produced by a Bunsen burner?
5. What happens to the elastic potential energy in the bow in the first photograph?
6. If energy cannot be destroyed, how can we 'waste' energy?
7. Draw a flow chart to show all the energy transfers in a wind-up torch, starting with food. Show how energy is wasted at each stage.
8. The rollercoaster carriages in the photograph are moved to the top of the first rise on the track by electric motors. Once they start falling for the first time, there is no more energy input.

    Explain why the rollercoasters can go up other rises on the track without the need for motors, and what happens to the energy originally transferred to the carriages by these electric motors.

P1 2.2 Efficiency and Sankey diagrams

Learning objectives
- explain what efficiency means
- calculate the efficiency of energy transfers
- represent energy transfers using Sankey diagrams
- interpret Sankey diagrams.

Efficiency
All energy transfers produce some forms of wasted energy. The **efficiency** of a device is a measure of the amount of energy that is usefully transferred. The higher the efficiency, the more of the input energy is transferred into useful forms of energy.

The energy transfers in a device can be represented using a **Sankey diagram.** Figure 1 shows a Sankey diagram for a light bulb. The widths of the arrows are proportional to the amounts of energy they represent.

Calculating efficiency
Efficiency can be calculated using the energy or the **power** transferred by a device. Power is the energy transferred each second, and is measured in **watts (W)** or **kilowatts (kW)**.

$$\text{efficiency} = \frac{\text{useful energy out}}{\text{total energy in}} \;(\times 100\%)$$

$$\text{efficiency} = \frac{\text{useful power out}}{\text{total power in}} \;(\times 100\%)$$

You can use joules or kilojoules in the energy version of the equation, as long as you use the same units for both numbers. You can use watts or kilowatts in the power version, as long as you use the same units for both numbers.

The efficiency can be quoted as a decimal number less than one, or as a percentage if you multiply your answer by 100%.

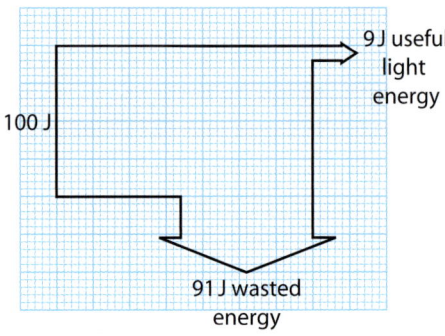

Figure 1 A Sankey diagram for a light bulb, showing the energy transferred each second.

Examiner feedback
The arrows in a Sankey diagram should be proportional to the amount of energy they represent. If the starting energy is 100 J, make the width of the overall arrow a multiple of 10 squares. This will make it easier to work out how wide to make the arrows representing the energy transfers.

Example 1
What is the efficiency of an electric kettle if it uses 500 kJ of electrical energy and transfers only 400 kJ of energy to the water in the kettle?

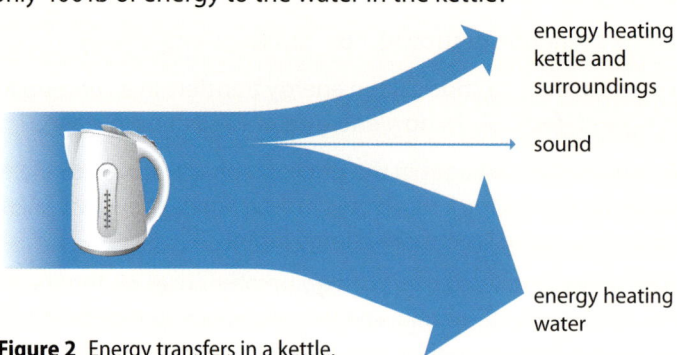

Figure 2 Energy transfers in a kettle.

$$\text{efficiency} = \frac{\text{useful energy out}}{\text{total energy in}} \;(\times 100\%)$$

$$= \frac{400\,\text{kJ}}{500\,\text{kJ}}$$

$$= 80\%$$

So the kettle only wastes 20% of the energy that is transferred to it.

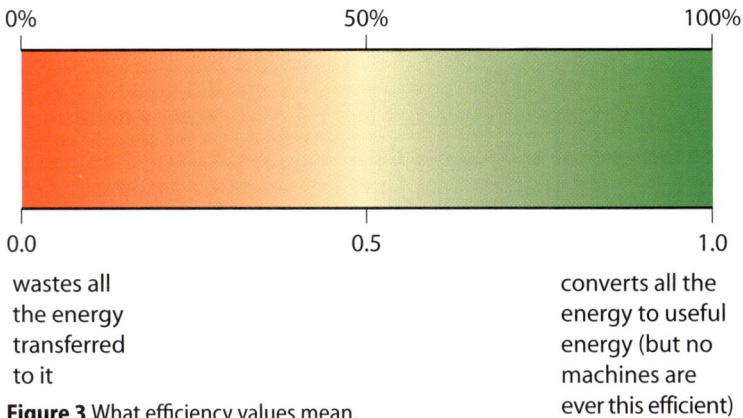

wastes all the energy transferred to it

converts all the energy to useful energy (but no machines are ever this efficient)

Figure 3 What efficiency values mean.

Examiner feedback

Some energy is always wasted, so the efficiency of a device can never be 1 (or 100%). If your answer gives a number bigger than 1 or a percentage bigger than 100%, check that you have put the correct numbers into the equation.

Science skills

The diagram shows an investigation to find the efficiencies of different bouncing balls. Some of the kinetic energy in the ball is transferred to heat energy as it bounces. This means that a ball never bounces to the same height from which it was dropped. The height of the ball is a measure of the gravitational potential energy stored in it. The higher the ball at the top of its bounce, the more efficient it is. The table shows the results for two different balls.

Drop	Bounce height/cm		
	Ball 1	Ball 2	Ball 3
1	59.0	38.0	49.5
2	60.5	35.5	47.0
3	58.0	38.5	47.5
4	60.0	37.0	48.0
5	57.5	31.5	49.0

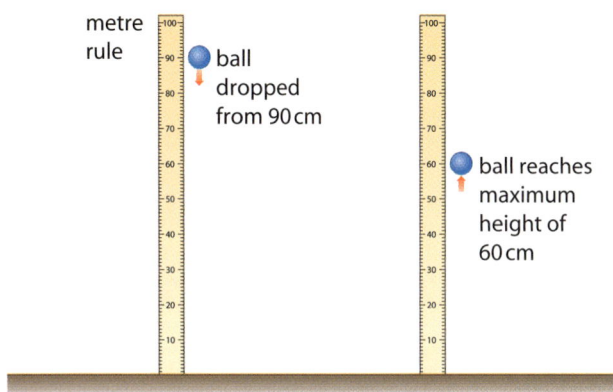

Figure 4 Bouncing balls.

a Find the mean and range of each set of data, ignoring any anomalous results.
b Suggest why there is a range of results for each ball.
c What was done in the investigation to improve reliability?
d For which ball are the results most precise? Explain your answer.

Questions

1. Look at the Sankey diagram in Figure 2. How could the kettle be made more efficient?
2. An electric immersion heater uses 50 kJ of electrical energy and transfers 45 kJ of heat to the water. **(a)** How efficient is it? **(b)** What forms of energy are wasted?
3. Draw a Sankey diagram to represent the immersion heater in question 2.
4. How efficient is the light bulb in Figure 1?
5. Your muscles waste about 75 J of energy for every 25 J they convert into movement. How efficient are your muscles?
6. An electric fan has an efficiency of 80%. If it produces 120 W of useful kinetic energy in the air, how much power is it using?
7. **(a)** What is the efficiency of the bouncing ball shown in Figure 4? **(b)** How high would you expect its second bounce to be? **(c)** What assumptions have you made in working out your answers?
8. Compare light bulbs and kettles in terms of energy transfers and efficiency and illustrate your answers with diagrams.

Energy and efficiency 21

P1 2.3 Reducing energy consumption

Learning objectives
- describe some ways of reducing energy consumption
- evaluate the effectiveness and cost effectiveness of some of these.

Figure 1 Switching off unused equipment can reduce wasted energy.

Reducing wasted energy

We all pay for the energy we use, so if we reduce waste we save money. Reducing the amount of fossil fuels we use also reduces the amount of carbon dioxide that enters the atmosphere. Carbon dioxide is thought to be leading to climate change.

One very easy way of reducing wasted energy is to keep our homes cooler and wear more clothes.

We should also switch off all appliances and lights that are not being used. All the energy transferred by a light bulb in an empty room is wasted energy. Appliances such as TVs or computers that are left on standby also waste energy.

Waste can also be reduced by using more efficient appliances. Modern low-energy light bulbs and LED lights are more efficient than old fashioned light bulbs. They cost more than normal bulbs. However, they also last longer so they will save more money in electricity bills and replacement costs than they cost to buy. They are cost effective.

All new appliances have an energy label that shows how efficient they are – see Figure 2. However, more efficient appliances are usually more expensive than less efficient ones. It is not usually cost effective to replace an old appliance that is still working with a new, more efficient one.

> **Science skills**
> Not only may buying a new, more efficient appliance cost more money, but throwing away an old appliance that still works may also result in more energy being used overall.
>
> **a** Why might replacing an old appliance with a new one not always result in reducing overall energy consumption and carbon dioxide emissions?

Energy label

Energy — Washing machine
Manufacturer
Model
More efficient
A
B ← B
C
D
E
F
G
Less efficient

Energy consumption kWh/cycle — **1.75**
Based on standard test results for 60°C cotton cycle
Actual energy consumption will depend on how the appliance is used

Washing performance	A**B**CDEF
A higher G Lower	
Spin drying performance	A**B**CDEF
A higher G Lower	
Spin speed (rpm)	1400
Capacity (cotton) kg	5.0
Water consumption l	5.5
Noise Washing	5.2
(dB(A)re 1 pW) Spinning	7.0

Further information is contained in product brochures

Figure 2 An energy efficiency label for a washing machine.

Transport and energy

Figure 3 shows how much energy it takes to move one passenger one kilometre using different forms of transport. Less energy would be used for transport if more people took the bus or train instead of using a car. Even more energy would be saved if more people walked or used a bicycle for short journeys; they would also be healthier.

Modern cars are usually more efficient than older ones, which means they can go further on a litre of fuel than older cars. Buying a new, more efficient car can save on fuel costs, but it may not be cost effective. It costs a lot to buy a new car, and it also takes a lot of energy to make a new car.

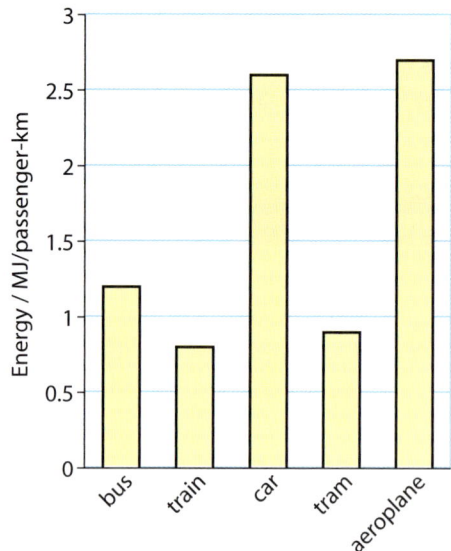

Figure 3 Different types of transport need different amounts of energy. These figures assume an average number of people in each form of transport.

Science skills

Some decisions about cutting energy use are made by individuals, but sometimes the government passes laws to make people use less energy.

Which of these ways of saving energy are decided by individuals, which are decided by the government, and which are a combination of both?

b Banning the sale of old-fashioned inefficient light bulbs.

c Explaining to people why it is important to reduce their energy use.

d Giving a grant for replacing an inefficient boiler with a new, efficient one.

Using wasted energy

Sometimes wasted energy can be reused. In many factories, large fans extract air from the building to remove fumes or smells, and to ensure a supply of fresh air. The removed air transfers energy with it, which is wasted as it spreads out and warms the surroundings. If the waste air is passed through a **heat exchanger**, some of the energy can be transferred to heat the air coming into the building and warm it.

Taking it further

As well as considering payback time in terms of costs, the energy payback time for an item can be considered. This takes into account all the energy used in manufacturing the item (including mining, processing and transporting raw materials, running the factory, transporting goods to shops, and so on), and compares it to the energy saved per year from using the new item. If your concern is for the environment then the energy payback time may be more relevant than the financial payback time.

Questions

1. Give two reasons why we should try to reduce wasted energy.

2. How will keeping our homes cooler reduce wasted energy?

3. What information would you need to allow you to work out whether buying a more expensive LED light instead of a normal bulb would save you money overall?

4. Jenny lives on her own and uses her tumble dryer once a week. Sam has three young children and uses her tumble dryer every day. Explain who is more likely to benefit from buying a new, more efficient tumble dryer.

5. The energy per passenger-km for cars in Figure 3 was calculated assuming each car carried two people. How would the energy change if:
   (a) all cars carried four people? **(b)** all cars had only one person in them?

6. Which of the values in question 5 would be more likely to be used by:
   (a) a car manufacturer selling cars? **(b)** a train company trying to persuade people to use the train? **(c)** Explain your answers.

7. How does fitting a heat exchanger to the air circulation system in a factory help to save money and help the environment?

8. What does 'cost-effective' mean? Explain some of the factors you would consider in deciding whether replacing a central heating boiler will be cost-effective.

Route to A*

Some questions in the exam award marks for using good English and for organising information clearly. For question 8, you could start by explaining the idea of payback time, and how this relates to cost-effectiveness. You could list factors that would help you to work out the total cost to install the new boiler and then go on to explain how you could work out how much money it would save compared to the boiler being replaced.

Energy and efficiency

Assess yourself questions

1. Figure 1 shows an insulated box used to keep food hot.

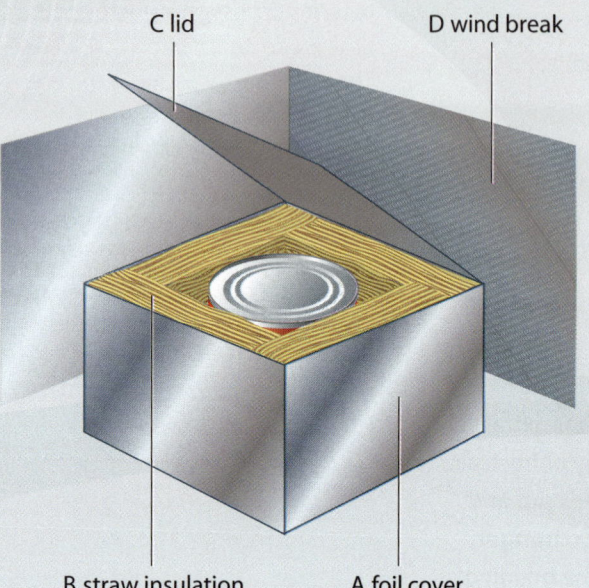

Figure 1 Insulated box.

Choose the correct parts, A–D, to answer the questions below:
   (a) What stops the box emitting infrared radiation?
   (b) What helps to stop heat being transferred by convection?
   (c) What helps to stop heat being transferred by conduction?
   (d) What stops the wind moving warmed air away from the box? *(4 marks)*

2. A student was testing different ways of insulating a food box. She carried out four different tests, each using materials in different ways. Look at tests (a)–(c) and decide which kind of variable was being used. Choose your answers from the box.
   (a) Foam of different thicknesses.
   (b) Foam, foil or bubble wrap.
   (c) One, two or three layers of foam. *(3 marks)*

   | categoric | continuous |

3. (a) Describe how a convection current will form in the air near a lit candle. Draw a diagram to illustrate your answer. *(4 marks)*
   (b) Sketch the convection current that would be formed by an ice cube floating in a glass of water. *(1 mark)*
   (c) Explain why the two convection currents are different. *(4 marks)*

4. (a) Explain what the terms 'payback time' and 'cost-effective' mean. *(2 marks)*
   (b) Describe how you would decide which type of insulation to add to a house. *(3 marks)*

5. Look at the house in Figure 2.

Figure 2 House with cooling features.

   Explain how each of the labelled features helps the house to keep cool. *(3 marks)*

6. Animal adaptations to maintaining the correct body temperature can involve their shape, the materials their body is made from, or their behaviour. Explain how these adaptations of elephants help to keep them cool.
   (a) Large ears. *(2 marks)*
   (b) No fur. *(2 marks)*
   (c) They often stand in the shade of trees. *(2 marks)*
   (d) They suck up water in their trunks and spray it over their bodies. *(3 marks)*

7. A 150 W fan produces 130 W of useful kinetic energy in the air.
   (a) How is the remaining 20 W of energy transferred? *(2 marks)*
   (b) Draw a Sankey diagram to represent the energy transfers in the fan. Draw your diagram on graph paper. *(2 marks)*
   (c) Calculate the efficiency of the fan. *(3 marks)*

8 Explain how putting a lid on a cup of soup will help to keep it hot. (5 marks)

9 A storage heater contains 10 kg of concrete, with a specific heat capacity of 900 J/kg·°C. At the end of its overnight heating period, the temperature of the concrete is 60 °C.

How much energy has been stored in the concrete? State any assumptions you had to make in working out your answer. (5 marks)

10 The apparatus shown in Figure 3 was used to investigate how well different-coloured materials absorb and emit infrared radiation. Table 1 shows the results of the investigation.

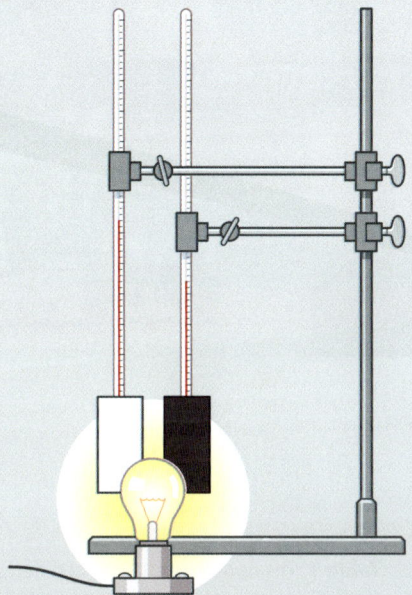

Figure 3 Experimental apparatus.

Table 1 Results of experiment.

Time/ min	Temperature/°C	
	Black	White
0	18	18
2	21	19
4	24	21
6	26	23
8	30	25
10	32	27
12	30	26
14	28	25
16	27	24
18	26	23
20	25	22

(a) Plot a graph to show these results. (4 marks)
(b) At what point do you think the bulb was switched off? Explain your answer. (2 marks)
(c) Write a conclusion for this investigation. (4 marks)

11 A school hall has a very high ceiling, and it gets very hot in the summer. Explain why cooling will be most effective if windows near the ceiling are opened as well as opening windows or doors at ground level. (4 marks)

12 A 1.5 kg block of aluminium is heated up using an immersion heater. 13 kJ of energy is transferred to the block. The specific heat capacity of aluminium is 899 J/kg/°C.

(a) Calculate the temperature rise (to the nearest degree) in the aluminium block. (3 marks)
(b) Explain why the temperature rise would actually be less than this. (1 mark)

13 A student takes a beaker full of crushed ice and heats it.

(a) Sketch a graph to show how the temperature of the ice changes as the ice melts and as the student continues to heat the water formed. Include significant temperatures on the graph. (3 marks)
(b) Explain the shape of your graph using kinetic theory. (4 marks)

14 A wine cooler consists of a container made from porous pottery. When it is used, the pot is soaked in water and a wine bottle is placed inside it. Explain how the wine cooler works. (5 marks)

15 A coolbox is used to keep food or drinks cold for picnics. Explain why the coolbox has the following features.

(a) A plastic rather than a metal outer case. (2 marks)
(b) Foam between the inner and outer cases. (2 marks)
(c) A white inner case. (2 marks)

16 Blocks of ice are put inside the coolbox to help to keep the contents cold.

(a) How does the ice help to keep the contents cold? (1 mark)
(b) Explain two ways (other than weight) in which ice is a better material to use for this purpose than a block of metal cooled to the same initial temperature. (4 marks)

17 How could you test a selection of coolboxes to find out which is the most effective at keeping food cool? Describe what you would do, and how you would make your test fair.

In this question you will be assessed on using good English, organising information clearly and using specialist terms where appropriate (6 marks)

P13.1 Electrical energy

Learning objectives
- describe some examples of energy transfers in electrical devices
- explain how to work out the amount of energy a device uses
- explain what power means.

Energy transfers in electrical appliances

Electricity is a very useful way of transferring energy, as electrical devices can be designed to bring about many different energy transfers. The photograph shows some appliances that transfer electrical energy into light, heat, sound and kinetic energy.

A lamp, an electric oven, headphones and the Segway. The Segway contains electric motors and moves forwards when you lean forwards. Can you work out the energy transfers in each case?

Science skills

a Explain what form of chart you would use to display this data.

b What advantages would this type of display have compared with the table?

Look at the data in Table 1.

c Suggest why no-one owned microwave ovens or telephone chargers in 1970.

d What economic factors might a person take into account when deciding to buy a new appliance?

e What environmental factors might they take into account?

f How might the factors in d and e depend on the type of appliance?

Table 1 The number (in 1000s) of different appliances owned in the UK, 1970 and 2000.

Year	1970	2000
fridges & freezers	10837	37006
washing machine	11728	19379
tumble dryer	134	8635
dish washer	221	6009
telephone chargers	–	3710
oven	7683	14428
hob	7615	11538
microwave	–	20144
kettle	10259	24117
toaster	4540	19623

The number of some types of electrical appliances owned (in thousands) in 1970 and 2010.

Energy and power

The amount of electrical energy a device uses depends on its **power** and how long it is switched on for. Energy is measured in joules (J). The power of an appliance is the rate at which it transforms energy, and is measured in **watts** (W). 1 watt = 1 joule of energy transferred each second.

$$E = P \times t$$
$$\text{energy transferred} = \text{power} \times \text{time}$$
$$\text{(joules, J)} \quad \text{(watts, W)} \quad \text{(seconds, s)}$$

Example 1

A 20 W light bulb is switched on for 5 hours. How much energy does it transfer?

5 hours = 5 × 3600 seconds
        = 18 000 seconds
$E = P \times t$
energy = power × time
       = 20 W × 18 000 seconds
       = 360 000 J (or 360 kJ)

Example 2

A 3 kW heater uses 8000 kJ of energy. For how many minutes was it switched on?

$E = P \times t$
energy = power × time
$$\text{time} = \frac{\text{energy}}{\text{power}}$$
$$= \frac{8\,000\,000 \text{ J}}{3000 \text{ W}}$$
= 2667 seconds
= 44.4 minutes or 44 minutes 24 seconds

> **Examiner feedback**
>
> Make sure that the units you use in these calculations are always the correct ones. In the formula to work out the energy transferred, if energy is in joules, power must be in watts. If you are given a value in kilowatts, convert it to watts by multiplying by 1000. The time must be in seconds. If you are given a time in minutes convert it to seconds by multiplying by 60. If you are given a time in hours, multiply by 3600.

> **Examiner feedback**
>
> In example 2, you could have left the energy in kJ and the power in kW and you would have got the same answer. However unless you are very confident with maths and equations, it is safest in an exam to always convert the values to the standard units (joules and watts, in this case) before putting the numbers into the equation.

Questions

1. What energy transfers are the following devices designed to bring about? **(a)** electric drill **(b)** fan heater **(c)** television.

2. How is energy wasted in the devices in question 1?

3. Name two electrical devices (other than those in question 1) that are designed to transfer electrical energy into: **(a)** heating; **(b)** light; **(c)** sound; **(d)** movement.

4. A 50 W radio is switched on for 3 hours. How much energy does it use?

5. A tumble dryer uses 2700 kJ of electrical energy when it is used for half an hour. What power is the tumble dryer?

6. A computer uses 2400 kJ of energy. Its power is 65 W. How long was it switched on for? Give your answer in hours, minutes and seconds to the nearest second.

7. An electric oven has a power of 3 kW. A cake takes 40 minutes to bake. **(a)** What is the maximum amount of energy the oven will use to bake the cake? **(b)** Explain why this is a maximum amount. (*Hint*: think about what the thermostat in an oven does.)

8. 'The increasing ownership of toasters could help to reduce the amount of electricity used.' Explain this statement. (*Hint*: think about how you would make toast if you did not have a toaster.)

P1 3.2 Paying for electricity

Learning objectives
- calculate the energy used by an appliance
- calculate the cost of using mains electricity.

The power of appliances

We use electricity for a lot of different things but it all has to be paid for. Electricity bills are worked out from the amount of energy used.

Many household devices transfer a lot of energy, and their power is usually measured in kilowatts (kW), where 1 kW = 1000 W. The **power rating** of an appliance is shown on a label.

Calculating the cost

A joule is quite a small amount of energy. It is impractical to quote energy use in thousands of kilojoules, so electricity companies use the **kilowatt-hour** (**kWh**). This is the amount of energy that is transferred by a 1 kW device in one hour. It is sometimes called a **Unit** of electricity.

$$E = P \times t$$
energy transferred = power × time
(kilowatt-hours, kWh) (kilowatts, kW) (hours, h)

Example 1

A 10 kW electric shower is used for a total of 90 minutes during a week. How many kilowatt-hours of energy does it transfer in one week?

energy = power × time
= 10 kW × 1.5 h
= 15 kWh

Electricity companies usually give their prices in pence per kWh. You can work out the cost of electricity by multiplying the energy by the cost per kWh.

total cost = number of kilowatt-hours × cost per kilowatt-hour
(in pence, p)   (in kWh or Units)   (in pence, p)

Example 2

An electric heater has a power rating of 2 kW. What is the cost of using the heater for three hours if one kWh of electricity costs 5p?

Energy in kWh = 2 kW × 3 h = 6 kWh

Cost in pence = 6 kWh × 5p = 30p

Example 3

It costs £2.62 to use a 3.5 kW tumble dryer. The unit price was 15p. How long was it used for? First calculate the energy used.

$$\text{number of kilowatt hours} = \frac{\text{total cost}}{\text{cost per kilowatt hour}}$$

$$= \frac{262p}{15p}$$

$$= 17.47 \text{ kWh}$$

Then calculate the time:

$$\text{time} = \frac{\text{energy}}{\text{power}}$$

$$= \frac{17.47 \text{ kWh}}{3.5 \text{ kW}}$$

$$= 4.99 \text{ hours}$$

This hair straightener iron has a power rating of 40 W.

Route to A*

Be careful with the units. There are two equations for calculating energy transferred: one uses joules, watts and seconds (see lesson P1 3.1) and the other uses kilowatt-hours, kilowatts and hours. Don't mix up the two sets of units.

You need to use the equation with kilowatt-hours if you are calculating the cost of electricity used.

Examiner feedback

Remember, in any calculation, make sure that you use the correct units. For example, if an appliance is switched on for 30 minutes, the value you use for time should be 0.5 hours.

Examiner feedback

Although the units 'watts' and 'kilowatt-hours' sound similar, remember that watts are used to measure power, and kilowatt-hours are used to measure energy transferred.

Electricity meters and bills

Each home has an electricity meter that records the amount of electricity used. Each electricity bill is based on the number of units used since the previous bill.

AQALec ELECTRICITY BILL

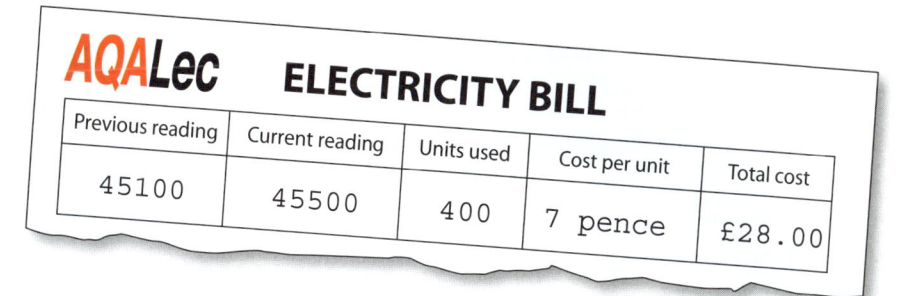

Previous reading	Current reading	Units used	Cost per unit	Total cost
45100	45500	400	7 pence	£28.00

Figure 1 An electricity bill.

A type of electricity meter fitted in many older homes.

Science skills

The electricity meter in the photograph on the right is a 'smart' meter. It can show the customer how much electricity is being used at different times of day, and how the electricity use compares with the previous day, week or month. This should help consumers to reduce the amount of electricity they use. The meter can send readings directly to the electricity company, so they do not need to employ people to read the meters.

a In what way does the electricity company benefit if its customers have smart meters?

b How could smart meters be a disadvantage for the electricity company?

c The government have said that all homes should have smart meters by 2020. Suggest why.

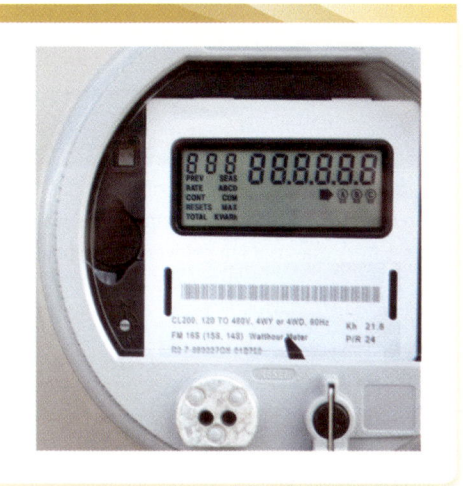

Questions

1. Explain why there are two different units for measuring energy used.
2. What is a Unit of electricity?
3. An electricity bill says the current reading is 11 654 Units, and the previous one was 10 763 Units. What will the electricity bill be if electricity costs 14 p per Unit?
4. A 3 kW electrical heater transfers 15 kWh of energy. How long was it switched on for?
5. How much energy is transferred to a 100 W bulb left on for 2 hours 15 minutes?
6. An electric lawnmower has a power rating of 1.2 kW. It takes 30 minutes to mow a lawn and costs 9 p. What is the price of electricity?
7. The cost of running an aquarium pump continuously is 8 p per week. If the price per kWh is 12 p, what is the power of the pump (to the nearest watt)?
8. Explain how electricity is charged for, and how to calculate the energy used by an appliance and the cost of the electricity.

Taking it further

Can you work out how many joules there are in a kilowatt-hour of electrical energy?

Electrical devices

P1 3.3 Using different devices

Learning objectives
- discuss the advantages and disadvantages of using different electrical appliances for a particular application
- consider situations where electricity or specific devices are not available.

Choosing a device
There are many different uses for electricity, and for each application there are often several different types of device that can be used. Some devices are more powerful than others. The photograph shows a low-power tubular heater. This is an alternative to using a 1 or 2 kW electric fire or fan heater.

Sometimes you can choose between completely different types of equipment. For example, many homes have both a conventional oven and a microwave oven. Microwave ovens heat food in a different way to conventional ovens, which means the food cooks much more quickly. Because the microwave oven itself does not get hot, less energy is wasted in heating the surroundings. A microwave oven has an efficiency of nearly 0.6, whereas a conventional oven has an efficiency of only about 0.15 (see lesson P1 2.2).

This tubular heater has a power of 120 W. It is being used to make sure the temperature in a conservatory does not fall below freezing point.

The cake on the left was cooked in a conventional oven. The one on the right was cooked in a microwave oven.

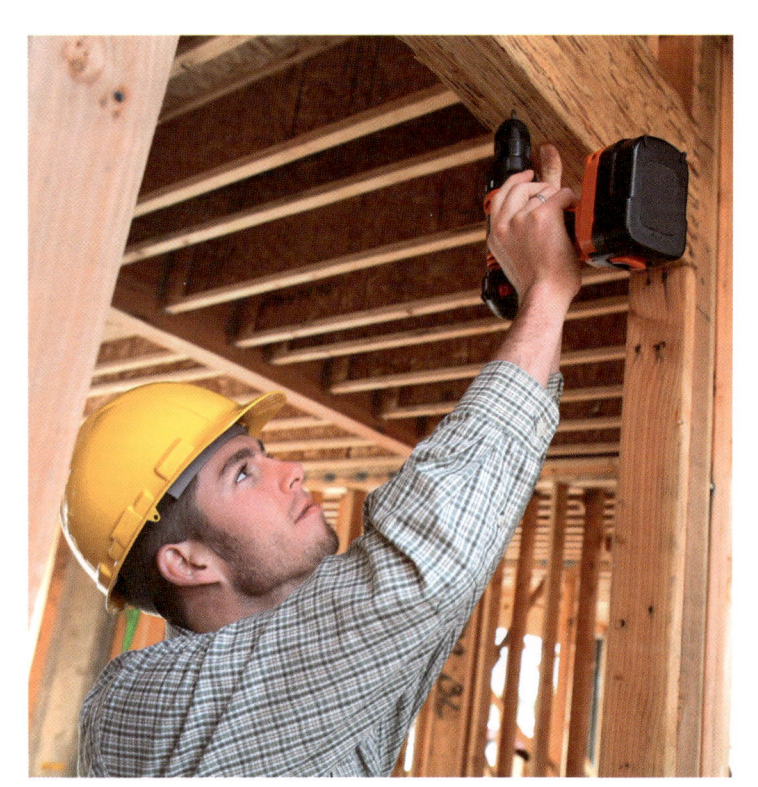

Working away from the mains supply
Sometimes electrical devices are needed where there is no mains electricity supply. If electricity is available nearby, **rechargeable batteries** can be used to power some types of equipment. If there are no facilities for recharging then **disposable batteries** can be used. However, disposable batteries are only suitable for low-power devices such as torches and radios.

In some parts of the world, disposable batteries are not available or are too expensive. In 1994 Trevor Bayliss invented a clockwork radio to be sold in Africa. The radio would work for about 15 minutes after being wound for two minutes. The clockwork radio allowed people to listen to educational and news broadcasts without having to buy batteries. Today there are also wind-up torches on sale, as well as radios and other devices powered by **solar cells**.

This worker is using a battery-powered drill, as there is no electricity supply on the construction site.

Science skills

Clockwork torches and radios are sold all over the world. How might a clockwork radio be useful to:

a a person living in the UK?

b someone living in a remote part of Africa?

This fan is powered by electricity made in a solar cell.

A mains-powered fan.

Questions

1. The tubular heater in the first photograph can be left on overnight. **(a)** How much will it cost to leave it on for eight hours, if electricity costs 15p per kWh? **(b)** How much would it cost to run a 2 kW electric fan heater for the same time?

2. What are some of the advantages and disadvantages of using a tubular heater instead of a fan heater?

3. **(a)** Give two reasons why a microwave oven would use much less energy than a conventional oven to cook a piece of food. **(b)** Suggest why people still use conventional ovens for cooking. Give as many reasons as you can.

4. An electrician is putting new wiring into an old house. Why might she need to use a battery-powered drill?

5. **(a)** Look at the photographs of the fans above. What are the advantages and disadvantages of the different types? **(b)** What are the advantages and disadvantages of a hand-held fan that you move yourself?

6. It takes 1.5 hours to cook jacket potatoes in a 2 kW conventional oven. It takes 20 minutes to cook the same-sized potatoes in an 850 W microwave oven. What is the difference in cost if electricity costs 16p per kWh?

7. You can buy refrigerators that work using bottled gas. These are more expensive than mains-powered fridges of a similar size. Suggest who might buy these fridges.

8. A woman has a battery-powered radio that she listens to when she is gardening. She has a clockwork radio that she takes on camping holidays. Suggest why she uses both kinds of radio, and whether or not a solar-powered radio might be better for one or both uses.

Electrical devices

P1 4.1 Power stations

Learning objectives
- describe how power stations work
- describe the different energy resources that can be used by power stations.

Inside a power station

Electricity is not a source of energy because it has to be generated using other forms of energy. Most of the electricity we use in the UK is generated in power stations. Energy stored in fuel is used to heat water and turn it into steam. The steam turns a turbine, and the turbine makes the generator turn. Figure 1 shows what happens inside a power station.

4 The water is cooled in a cooling tower before being sent back to the furnace.

hot waste gases

2 The steam is used to spin a **turbine**, which is like a giant fan.

electrical cables

cooling towers

water input

coal dust

steam out

3 The turbine is attached to a **generator**. The spinning turbine makes the generator turn. The generator converts kinetic energy into electrical energy.

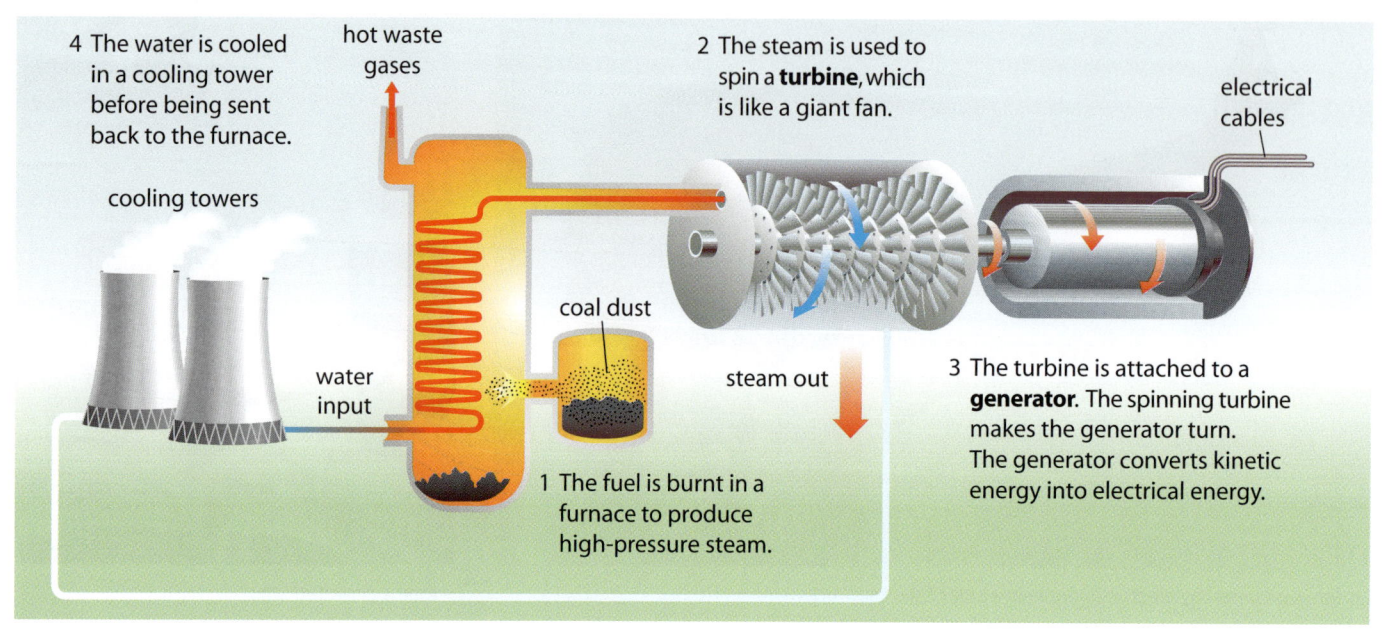

1 The fuel is burnt in a furnace to produce high-pressure steam.

Figure 1 A coal-fired power station.

Science in action

Some gas-fired power stations are 'combined cycle gas turbine' or 'CCGT' power stations.

When natural gas is burnt, the hot gases produced drive a turbine directly, but then they are also passed through a heat exchanger where they heat water, changing it to steam. This steam is used to drive a different turbine. A CCGT power station is more efficient than other kinds of gas-fired power stations.

In some power stations that use natural gas as the energy source, the hot waste gases from burning are at a high pressure and are used to drive the turbine directly. These are called **gas turbine** power stations.

water vapour from cooling towers

waste gases from burning fuel emitted from this chimney

A coal-fired power station.

Energy resources for power stations

Most of the power stations in the UK use **fossil fuels**. Fossil fuels are being formed underground continuously but very slowly. It takes millions of years for these fuels to form, and we are using them up much faster than they are being formed. These fuels are called **non-renewable** resources, because once we have used up the ones that exist at the moment there will be no more left.

Nuclear fuels

Nuclear power stations generate electricity in a similar way to a fossil-fuelled power station but they use **uranium** or **plutonium** as fuel. These elements are **radioactive**. They do not burn in a chemical reaction like fossil fuels do. Instead, the atoms themselves split up to make new elements, releasing energy which is used to make steam. This kind of reaction is called **nuclear fission**. Fission produces a lot of energy from a small amount of fuel, so a nuclear power station has lower fuel costs than a fossil-fuelled one. Supplies of nuclear fuel are likely to last much longer than supplies of fossil fuels.

Biofuels

Biomass is biological material obtained from living things, or from things that have recently died. Biomass includes wood and other plant material and animal waste. Biomass is a **renewable resource** because new plants can be grown to replace the ones used.

Biofuels are fuels made using biomass. Biofuels include:
- straw, nutshells, woodchips and other waste materials
- plants such as willow or *Miscanthus* grass grown for use as biofuel
- ethanol, made from **fermented** plant material such as sugar cane
- biodiesel, made from various plant oils
- methane, made by the fermentation of animal wastes in **sludge digesters**.

Some power stations in the UK can burn biofuels together with fossil fuels.

Examiner feedback

You must be aware of the effects on the environment of using different energy resources. Nuclear fuels produce very little carbon dioxide but they generate radioactive waste, which must be kept safe for many years.

Route to A*

Both fossil fuels and biofuels use substances that were originally part of living things. The difference is that the substances in biofuels have just been grown. The substances in fossil fuels come from things that lived millions of years ago, and have been changed over millions of years of being buried underground.

Questions

1. Explain why electricity is not a source of energy.
2. Explain why fossil fuels are referred to as non-renewable fuels.
3. Why are biofuels referred to as renewable fuels?
4. **(a)** Name two nuclear fuels. **(b)** Describe two differences between a fossil-fuelled and a nuclear power station.
5. All the power stations on these pages use stored energy to make steam. Which kinds of stored energy are used?
6. Draw a flow chart to show all the stages in a coal-fired power station.
7. Look at Figure 2. Suggest how and why a similar chart for 2050 might differ from Figure 2.
8. Describe three different ways in which natural gas can be used in power stations, and explain which is the most efficient.

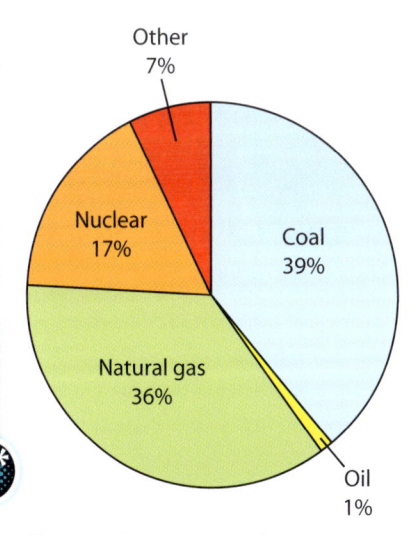

Figure 2 Energy sources for generating electricity in the UK in 2007. Coal, oil and natural gas are all fossil fuels. 'Other' includes hydroelectricity, wind power and other fuels such as biomass.

Other 7%
Nuclear 17%
Coal 39%
Natural gas 36%
Oil 1%

Generating electricity

P1 4.2 Comparing power stations

Learning objectives
- list some of the environmental effects of different energy resources used in power stations
- compare different kinds of power stations in terms of running costs, pollution and safety.

Problems with fossil fuels

There are several different fuels that can be used in power stations. Each type of fuel has advantages and disadvantages. Table 1 shows some of the pollution caused by coal-fired power stations.

Table 1 Pollution problems with coal-fired power stations.

Waste entering atmosphere	What problems does it cause?	What can be done?
carbon dioxide	contributes to global warming	capture it and store it so it does not go into the atmosphere
sulfur dioxide	causes acid rain	remove it from the waste gases, or remove sulfur from the coal before it is burnt
nitrogen oxides	cause acid rain	use furnaces that reduce the amount produced
smoke and dust	can be harmful to health	remove from the waste gases

Natural gas is cleaner and more efficient than coal as it does not contain sulfur. Power stations that burn natural gas emit less carbon dioxide for each kilowatt hour of electricity they produce.

Most of the measures in the last column of Table 1 are used in UK power stations, except for capturing the carbon dioxide emissions. Several companies are developing **carbon capture and storage** schemes. One possible type of storage is under the North Sea, where oil and gas have been extracted.

Biofuels

Crops take in carbon dioxide from the atmosphere when they grow. If the crop is burnt, the same amount of carbon dioxide gets put back into the atmosphere. This means that in using biofuels, the total amount of carbon dioxide in the atmosphere has not changed overall.

That is not the whole story, however. Energy is needed to make fertiliser and to plant, harvest and transport the crops. Most of this energy is obtained by burning fossil fuels. So some carbon dioxide *is* added to the atmosphere, although not as much as if the same energy had been released from burning fossil fuels directly.

At present coal is cheaper than biofuel for power stations in the UK.

Nuclear power

Nuclear power stations do not emit any carbon dioxide or other gases. However, there are other potential problems with nuclear power stations. The waste they produce is radioactive, and some of it will be hazardous for thousands of years. The waste must be sealed into concrete or glass and buried safely so the radioactivity cannot damage the environment. A nuclear power station also needs to be carefully **decommissioned** (dismantled safely) at the end of its life so that no radioactivity escapes into the environment. It costs a lot more to build and to decommission a nuclear power station than a fossil-fuelled one.

Coal is transported to power stations by rail.

There are not many accidents in nuclear power stations, and the power stations are designed to contain any radioactive leaks. However, if a major accident occurs it can have very serious consequences.

Science skills

a What economic, social and environmental issues could be raised by plans for a new power station?

b Who should make the decision whether or not to build a new power station, and what type it should be?

An accident at the Chernobyl nuclear reactor in the Ukraine contaminated land for miles around. Radioactive dust even reached the UK.

Questions

1. List the ways in which coal-fired power stations can cause pollution.
2. Describe how pollution from fossil-fuelled power stations is currently being dealt with in the UK.
3. Describe two advantages of using natural gas instead of coal to generate electricity.
4. Explain some advantages and disadvantages of nuclear power.
5. (a) Suggest why a nuclear power station costs more to build than a fossil-fuelled power station.
   (b) Why is decommissioning it properly very important?
6. How can a nuclear accident affect people in parts of the world very distant from where it occurred?
7. Power companies were required by law to take the measures shown in Table 1 to reduce pollution from coal-fired power stations. Suggest why it was necessary to make such laws.
8. Biofuels are often described as 'carbon neutral'. Suggest what this means, and why it is not actually correct.

Generating electricity 35

P1 4.3 Electricity from renewable resources

Learning objectives
- describe the different ways in which renewable resources can be used to generate electricity.

Wind and water

Wind and water can be used to generate electricity by turning turbines directly. Wind turbines can be built on land or at sea but need to be placed in windy locations. They only produce electricity when the wind is blowing.

Water can be used to turn turbines in different ways. The spinning turbine turns a generator to produce electricity.

- **Hydroelectricity** can be produced by building dams in hilly areas to trap water in reservoirs. The water flows downhill and turns turbines at the bottom.
- **Tidal power** involves building a **barrage** across a river estuary. The water turns turbines as it flows in and out. **Tidal stream turbines** are a bit like underwater wind turbines. They are placed where strong tidal currents flow. This technology is still being developed. Tidal power is not available all the time but it is available at predictable times.
- **Wave power** uses the motion of waves to generate electricity. One way of doing this is to make the waves force air through a tube built on the coast. The moving air makes a turbine spin. Wave power is only available when there are high waves. The photograph on the left shows a different type of wave power generator, which is anchored out at sea. It floats on the surface and bends as waves pass beneath it.

The Pelamis Wave Energy Converter being tested in Scotland. These wave energy machines can be anchored out at sea.

Solar power

Solar cells contain chemicals that convert light energy into electrical energy. They produce electricity directly from the Sun's radiation. At present solar cells are expensive and not very efficient. New materials are being developed all the time that should improve efficiency.

Examiner feedback

Some students think that solar cells will only be widely used when their efficiency is nearly 100%. This is not correct. There are many reasons why solar cells are not in widespread use today, but cost is likely to be the most important reason.

Solar cells are very useful for producing electricity in remote locations. The solar cells on this buoy charge a battery. Electricity from the battery is then used at night to power a light on the buoy.

Solar power can also be used to turn turbines. One way of doing this is to use an array of mirrors to focus energy from the Sun on a furnace at the top of a high tower. The concentrated energy heats water to make steam.

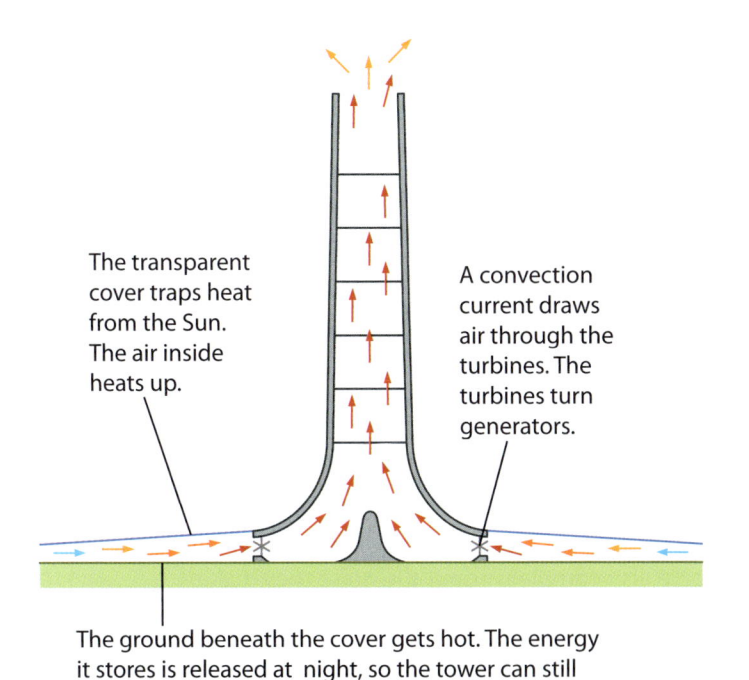

The transparent cover traps heat from the Sun. The air inside heats up.

A convection current draws air through the turbines. The turbines turn generators.

The ground beneath the cover gets hot. The energy it stores is released at night, so the tower can still generate electricity at night.

Figure 1 A solar tower uses convection currents to turn turbines.

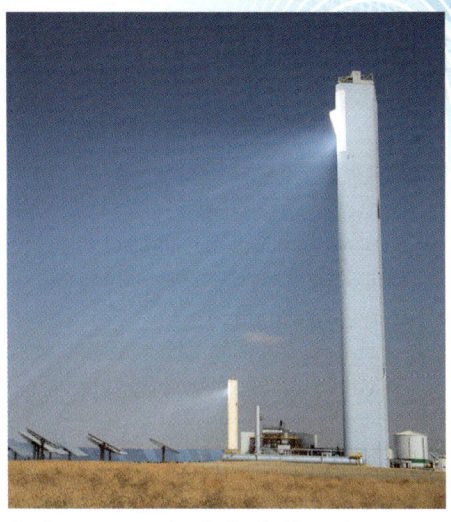

A solar power station in Spain. The mirrors concentrate sunlight on the furnace at the top of the tower, where water is heated to make steam.

Solar towers can also be built to use energy from the Sun to create convection currents. These currents then turn air turbines. Figure 1 shows how this type of solar tower works.

Geothermal energy

Hot rocks can also be used to generate electricity. In some volcanic areas hot water and steam rise to the surface, or pipes can be drilled into the ground to allow the steam to rise. The steam can be used to drive turbines, which drive generators. This is known as **geothermal energy**. Hot water produced in volcanic areas can also be piped to nearby houses to heat them directly.

Route to A*

Geothermal energy is not renewable in the same sense as the other sources on these pages, as eventually the hot rocks will cool down. However the supply of heat will last much longer than supplies of fossil fuels so geothermal energy is often included when talking about renewables.

Questions

1. How can electricity be produced using the wind?
2. How can electricity be produced directly using the Sun's radiation?
3. Describe four different ways in which water can be used to generate electricity.
4. Look at all the renewable resources on this page. Which ones can generate electricity: **(a)** all the time? **(b)** only some of the time?
5. **(a)** Which resources can produce electricity at predicable times? **(b)** Why is this important?
6. Describe two different ways in which solar towers can be used to generate electricity.
7. Why are solar towers not likely to be used in the UK?
8. Describe how a geothermal power station works and compare it with a fossil-fuelled power station.

Generating electricity

P1 4.4 Renewables and the environment

Learning objectives
- describe the effects that different renewable energy resources have on the environment
- evaluate different methods of generating electricity using renewable resources.

People often think of renewable energy resources as 'clean' sources of energy, because most of them do not add polluting gases to the atmosphere. However, they can affect the environment in other ways.

Visual and noise pollution

One objection that many people have to wind turbines is that they cause visual pollution (they spoil the view). Fossil-fuelled power stations are not pretty, but people have got used to them, and they are usually built in areas that already have industrial buildings. Wind farms are often built in places where people go to enjoy the countryside, because the winds are usually stronger and steadier there. Some people also complain about the noise they make.

Wildlife

The flooding of land for reservoirs for hydroelectric power stations destroys wildlife habitats. Growing crops for biofuels could also damage habitats if previously unfarmed land is ploughed up or rainforests are cleared.

Tidal barrages are huge dams that change the flow of rivers. This may affect birds and other wildlife that live or feed on tidal mudflats, and may affect the migration of fish. The first, and only large, tidal power station is built across the estuary of the Rance River, in France. It has been operating since 1966.

Some people object to wind farms because some birds are killed. This problem can be reduced by not siting wind farms on bird migration routes.

Do these **wind turbines** spoil the view?

Dunlin feed on animals that live in the mud. These may not survive if the flow of water in the estuary is changed.

Building a dam across a river can prevent the migration of fish such as salmon. A fish ladder can help them to get past the dam.

Land use

Biofuels can be used to generate electricity, and they can also be used as fuel for vehicles. Growing biofuels uses land. Some of this land could otherwise be used for growing food so food prices could be affected. If food prices rose, this would particularly affect the developing world.

This is also true of hydroelectricity, as the reservoirs flood large areas of land. Unlike biofuel crops, a new reservoir could provide habitats for different kinds of wildlife, and a valuable leisure amenity.

Wind farms do not have such a great effect on the land, as farming can still take place around them.

Waste gases

The main problem with fossil-fuelled power stations is that they emit carbon dioxide into the atmosphere. In geothermal power stations, the hot water rising from the depths of the Earth often contains some dissolved gases, such as carbon dioxide and methane. These gases can escape into the atmosphere and contribute to global warming. However, a geothermal power station only produces about one-tenth as much carbon dioxide as a coal-fired power station for the same amount of electricity generated.

The reservoirs created for hydroelectric power stations can also pollute the atmosphere. Carbon dioxide and methane are released for a while after the land is first flooded, as plants die and rot.

Science skills

New wind farms or other renewable resources need planning permission. Which of the possible objections on these pages are likely to be based on:

a Scientific evidence?

b Opinion?

Route to A*

If you are asked to compare different ways of doing things, such as in question 8, try to consider all the possible factors. For example, large rivers may already have roads nearby, whereas building a new dam in the hills might also involve building access roads so that construction and maintenance machinery and materials can be taken to the dam.

Questions

1. Why are some people more concerned about the visual impact of wind turbines than power stations?
2. Some wind farms are built in the sea. What problems could this cause?
3. What effects might wind turbines on land have on: (a) wildlife? (b) farming?
4. What effects could the growing of biofuel crops have on the environment?
5. What effects might a tidal barrage have on scenery, shipping and wildlife?
6. Suggest how a wave power generator (see the photograph in P1 4.3) might affect the environment.
7. Tidal power could be obtained using tidal stream turbines or by building a barrage across an estuary. Explain which option will: (a) have the greatest effect on wildlife; (b) be the most expensive to build; (c) be the most expensive to maintain.
8. Hydroelectric power stations can be built next to dams on rivers, or a dam can be built in the hills to make a new reservoir. Compare the advantages and disadvantages of these two options.

P1 4.5 Electricity distribution and voltage

Learning objectives
- describe how electricity is distributed from power stations to consumers
- explain why transformers are used in the National Grid
- explain why electricity is transmitted at very high voltages when distributed through the National Grid
- evaluate the advantages and disadvantages of overhead power lines and underground cables.

The National Grid

All power stations and almost all users of electricity are connected by a system of wires and cables called the **National Grid**. This allows electricity to be distributed to most parts of the UK.

Electricity passing through a wire will heat it up. The warming of the **transmission lines** in the National Grid is wasted energy. If the **voltage** of the electricity is increased, the current will be lower so less energy is wasted. Figure 1 shows the different voltages used in the National Grid.

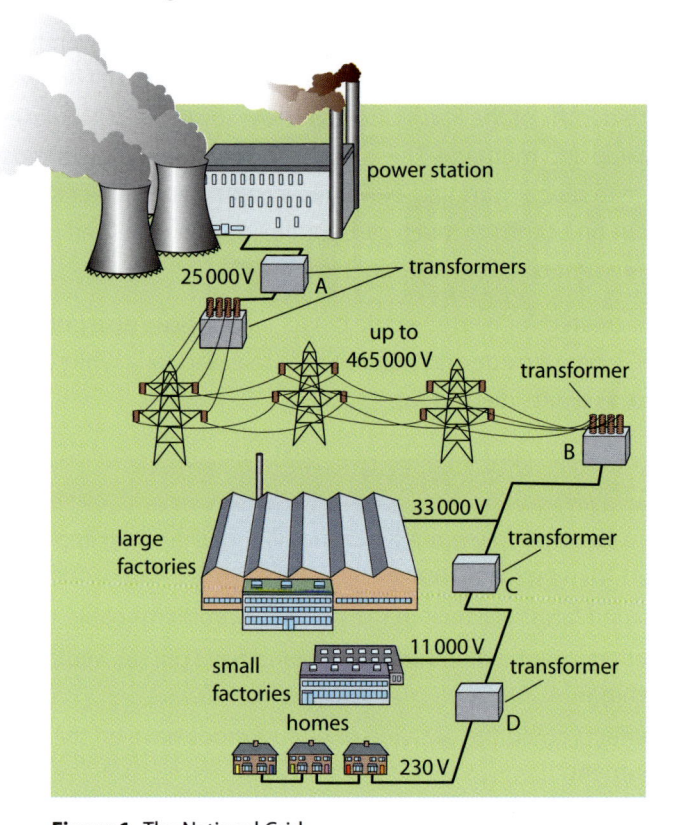

Figure 1 The National Grid.

Transformers

Voltage is changed using **transformers**. A **step-up transformer** increases the voltage and reduces the current. A **step-down transformer** makes the voltage lower but increases the current.

The relationship between power, voltage and current is given by the equation below.

$$P = V \times I$$
$$\text{power} = \text{voltage} \times \text{current}$$
$$\text{(watts, W)} \quad \text{(volts, V)} \quad \text{(amps, A)}$$

If a transformer doubles the voltage, the current is halved.
This means that the power stays the same, as long as no energy is wasted in the transformer.

Science skills

A student used a **resistor** as a model of transmission lines. The table shows the results of an experiment to measure the energy transferred in the resistor with different currents.

Current/A	Power/W
0.0	0.0
0.2	0.2
0.4	0.8
0.6	1.8
0.8	3.2
1.0	5.0
1.2	7.2
1.4	9.8
1.6	12.8
1.8	16.2
2.0	20.0

a Plot a graph to show this data.

b Write a conclusion for the investigation.

Renewable resources and the National Grid

The National Grid allows electricity to be distributed to most places in the UK. It was set up when most of our electricity was generated in a relatively small number of big power stations. Today there are a lot more, smaller sources of electricity, such as wind farms and hydroelectric power stations. These all need to be connected to the National Grid if they are to be useful. However, sometimes this can cost more than it is worth for the amount of electricity produced.

Overground or underground?

Most of the transmission lines in the National Grid are suspended from pylons. These wires do not have to be insulated. They can be damaged by lightning, high winds or icy weather. However, it is easy to find and repair damaged sections of power line.

Underground cables can be used in scenic areas, where rows of pylons would spoil the view. Underground cables are less easily damaged by severe weather. However they need to be well insulated, they are more expensive to install, and finding and repairing faults is more difficult and takes longer.

This house has its own small hydroelectricity supply from a nearby river. However, it would cost too much to connect it to the National Grid, so the owner cannot sell any spare electricity.

Science skills

New wind farms are being built in the north west of Scotland, and the transmission lines shown in the photograph need to be upgraded. The plan is to replace the pylons with much bigger ones. These pylons are very close to the Cairngorms National Park. Protesters say that the new transmission lines should be buried.

c Who should make the decision about what sort of new power lines are installed?

d Who should pay the extra cost if underground cables are installed?

The pylons in this photograph carry electricity south from power stations in the north of Scotland.

Questions

1. Why is the voltage increased before electricity is sent through the National Grid?
2. Why is the voltage then reduced before electricity is supplied to homes?
3. Look at Figure 1. The transformers are labelled A–D. For each transformer, say whether it is a step-up or step-down transformer.
4. Which of these electricity supplies provides the most power: 2 A at 230 V or 18 A at 20 V? Explain your answer.
5. A step-down transformer halves the voltages of the electricity supplies in question 4. What will the new currents be?
6. An advert for solar cells claims that any electricity that the homeowner does not use can be sold to the National Grid. Explain why this claim is not entirely correct.
7. What are the advantages and disadvantages of burying power cables underground?
8. Explain why the following statement is partly correct and partly incorrect: 'A step-up transformer increases the energy provided by the electricity supply.' Use data from Figure 1 to support your answer.

Generating electricity 41

P1 4.6

Meeting the demand

Learning objectives
- describe some of the ways in which the electricity supply can be matched to the demand
- know that different power stations have different start-up times.

The demand for electricity

The demand for electricity changes during the day and also during the year. Figure 1 shows some typical examples.

The demand also changes from minute to minute. If there is a popular programme on TV, millions of people sit down to watch it and the overall demand for electricity falls. At half-time in a football match, or when the adverts come on, thousands (or even millions) of people get up and switch on lights or kettles, and the demand can shoot up by over 2 MW within a minute or two. This sudden change is called a **TV pick-up**.

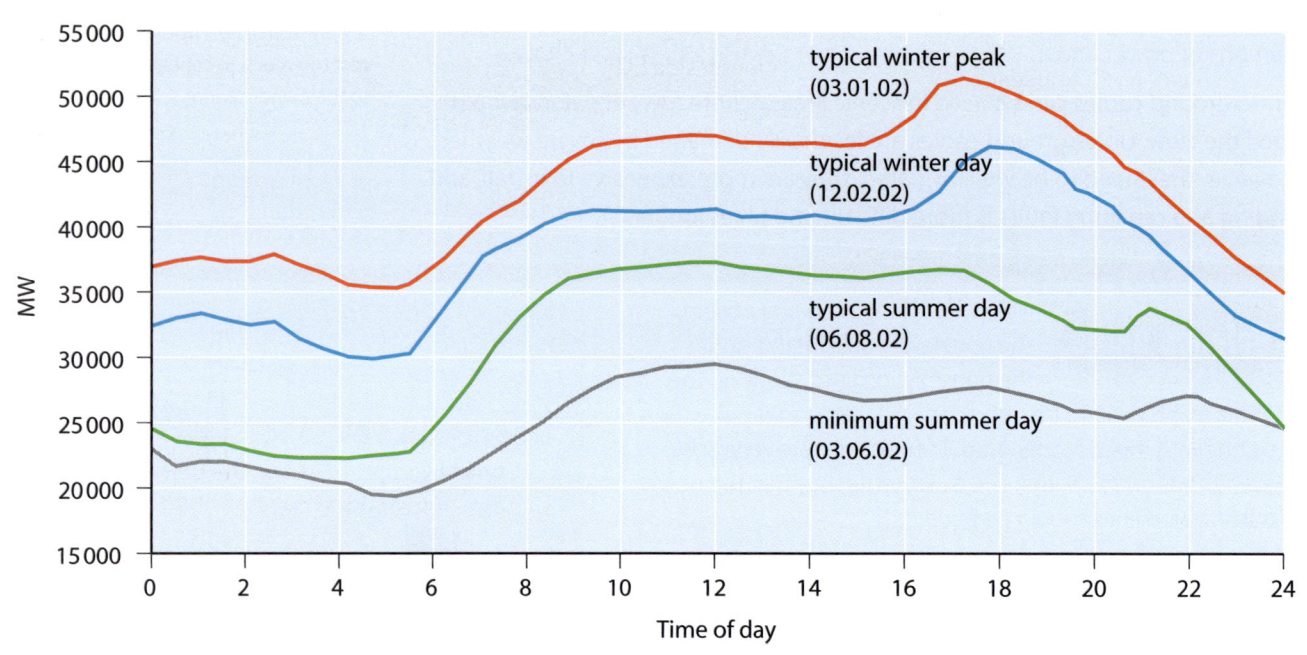

Figure 1 A comparison of the electricity demand through the day in summer and in winter.

Power engineers need to predict these changes because it is not easy to suddenly increase the amount of energy generated. It can take hours to start up a power station from cold, although gas-fired power stations can start up more quickly than coal-fired ones. Power stations are often kept running below their full generating capacity. This can waste some energy but it means that the amount of electricity generated can be increased within minutes instead of hours.

Hydroelectric power stations are very useful because they can start producing their maximum amount of electricity within a minute. Supplying enough electricity will be even more complicated when more renewable resources are used. Many sources of renewable energy are not **reliable**. This means they are only available some of the time, and we cannot always predict when they will be available.

Pumped storage

Power stations run more efficiently when they are generating their maximum amount of electricity, so sometimes more electricity is being generated than is needed. Some of this energy can be stored using a pumped-storage power station (see Figure 2).

Taking it further

Potential energy is calculated using the formula $E_p = m \times g \times h$, where E_p is the potential energy, m is the mass, g is the acceleration due to gravity and h is the height above a datum level. Can you use this equation to explain why a hydroelectric power station generates more electricity per cubic metre of water than a tidal power barrage, and why a tidal barrage has to trap a much larger volume of water than a hydroelectric dam?

When there is plenty of electricity being generated, the turbines act as pumps and pump water into the top reservoir.

upper reservoir

When there is a sudden demand for electricity, water runs down the pipes and drives turbines and generators.

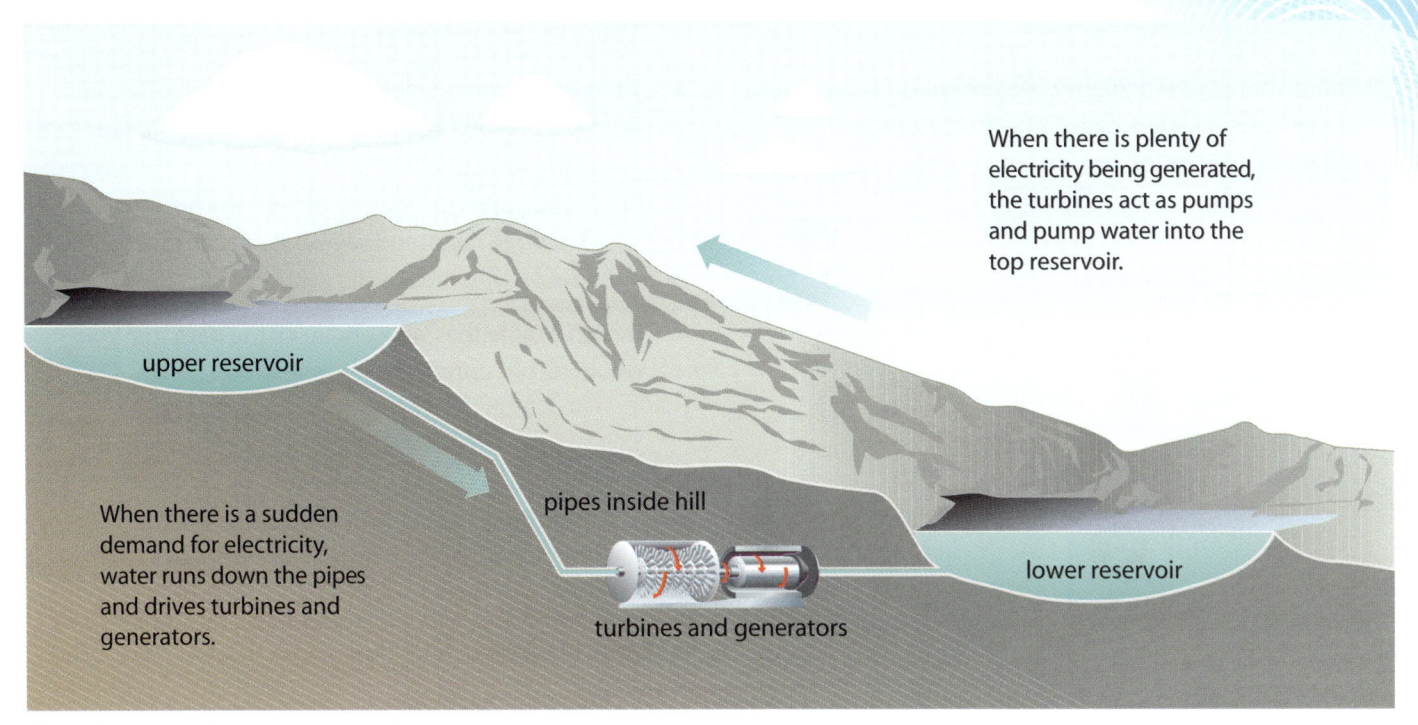

pipes inside hill

turbines and generators

lower reservoir

Figure 2 A pumped-storage power station.

Electricity tariffs

An electricity **tariff** is the amount that customers pay for electricity. Electricity companies try to reduce the demand for electricity during the day by increasing the price. Customers on tariffs such as 'Economy 7' pay a lower price for electricity used during seven hours overnight. Storage heaters (see lesson P1 1.7) heat up during the night because this is when cheap electricity is available.

Recharging an electric car at home could almost double the amount of electricity a home uses. Electricity companies are developing 'smart' controllers that only let electric cars recharge when there is enough supply available.

Electric cars will be recharged from the mains supply.

Questions

1. Look at Figure 1. Explain the demand for electricity on a typical winter day.

2. **(a)** Why is there a peak in demand in the early evening in winter but not in summer? **(b)** Why is there more demand for electricity in winter than in summer?

3. **(a)** Why do power engineers need to know what weather is forecast for the next few hours? **(b)** Why do they sometimes need to know what the TV schedules are?

4. Why can't power engineers just use hydroelectricity to meet sudden demands? (*Hint:* you may need to look back at Lesson P1 4.1.)

5. Other than hydroelectricity, which renewable resources are available at predictable times?

6. When might wind power be available but not solar power?

7. Look at Figure 1. Explain when a pumped-storage power station would be: **(a)** pumping water up to the top reservoir; **(b)** generating electricity.

8. Explain why electricity is often cheaper to use from about 11 pm to 6 am.

Generating electricity   43

ISA practice: keeping drinks hot

Hot drinks are placed in many different types of containers. You have been asked to investigate the best type of container to keep drinks hot.

The four different drinks containers: a glass, a ceramic mug, an insulated mug and a plastic mug.

Your task is to investigate four different cups to find out which one keeps a drink hot for longest.

Hypothesis
It is suggested that there is a link between the material used in the cup and the time it takes for a drink to cool.

Section 1

1. In this investigation you will need to control some of the variables.
   (a) Name one variable you will need to control in this investigation. *(1 mark)*
   (b) Describe briefly how you would carry out a preliminary investigation to find a suitable value to use for this variable. Explain how the results will help you decide on the best value for this variable. *(2 marks)*

2. Describe how you would carry out the investigation. You should include:
   - the equipment that you would use
   - how you would use the equipment
   - the measurements that you would make
   - how you would make it a fair test.

   You may include a labelled diagram to help you to explain your method.

   In this question you will be assessed on using good English, organising information clearly and using specialist terms where appropriate. *(6 marks)*

3. Think about the possible hazards in the investigation.
   (a) Describe one hazard that you think may be present in the investigation. *(1 mark)*
   (b) Identify the risk associated with the hazard you described in (a), and say what control measures you could use to reduce the risk. *(2 marks)*

4. Design a table that will contain all the data that you would record during the investigation. *(2 marks)*

Total for Section 1: 14 marks

Section 2
A group of students, Study Group 1, carried out an investigation into the hypothesis. The students used the same volume of hot water in each container. They only had time to test the glass and the ceramic mug when they started their investigation. They tested the other mugs the next day.

Figure 1 shows the results they obtained.

Time (min)	Glass container temp (°C)	Ceramic mug temp (°C)	Metal mug temp (°C)	Plastic foam mug temp (°C)
0	85	85	85	85
1	83	81	81	82
2	82	79	79	80
3	80	76	76	78
4	78	74	74	77
5	76	72	71	75
6	75	70	69	73
7	73	69	67	72
8	72	66	65	71
9	71	65	64	69
10	69	63	60	67

Figure 1 Results for Study Group 1.

5. (a) (i) What is the independent variable in this investigation?
       (ii) What is the dependent variable in this investigation?
       (iii) Name one control variable this investigation. *(3 marks)*
   (b) Plot a graph to show the link between the type of cup and the temperature loss. *(4 marks)*
   (c) Do the results support the hypothesis? Explain your answer. *(3 marks)*

Below are the results from three other study groups. Table 1 shows the results from another group of students, Study Group 2.

Table 1 Results from Study Group 2.

Type of cup	Temperature/°C		Change of temperature/°C
	At the start	After ten minutes	
glass	80	64	16
ceramic	80	58	22
metal	80	56	24
plastic foam	80	63	17

Table 2 shows the results of a third group of students, Study Group 3. Figure 2 is a graph produced by Study Group 4, a group of scientists in a research laboratory. The scientists used metal mugs of four different sizes and investigated how long each mug took to cool down after being filled with hot water.

Table 2 Results from Study Group 3.

Type of cup	Change of temperature after 15 minutes/°C			
	Test 1	Test 2	Test 3	Mean
glass	22	23	20	22
ceramic	31	30	29	30
metal	34	35	32	34
plastic foam	22	31	20	24

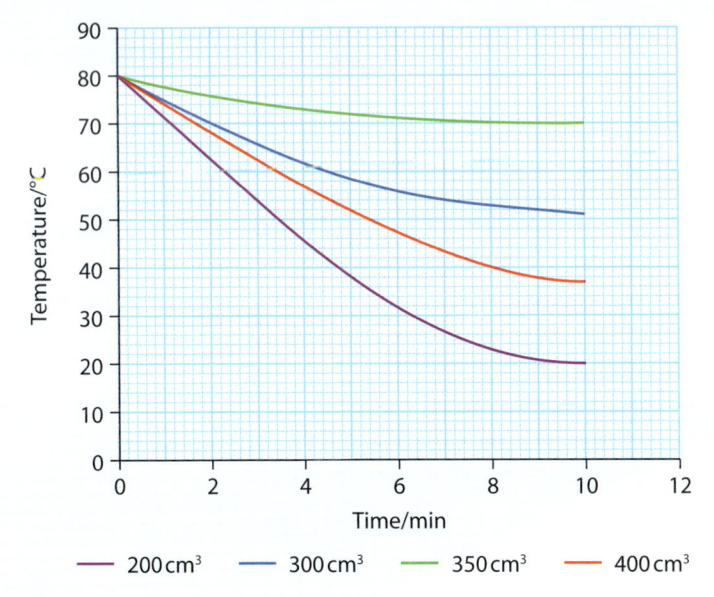

Figure 2 Study Group 4's results.

6 Describe one way in which the results of Study Group 2 are similar to or different from those of Study Group 1, and give one reason why the results are similar or different.
(3 marks)

7 (a) Draw a sketch graph or chart of the results from Study Group 2. *(3 marks)*
 (b) Does the data support the hypothesis being investigated? To gain full marks you should use all of the relevant data from Study Groups 1, 2 and 3 to explain whether or not the data supports the hypothesis. *(3 marks)*
 (c) The data from the other groups only gives a limited amount of information. What other information or data would you need in order to be more certain as to whether or not the hypothesis is correct? Explain the reason for your answer. *(3 marks)*
 (d) Use the results of Study Groups 2, 3 and 4 to answer this question. What is the relationship between the material of the drinks container and the length of time the drink remains hot?
 How well does the data support your answer?
(3 marks)

8 Look back at the investigation method used by Study Group 1. If you could repeat the investigation, suggest one change that you would make to the method, and explain the reason for the change. *(3 marks)*

9 A company wants to make drinks containers that will lose no more than 20 °C in 10 minutes. How could the results of this investigation help the company to decide on the best size and material for the drinks container?
(3 marks)

Total for Section 2: 31 marks
Total for the ISA: 45 marks

Assess yourself questions

1. Which of these statements apply to using biofuels to generate electricity? Select two answers. *(2 marks)*
   - A They can be burnt in power stations in a similar way to fossil fuels.
   - B They do not produce any carbon dioxide when they burn.
   - C Burning biofuels adds less carbon dioxide to the air overall than burning fossil fuels.
   - D Burning biofuels in a power station does not add any carbon dioxide to the air overall.
   - E The carbon contained in biofuels was taken out of the atmosphere by respiration when the plants grew.

2. A TV uses 90 W of power when it is switched on. Electricity costs 16.5p per Unit.
   - (a) What is 90 W in kW? *(1 mark)*
   - (b) How much energy (in kWh) does the TV use in six hours? *(2 marks)*
   - (c) How much does this electricity cost? *(1 mark)*
   - (d) Why should you switch a TV off when it is not being used, instead of putting it on standby? *(1 mark)*

3. (a) Write down two disadvantages of using energy from uranium to generate electricity. *(2 marks)*
   (b) Write down two advantages of using uranium. *(2 marks)*

4. (a) What is a TV pick-up? *(2 marks)*
   (b) Why do power engineers need to use weather forecasts? *(2 marks)*
   (c) Which kind of power station can start generating in the shortest time if there is an increase in demand? *(1 mark)*

5. Write down one energy resource that matches each of these descriptions.
   - (a) Available at any time. *(1 mark)*
   - (b) Produces carbon dioxide. *(1 mark)*
   - (c) Availability depends on the weather. *(1 mark)*
   - (d) Available at predictable times, but not all the time. *(1 mark)*

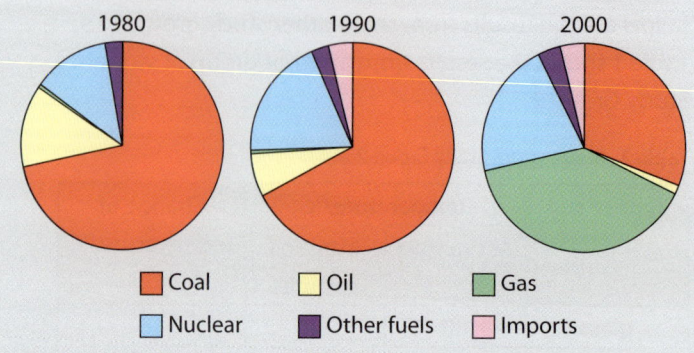

Figure 1 Pie charts of energy resources used to generate electricity.

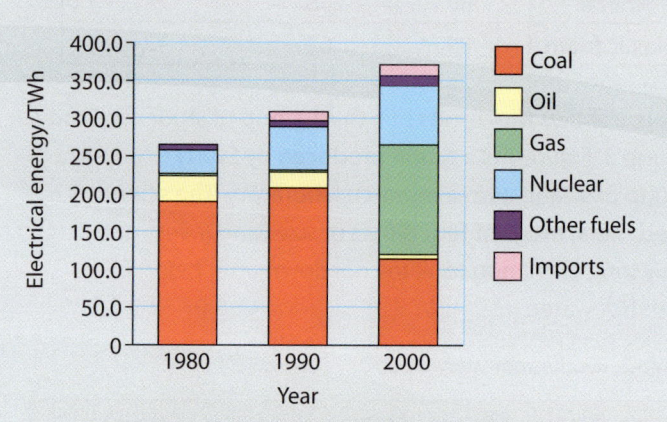

Figure 2 Bar charts of energy resources used to generate electricity.

6. Figures 1 and 2 use two types of chart to show the different energy resources used to generate electricity in the UK in three separate years.
   - (a) What information does Figure 2 provide that Figure 1 does not? *(1 mark)*
   - (b) Describe three changes between the energy resources used in 1980 and in 2000. *(3 marks)*
   - (c) Suggest reasons for these changes. *(3 marks)*

7. Eilean Dubh is a small island off the coast of Scotland, with no mains electricity supply. There are only a few houses on the island, and their total energy use averages 30 000 kWh per year.

   The islanders currently use a diesel generator to provide their electricity. This costs 20p for every kilowatt hour of electricity generated.

   They are considering investing in a renewable source of energy. Some details about two alternative energy sources are shown in the table below.

	Capital cost	Maximum output/kW
wind turbine	£25 000	6.0
solar cells	£40 000	7.5

   (a) What is the maximum possible output of the wind turbine over one year in kWh? *(3 marks)*

(b) The wind turbines are likely to produce only about one-third of this amount. Why is this? *(2 marks)*

(c) If the solar cells generate about 7000 kWh per year, and last for 20 years, how much will each Unit of electricity cost? *(5 marks)*

(d) The electricity from the wind turbine is likely to cost about 13p per unit. Other than cost, suggest what advantage the wind turbine has over the solar cells. *(1 mark)*

(e) If the islanders could get all their electricity from the wind turbine, what would be the payback time for installing the turbine? *(4 marks)*

8 (a) Give two reasons why using a microwave oven instead of a conventional oven can help to reduce the amount of energy used. *(2 marks)*

(b) How can homeowners make sure they buy the most efficient appliances? *(1 mark)*

9 A ready meal takes an hour to cook in a 3 kW conventional oven. The same meal can be cooked in 15 minutes in a microwave oven. The oven uses 850 W to cook food.

(a) Electricity costs 14p per unit. How much does it cost to cook the meal in the conventional oven? *(3 marks)*

(b) How much money does a homeowner save if he uses the microwave oven to cook the same meal? *(3 marks)*

(c) A cheap microwave oven costs £50. The homeowner has meals like this about twice a week. What is the payback time for the microwave oven? *(2 marks)*

10 Here are some opinions about hydroelectricity.

A Hydroelectric power stations do not contribute to global warming.

B Hydroelectric power stations are useful because they can start and stop quickly.

C Pumped storage power stations can store electricity.

(a) (i) Suggest why most people would think that statement A is correct. *(1 mark)*

(ii) Explain why it is not quite correct. *(1 mark)*

(b) (i) How does the start-up time of a hydroelectric power station compare to that of a gas-fired and a coal-fired power station? *(1 mark)*

(ii) Why is it useful to have some power stations that can start up quickly? *(2 marks)*

(c) Describe two differences between a pumped storage power station and a normal hydroelectric power station. *(2 marks)*

(d) In what form is energy stored in a hydroelectric power station? *(1 mark)*

(e) At what time of day is a pumped storage power station usually storing energy? Explain your answer *(4 marks)*

(f) Explain why opinion C is not correct. *(1 mark)*

11 (a) What does a transformer do? *(1 mark)*

(b) Explain the difference between a step-up and a step-down transformer. *(1 mark)*

(c) What is the National Grid? *(1 mark)*

(d) Explain why the National Grid is needed, instead of just connecting each town only to its nearest power station. *(3 marks)*

(e) Why is electricity transmitted around the country at very high voltages? *(1 mark)*

12 It costs £9000 to install a set of solar cells in the roof of a house. The suppliers of the solar cells say that the owners should be able to sell approximately £630 of electricity to the grid each year. What is the payback time for the solar cells? *(3 marks)*

13 Renewable energy resources can have environmental effects. Give one possible environmental effect of each of the following resources.

(a) Hydroelectricity. *(1 mark)*

(b) Wind power. *(1 mark)*

(c) Tidal power. *(1 mark)*

(d) Biofuels. *(1 mark)*

14 Many people think that biofuels do not add carbon dioxide to the atmosphere.

(a) Explain why they think this. *(2 marks)*

(b) Explain why this idea is not usually correct. *(3 marks)*

15 Carbon dioxide and sulfur dioxide can both be emitted when fossil fuels are burnt.

(a) Name one environmental effect of each of these pollutants. *(2 marks)*

(b) Describe how the emissions of these pollutants can be reduced. *(2 marks)*

16 Most people who own gardens use a powered mower to cut their lawns.

(a) Suggest two advantages of a petrol-engined mower compared to a mower with an electric motor. *(2 marks)*

(b) Suggest two disadvantages. *(2 marks)*

GradeStudio Route to A*

Here are three students' answers to the following question:

Solar Impulse is a solar-powered plane. It has the same wingspan as the Airbus 340 passenger plane and the same mass as a family car. *Solar Impulse* has 12 000 solar cells mounted on its wings to power its four engines. It also has rechargeable batteries.

In July 2010, *Solar Impulse* flew continuously for 26 hours, carrying just the pilot. It reached a speed of 70 km per hour.

Outline the advantages and disadvantages of using a solar-powered plane rather than an Airbus 340 to carry passengers.

In this question you will be assessed on using good English, organising information clearly and using specialist terms where appropriate.

(6 marks)

Read the three different answers together with the examiner comments. Then check what you have learnt and try putting it into practice in any further questions you answer.

B Grade answer

Student 1

A solar-powered plane uses energy from the Sun. It doesn't carry fuel. It weighs less than a normal passenger plane. The solar cells power the engines and recharge the batteries. No gases are given off.

- It is better to say 'carbon dioxide'.
- The correct scientific word is 'emitted'.

Examiner comment

This candidate has lifted information from the question but has not really developed it. They have outlined one or two advantages but have given no disadvantages. They have not stated that a renewable energy source is used. The significance of a 26-hour flight has been missed.

A Grade answer

Student 2

A better answer would explain the advantages of this fact.

The solar-powered plane uses a renewable energy source. In flight no carbon dioxide is emitted. Although the plane has a small mass, it only carries one person, but the Airbus has a crew and lots of passengers. The Solar Impulse has a lower speed than the Airbus.

A better answer would point out that journey times are therefore longer.

Examiner comment

This candidate has mentioned that the energy source is renewable. They have also mentioned that the polluting gas is carbon dioxide. Disadvantages of the solar plane are included, as the question requires. Two points are mentioned that could be developed further for a better answer. This candidate has also failed to mention the significance of a 26-hour flight.

AIM HIGH
FOR THE TOP GRADES

A* Grade answer

> The solar-powered plane uses energy from the Sun, which is a renewable energy source. The Airbus uses a fossil fuel, which, when ignited, emits carbon dioxide – a greenhouse gas that contributes to global warming.
>
> The solar cells use energy from the Sun to power the engines and to charge the batteries so that the batteries can be used to power the plane when it is dark. Solar cells are inefficient, so Solar Impulse needs 12 000 of them. The plane only carries one person so imagine the number of solar cells that would be needed to power a plane carrying hundreds of passengers.
>
> Solar Impulse is much slower than an Airbus, so journey times would be longer, which would not be good for the passengers. Although Solar Impulse is more environmentally friendly than Airbus and wouldn't use up non-renewable fossil fuel, it is not a practical option for carrying large numbers of passengers.

- Answer includes the environmental consequence of using aviation fuel.
- The candidate has picked up on the significance of a 26-hour flight.
- A good summarising sentence.

Examiner comment

This candidate has covered the main advantages and disadvantages of the solar-powered plane over an Airbus 340. They recognise that the energy source is renewable and that flying the plane does not contribute to global warming. They realise the significance of a 26-hour flight and that the batteries need to be charged during daylight hours so that they can power the plane during darkness. They have recognised the practical difficulties: the need for vast numbers of solar cells to make a plane carrying hundreds of passengers airborne, and the longer journey times because of a lower speed. The answer is completed with a succinct summary.

MOVING UP THE GRADES

- Read the information in the question very carefully.
- Make sure you know what you are being asked to do.
- The question is worth 6 marks and your use of language and grammar is important, so remember to check your spelling.
- Jot down the points as they occur to you.
- BUT organise the points into a logical order before starting your answer.

P1 Waves and the Universe

Information reaches our eyes and ears through light and sound, and both of these behave as waves. In chapter 5 you will find out about wave behaviour. Not just water waves, although they are useful because they are easy to see, but also different waves including light, other electromagnetic waves, and sound.

As well as using sound waves to communicate with those close to us, we can use electromagnetic waves for TV, radio and mobile phones. This allows us to communicate with people everywhere, including on the other side of the world or even in space. Different electromagnetic waves have different properties, and you will find out about some of these and how these properties make them suitable, or unsuitable, for communications.

In 1835, a French philosopher, Auguste Comte, said that the stars were so far away that we would never be able to find out what they were made of. Yet less than half a century later, scientists had discovered that the light and other electromagnetic waves from the stars carry information about their chemical composition. The waves also carry information about how the galaxies are moving and how far away they are. In chapter 6 you will find out how this information is carried, and the theories scientists now have, as a result of this evidence, about the beginning of the Universe.

Test yourself

1. How are sounds made?
2. Draw a diagram of a lamp and an eye. Draw rays to show how light from the lamp reaches the eye.
3. What do we call materials that (a) transmit light? (b) absorb light?
4. What colours are in the spectrum of white light?
5. Explain which of these are stars: (a) Venus; (b) the Sun; (c) Halley's comet; (d) Pluto; (e) the Pole Star.

Objectives

By the end of this unit you should be able to:
- explain how transverse and longitudinal waves behave
- explain, and draw diagrams showing, reflection, refraction and diffraction
- interpret wavelength and frequency data to identify types of electromagnetic waves
- explain how radio waves, microwaves, infrared and visible light are used for communications
- explain the Doppler effect and red shift
- explain the Big Bang theory of the Universe.

P1 5.1 What is a wave?

Learning objectives
- describe transverse and longitudinal waves
- draw diagrams of transverse and longitudinal waves
- explain that a wave transfers energy but the medium does not move
- analyse data on wave speeds.

Describing a wave

An **oscillation** is a repeated pattern of movement, which could be backwards and forwards, side to side, or up and down. A **wave** is an oscillation that travels from one place to another. Most waves travel through some material, called the **medium.** The medium does not move but the oscillations pass through it. For example, a cork bobbing up and down on the waves is not carried along by the waves – it just goes up and down. Energy is transferred by the wave and if the oscillations are bigger, or faster, more energy will usually be transferred. The energy of the water waves in the photograph is enough to erode the rocks.

Longitudinal and transverse waves

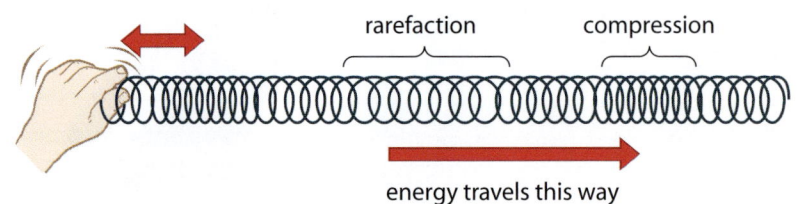

Figure 1a Waves in a spring can be longitudinal…

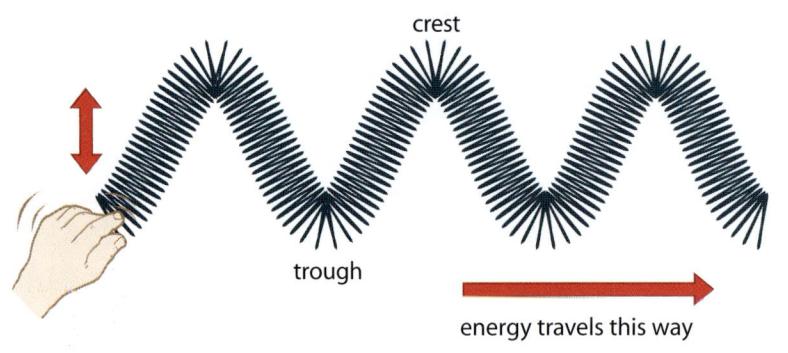

Figure 1b …or transverse.

Storm waves pounding rocks.

Figure 1 shows how waves can be sent along a slinky spring in two different ways. In Figure 1a the spring has been pushed forward and pulled back and pulses are travelling along it so that the coils squash together, in a **compression**, and spread out, in a **rarefaction**. This type of wave is called a **longitudinal wave**. The oscillations are parallel to the direction of energy transfer.

In Figure 1b the spring has been moved to one side and then the other, causing a **crest** and a **trough** to travel along the spring. This type of wave is called a **transverse wave**. The oscillations are perpendicular to the direction of energy transfer.

Examiner feedback

In an examination you must be able to explain the differences between longitudinal and transverse waves.

Examples of mechanical waves

The waves in the spring are examples of **mechanical waves**, which can be transverse or longitudinal and travel through solids, liquids or gases. Water waves and the waves in the rope in Figure 2 are transverse waves.

A **shock wave** is caused by an explosion or similar event like an earthquake. They transfer a lot of energy and move very fast. Shock waves through the air are longitudinal. However, those that travel through the solid Earth can be transverse or longitudinal.

Sound waves

Sound waves are always longitudinal waves. They need a medium to travel through and so cannot travel through a vacuum, or we would hear the Sun. Sound can travel through solids, liquids and gases.

Electromagnetic waves

Electromagnetic waves include visible light and range from **radio waves**, which have the least energy, to **gamma rays** with the most. They can all travel in a **vacuum** and through space. Scientists spent many years trying to decide how light travelled through a vacuum. Now they know that all electromagnetic waves behave as transverse waves – oscillations of an electric and a magnetic field.

Figure 2 Moving your hand up and down sends waves along the rope.

Science skills

The table shows the speed of longitudinal shock waves through some different rocks.

Rock	Wave speed m/s
granite	5700
basalt	6400
limestone	6000
sandstone	2900
sand	1500
clay	1800

a Which variable is the independent variable?
b What type of variable is:
i the rock type?
ii the wave speed?
c What is the range of wave speeds in these rocks?
d Plot a graph of this data.
e What is the mean value of the wave speed?

Science in action

The seismometer

The seismometer is a sensitive instrument used to detect shock waves travelling through the Earth. Early seismometers looked like the one above. It is placed in the basement of a building, on solid ground, away from traffic and other vibrations. It picks up transverse and longitudinal waves caused by explosions or earthquakes. The longitudinal waves travel faster and arrive first. The further away the earthquake, the longer the delay before the transverse waves arrive. The delay is used to calculate the distance to the earthquake. Using distances from three seismometers in different locations scientists can work out the exact position of the earthquake.

Questions

1. Give an example of: **(a)** a longitudinal wave; **(b)** a transverse wave.
2. How are transverse and longitudinal waves different?
3. Explain what is meant by the words 'compression' and 'rarefaction'.
4. Explain what is meant by the words 'crest' and 'trough'.
5. After an explosion all the windows in a nearby building are broken. How did this happen?
6. Describe and explain the similarities and differences between sound waves and light waves.

P1 5.2 Measuring waves

Learning objectives
- draw a diagram to show the amplitude and wavelength of a wave
- calculate the speed of a wave given its frequency and wavelength
- analyse data relating wave speed to depth of water.

Wavelength
Figure 1 shows a transverse wave. You can see that the pattern repeats. One complete wave is called a **cycle**. The length of one complete wave is called the **wavelength**. It is the distance from any point on the wave to the place where the pattern repeats. The same is true for a longitudinal wave, as shown in Figure 2.

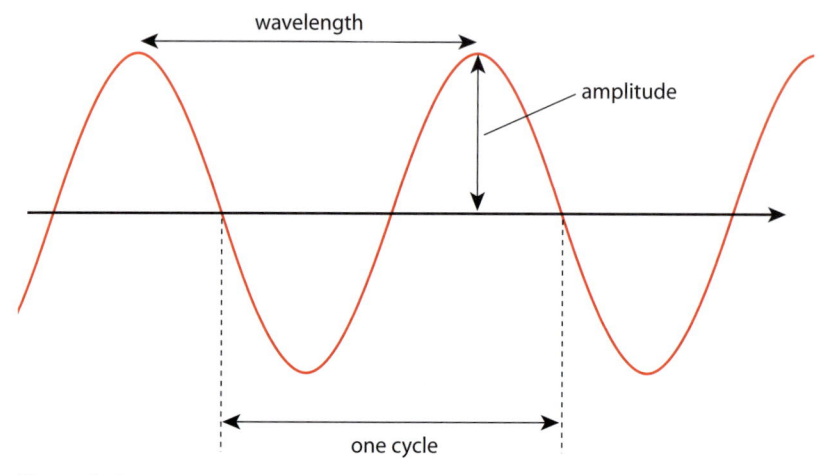

Figure 1 A transverse wave.

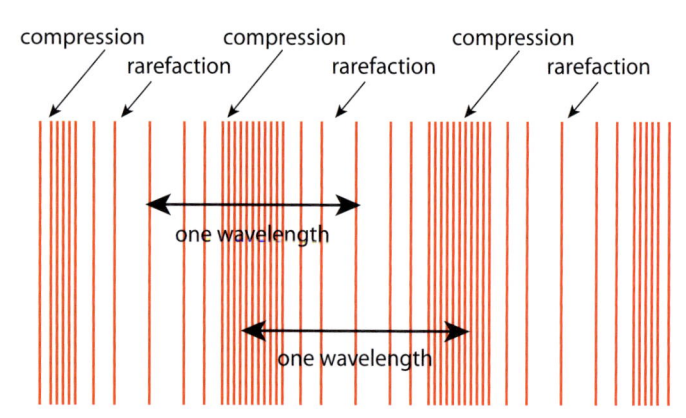

Figure 2 A longitudinal wave.

Amplitude
The **amplitude** is the maximum displacement (the height of a crest or the depth of a trough) that a point moves away from its position when there is no wave.

Frequency
Frequency is the number of cycles passing a point in one second. This depends on the source of the waves. If you are making waves in a spring, moving your hand faster increases the frequency of the waves. The unit 'one cycle per second' is called one **hertz**, Hz.

Wave speed
The wave speed depends on the medium. For example, light travels faster in a vacuum than it does through glass. In Figure 3 waves are being sent along a rope. The girl can't make the waves go faster by waving her hand faster – she just makes more, smaller waves.

Figure 3 Wave speed doesn't change when frequency is increased.

Examiner feedback
One common mistake is to take one wavelength as the distance between the two points either side of a crest, or a trough, of a wave. However, this is only half a wavelength. Another mistake is to take the amplitude as the distance between a crest and a trough; this is twice the amplitude.

The wave equation

For all waves, there is a relationship between the frequency, the wavelength and the wave speed.

$$v = f \times \lambda$$

wave speed = frequency × wavelength
(metres per second, m/s)　(hertz, Hz)　(metres, m)

As the frequency is increased more waves travel away from the source, but if the medium is the same, the speed is unchanged, so the wavelength is shorter.

Science skills

To find out how the speed of water waves changes with the depth of the water, some scientists measured the speed of waves in a tank of water. They changed the depth by adding more water. They made the waves by dipping a metal bar in the water at a regular rate of 2 Hz.

a In this experiment what is:
  i the dependent variable
  ii the independent variable
  iii a variable that is kept the same?

b Plot a graph to show how the wave speed changes with the depth of water.

c Are there any anomalous points? If so, which points are anomalous?

d A student says: 'The speed of waves is proportional to the depth of the water.' Explain whether you agree.

e Suggest how the students could have measured:
  i the depth
  ii the speed.

Depth of water/cm	Speed of waves / cm/s
0	0
1	30
2	45
3	55
4	62
5	63
6	77
8	89
10	99

Examiner feedback

In calculations you may have to rearrange the equation, and change units from, for example, centimetres to metres. Take care and read the question carefully.

Example 1

A radio wave has a frequency of 200 000 Hz and a wavelength of 1500 m.
What is its speed?

speed = frequency × wavelength
speed = 200 000 Hz × 1500 m
speed = 300 000 000 m/s.

Example 2

Water waves are travelling at 10 m/s and one reaches the beach every five seconds. What is their wavelength?

1 wave in 5 s = 1 ÷ 5 waves in 1 s
frequency = $\frac{1}{5}$ s = 0.2 Hz

wavelength = $\frac{\text{wave speed}}{\text{frequency}}$

wavelength = $\frac{10 \text{ m/s}}{0.2 \text{ Hz}}$

wavelength = 50 m.

Questions

1. Ten waves pass a point on a rope in 4 s. What is their frequency?
2. Five waves measure 25 cm and pass a point in 1 s. What is: **(a)** the wavelength? **(b)** the frequency?
3. Waves in a spring have a frequency of 8 Hz and a travel at a speed of 4 m/s. What is their wavelength?
4. Light waves have a wavelength of 0.0000005 m and a frequency of 600 000 000 000 000 Hz. What is the speed of light?
5. Water waves with wavelength 1.5 cm travel across a tank at 0.021 m/s. What is their frequency?
6. If the frequency of waves is doubled what happens to: **(a)** the wave speed? **(b)** the wavelength?
7. Longitudinal waves travel through steel at 6000 m/s. If the frequency is 2000 Hz what is the distance between the centre of a compression and the centre of a rarefaction?
8. Draw a diagram of a transverse wave and use it to explain what is meant by the wavelength, amplitude, frequency and wave speed of a wave, and the units each of these are measured in.

Waves

P1 5.3 Wave behaviour

Learning objectives
- explain that waves can be reflected, refracted and diffracted
- explain why some waves are diffracted more than others
- draw diagrams of waves being refracted, reflected and diffracted.

Studying waves
When waves are **transmitted**, for example light passing through glass, they are travelling through a **medium**. In some materials the energy of some waves is **absorbed** so the waves die away. For example, sound waves are not transmitted through thick foam. The energy is transferred to the foam which heats up slightly.

All waves can be **reflected, refracted** and **diffracted**. These different kinds of wave behaviour are easy to see with water waves.

Science skills
A **ripple tank** is a shallow tank of water with a glass bottom and a light over the top. This casts shadows of the waves on the screen under the tank. To prevent waves from reflecting off the sides they are gently sloping and made of a material that absorbs energy. A small dipper oscillates to make the waves. You can experiment with one or two wave sources making circular waves, or a long flat dipper to make plane waves.

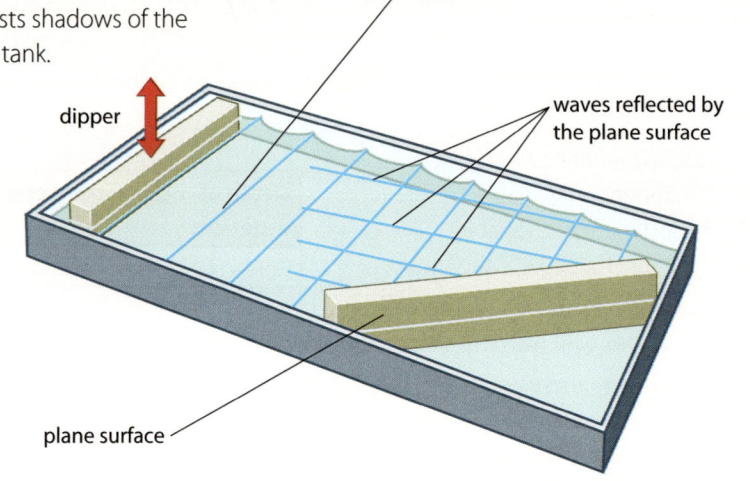

Figure 1 A ripple tank used to produce plane waves.

Reflection
When waves strike an interface (boundary) between materials, instead of being absorbed or transmitted, they may be **reflected**. Figure 2 shows plane (flat) waves being reflected by a barrier. Three lines are drawn to show what happens to the direction of the wave. The first is a perpendicular line, called the **normal**, crossing the barrier. The other two (arrowed lines) show the direction of the waves and are perpendicular to the **incident** and the reflected plane waves. When waves are reflected the **angle of incidence i = the angle of reflection r**.

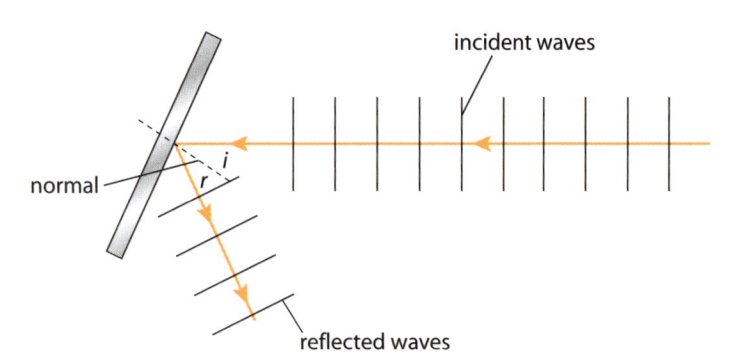

Figure 2 Water waves reflected by a barrier.

Examiner feedback
Make sure you don't confuse diffraction and refraction. Diffraction is spreading out of waves, and only happens to waves. Refraction is a change of direction of waves. Reflection and refraction may also happen to a stream of particles.

Refraction
When waves cross an interface between two materials they may change direction. This is called **refraction**. Figure 3 shows water waves being refracted towards the normal as they pass from deep to shallow water. Waves travelling along the normal are not refracted. If the direction of the water waves is reversed they follow the same path, and are refracted away from the normal as they cross the interface from shallow to deep water.

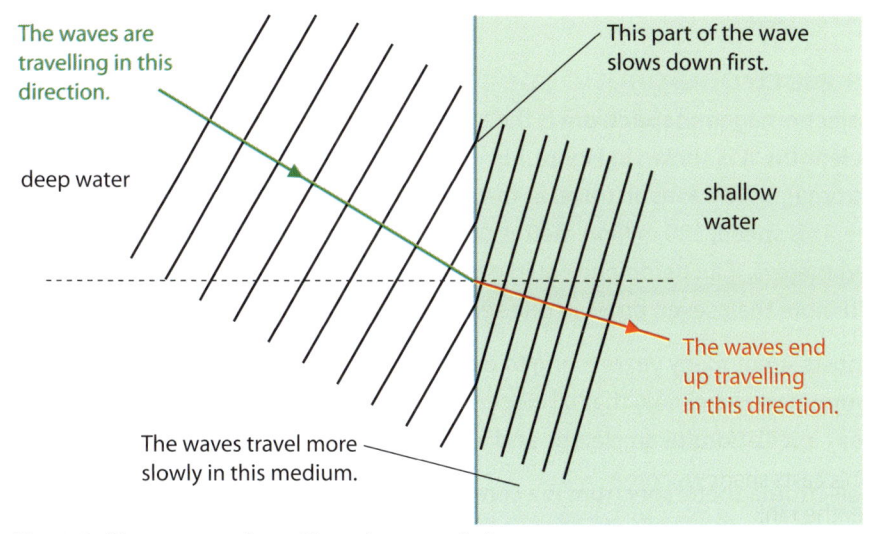

Figure 3 Water waves refracted by a change to shallow water.

The atmosphere

The atmosphere is not uniform. It has parts that have different temperatures and parts that may contain dust, water vapour or droplets. As waves are transmitted, some may be absorbed, and at interfaces between the different layers some may be refracted. For example, light is absorbed by clouds but radio waves are not. Mirages are caused by hot layers of air refracting light from the sky so that it appears to come from the ground and looks like a reflection from water.

Diffraction

Diffraction is the spreading out of waves when they pass an edge, as in Figure 4(a), or through a gap, as in Figure 4(b), 4(c) and 4(d). Diffraction is greatest when the gap is the same size as the wavelength of the wave, as shown in Figure 4(d). The wavelength of light is very small, about half a millionth of a metre, so light doesn't spread round corners unless the hole is very tiny.

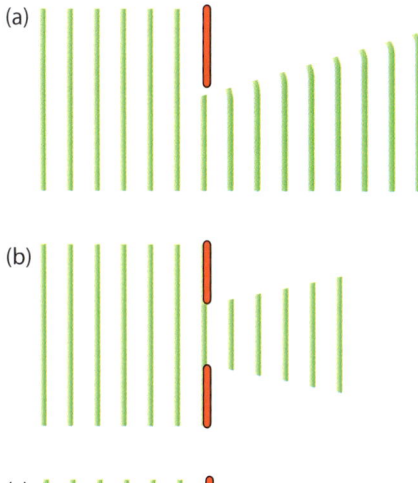

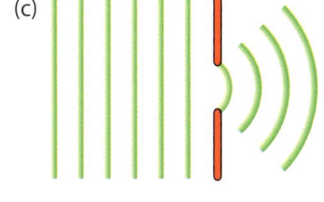

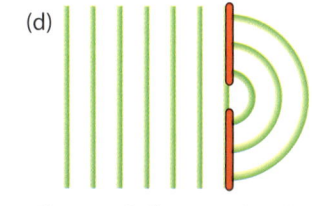

Figure 4 Diffraction of waves.

Questions

1. Draw a diagram and explain what happens when water waves hit a straight barrier at an angle.
2. Waves are refracted at an interface. What does 'refraction' mean?
3. How would you show that an unknown radiation was a wave and not a stream of particles?
4. Draw diagrams and use them to explain how diffraction depends on wavelength.
5. Light from the stars twinkles because it is refracted as it passes through the atmosphere. Explain what this means, and why it happens.
6. Figure 5 shows how scientists investigate layers of rock by detonating an explosion and detecting the reflections. Explain how the depth of an interface between two rock layers can be worked out.

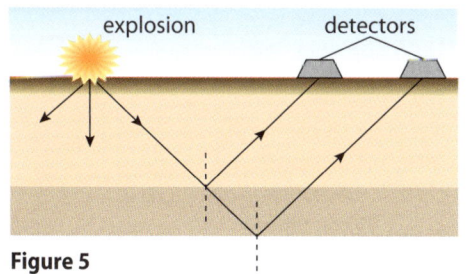

Figure 5

7. The waves on many beaches always seem to arrive parallel to the shore. This is because waves are refracted towards the normal as they enter shallower water. Draw a diagram to explain this effect.
8. Sir Isaac Newton said that light was not a wave because shadows had sharp edges. Explain why waves do not give shadows with sharp edges, and why scientists today say that light is a wave.

Waves 57

P15.4 Electromagnetic waves

Learning objectives
- list the types of waves in the electromagnetic spectrum, in order of energy, frequency and wavelength.
- Calculate frequencies and wavelengths of electromagnetic waves.
- Explain that radio waves, microwaves, infrared and visible light are used for communication.

The electromagnetic spectrum

The electromagnetic **spectrum** is the complete range of electromagnetic wavelengths. It is shown in Figure 1 in order of increasing energy. Electromagnetic waves all travel at the same speed in a vacuum and through space. This speed, 300 million metres per second, or 3×10^8 m/s, is the fastest speed there is. If an aeroplane could go at this speed it would go around the world more than seven times in one second.

Scientists spent many years trying to decide how light travelled through a vacuum. Now they know that all electromagnetic waves behave as transverse waves – oscillations of an electric and a magnetic field.

The electromagnetic spectrum is a continuous range of wavelengths, there are no gaps. As the energy increases, the frequency of the waves increases and the wavelength decreases, as shown in Figure 2. Electromagnetic waves with different wavelengths have some very different properties. For example, long wavelength radio waves are transmitted through brick and stone, but light is not. This is why different parts have different names, but there is no sharp division between the different parts of the spectrum. Table 1 shows some typical wavelengths. You can work out frequency from the wavelength and the speed of 300 000 000 m/s using the wave equation.

Table 1 Typical wavelengths in the electromagnetic spectrum.

Electromagnetic waves	Typical wavelengths
radio waves	1 m, 3 km
microwaves	1 cm, 10 cm
infrared (IR)	1 mm, 1 millionth of a metre
visible light: red, orange, yellow, green blue, indigo, violet	from about 7×10^{-7} m to 4×10^{-7} m; 0.51 millionths of a metre

Science skills Figure 2 shows how the wavelength of electromagnetic waves changes as the frequency changes.

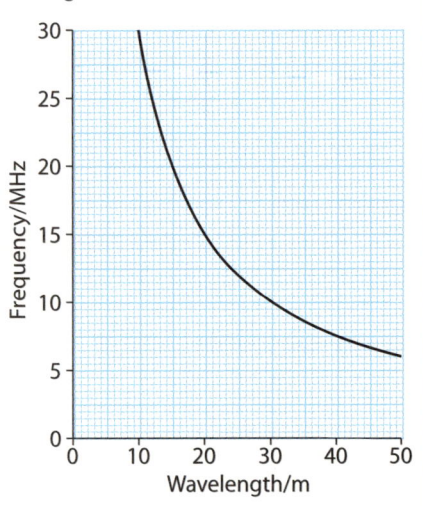

Figure 2 Change of wavelength with frequency.

a What is the wavelength when the frequency is 20 MHz?

b What happens to the wavelength when the frequency doubles?

c Use a pair of values from the graph to calculate the speed of the waves.

All electromagnetic waves travel at the speed of light in a vacuum.

low frequency / long wavelength → high frequency / short wavelength

radio waves | microwaves | infrared | visible light | ultraviolet | X-rays gamma-rays

1 m–1 km | 1 cm | 0.01 mm | 400–700 nm | 100 nm | 0.01 nm–1 nm

increasing energy

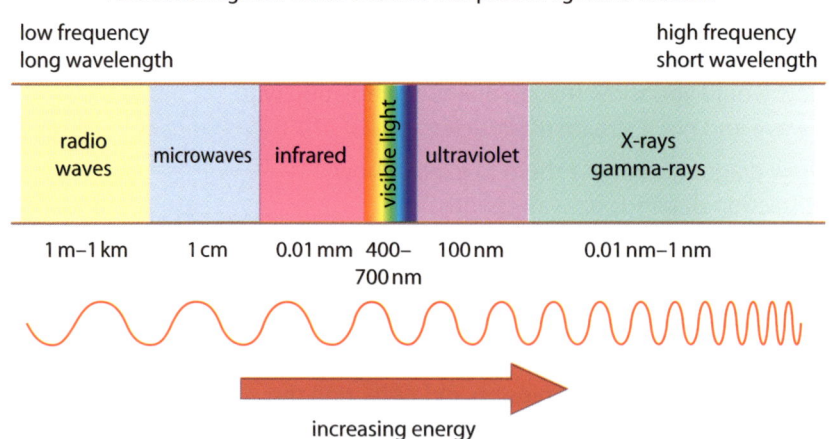

Figure 1 The spectrum of electromagnetic waves.

Are electromagnetic waves safe?

All electromagnetic waves have a heating effect when absorbed, and this is greater if the waves are carrying more energy. The **intensity** of a wave is a measure of the energy arriving on a unit area per second. For example, light is all around us and is normally quite safe. However, the more intense light from the Sun, or a laser, can damage eyes. Laser users wear eye protection.

Transmission through the atmosphere

- Radio waves pass through the atmosphere, and long waves are not absorbed by walls, so we use radio waves for broadcasting radio programmes and other information.
- Microwaves do not spread out like radio waves, they are very directional and there has to be a line-of-sight between transmitter and receiver. Some wavelengths are absorbed by water, so they are not so suitable for transmitting information.
- A lot of infrared radiation is absorbed by water vapour and gases in the atmosphere, so infrared is only used for very short distances.
- Light is transmitted through the atmosphere, but some is reflected from particles and if there are a lot of water droplets in the air, such as in clouds or fog, then the light is reflected so much a signal will not get through.
- Ultraviolet, X rays and gamma rays are absorbed by the atmosphere.

Science in action

Information is recorded onto a Blu-ray disc as a code of small bumps. When the disc is scanned with a blue-violet laser the bumps change how much light is reflected. This pattern is decoded to reproduce the information. DVDs use red lasers; the shorter blue wavelength allows Blu-ray discs to use smaller bumps so that more information fits onto the disc.

Blu-ray uses a 4.05×10^{-7} wavelength laser.

Questions

1. Which waves are more suitable for broadcasting a signal over a wide area?
2. Infrared waves from a remote control have a frequency of 3.19×10^{14} Hz. What is the wavelength?
3. Sodium lights give out yellow light with wavelength 0.000 000 59 m. What is the frequency?
4. Sun screens are all rated using the same test to see how much UV is prevented from reaching the skin. Why is it important to use the same test?
5. What electromagnetic waves have a typical frequency of about:
   (a) 100 million million Hz? (b) 1 000 million million Hz?
6. Look at Figure 3.

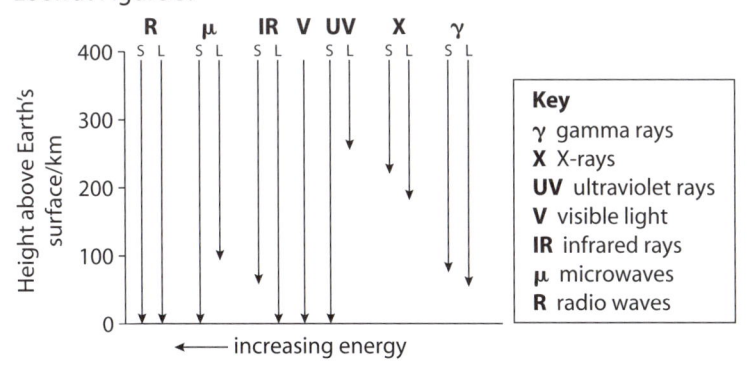

Figure 3 Schematic representation of absorption of short (S) and long (L) wave types of electromagnetic radiation by the atmosphere.

(a) Which waves are absorbed by the atmosphere? (b) For which waves is this an advantage? Explain your answer.

7. Describe the electromagnetic spectrum.

Route to A*

The speed of light can be written as 300 000 000 m/s or in standard form as 3×10^8 m/s, but also as 3×10^5 km/s, so take care with the units in questions. Changing all the numbers to standard form is a useful way to avoid unit problems. To calculate the frequency of infrared radiation with a wavelength of 1 mm:

Wavelength = 1×10^{-3} m

Speed of light = 3×10^8 m/s

Use the wave equation: $v = f\lambda$.

Rearranging, frequency $f = \dfrac{v}{\lambda}$.

$f = \dfrac{v}{\lambda} = \dfrac{3 \times 10^8}{1 \times 10^{-3}}$.

Therefore frequency = 3×10^{11} Hz

This is an acceptable answer, but you could also write 300 000 000 000 Hz.

P1 5.5 Radio waves and microwaves

Learning objectives
- describe how microwaves and radio waves are used in communications
- explain why microwaves are used to communicate with satellites
- explain the dangers of powerful microwave and radio transmissions
- evaluate the use of different types of waves for communication.

Radio communications
Radio waves are used to broadcast radio and television signals from transmitters.

Radio waves are received by TV aerials.

The information, for example sound or pictures, is converted to an electrical signal and then added to the radio waves that are transmitted in all directions. For a receiver to pick up radio waves, the aerial must be made of metal so it absorbs the waves. When it does so, the radio waves produce an alternating current in the aerial with a frequency which is the same as the radio wave itself. The original electric signal is recovered and used to reproduce the information; for example, it can be changed into the sound that comes from a loudspeaker. Each TV channel and radio programme is allocated a frequency band, a small range of frequencies, so that there is no interference between the different users.

Receiving signals
Microwaves and radio waves are absorbed by very thick or dense objects, like hills for example. However, long wave radio waves, especially those with wavelengths of about 1000 m, can be diffracted along valleys and around hills, as shown in Figure 1. If you live somewhere that does not have a clear straight path, or line of sight, to the transmitter, you can still receive radio waves, but microwaves are not diffracted by such large objects.

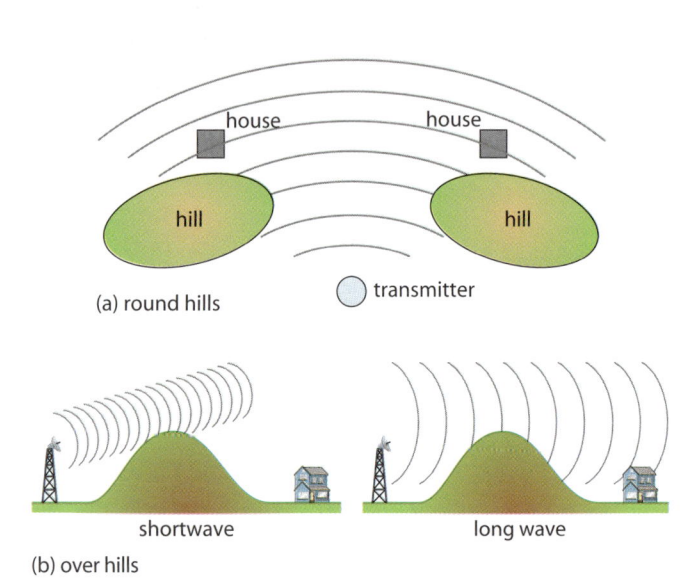

Figure 1 Radio waves can be received because of diffraction.

Microwaves
Satellites are used to transmit information quickly around the world, as shown in Figure 2. Some areas do not get good reception of radio signals but can receive signals from a satellite. A satellite can also provide a wide area with satellite TV. Many radio frequencies are reflected by the **ionosphere**, which is a high and electrically charged layer of our atmosphere. This means they cannot be used to communicate with satellites. Microwaves are used instead, as these can pass easily through the whole atmosphere.

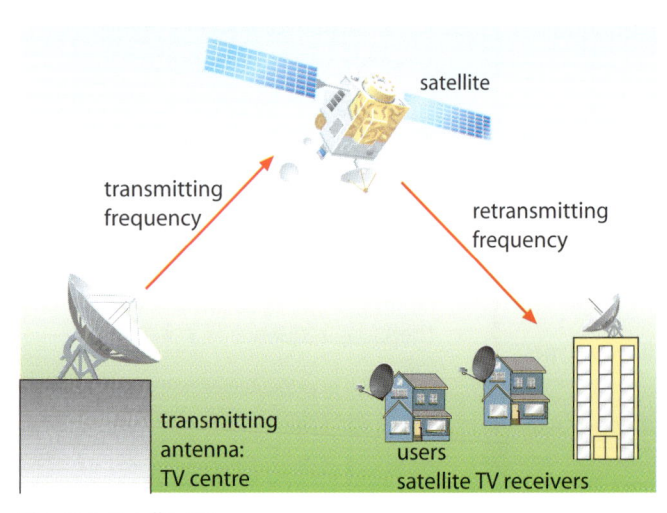

Figure 2 Satellite TV.

Dangers of microwaves and radio waves

We cannot detect **microwaves** or radio waves, so we must be careful not to expose our bodies to dangerous levels of these radiations. People are not allowed near powerful transmitters, like the one in the photograph, when they are switched on. Microwaves are reflected by metal and radio waves are absorbed or reflected, so metal can be used to screen rooms from these radiations.

Microwaves with a frequency of about 2450 million Hz are particularly dangerous. They make water molecules vibrate strongly, so they have a big heating effect on anything containing water. This is the frequency used in microwave ovens to cook food.

Science in action

Microwave ovens can be used to cook any food that contains water. The microwaves penetrate deep inside the food and cook it all the way through. The metal walls of the oven reflect the microwaves, which are then absorbed by the food. The door contains a metal mesh to reflect microwaves too.

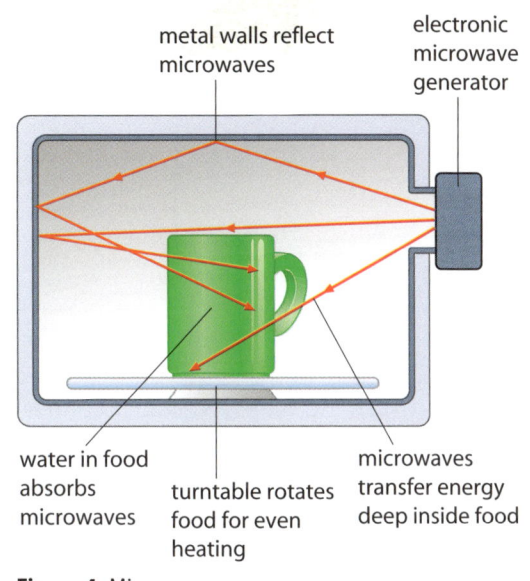

Figure 4 Microwave oven.

Transmitter towers.

Examiner feedback

It is important to remember when microwaves and radio waves are used and why they are used for different applications.

Practical

You can use a microwave transmitter and receiver to check whether microwaves obey the law of reflection, and see what materials absorb them.

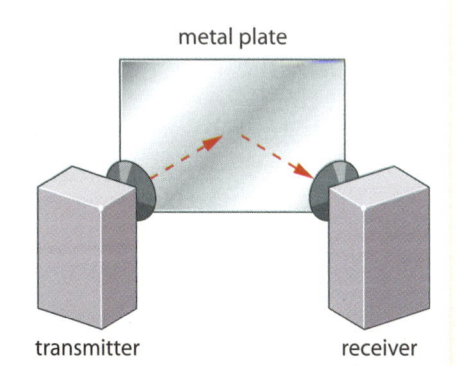

Figure 3 The angle of incidence equals the angle of reflection.

Questions

1. A radio station broadcasts on 2 million Hz, a TV station broadcasts on 2000 million Hz, and the emergency services use a radio frequency of 200 million Hz. Which uses the longest wavelength?
2. Why do microwave ovens have a safety lock to prevent them operating while the door is open?
3. A radio aerial receives a radio broadcast. Describe two things that happen to the metal aerial.
4. BBC 4 long wave radio broadcasts at 198 kHz. What is the wavelength?
5. Radio 1 is broadcast with a wavelength of 3.01 m. What frequency is this?
6. Describe the different ways that a television signal might reach your TV set.
7. Explain why radio waves can be received over a large area but microwaves need repeating transmitters on hills and buildings.
8. A student says that we should not use microwaves for communications because microwaves cook meat and so they will cook us. Explain to the student what is wrong with this conclusion.

Waves

P1 5.6 Mobile phones

Learning objectives
- describe how microwaves are used in mobile phones
- explain how Bluetooth is used
- analyse data on safety of mobile phones
- evaluate the possible risks of using mobile phones.

Mobile phone networks

Mobile phones use microwaves and a cellular network system, as shown in Figure 1. The phone communicates with a local mast or base station. The mast sends another microwave signal to a central base, which sends the signal on to the base station or mast for the receiving phone. Mobile phones use powers of up to about 2W. Whenever the phone is switched on it keeps in touch with the base station by sending messages and it uses more power if reception is bad, for example in a tunnel.

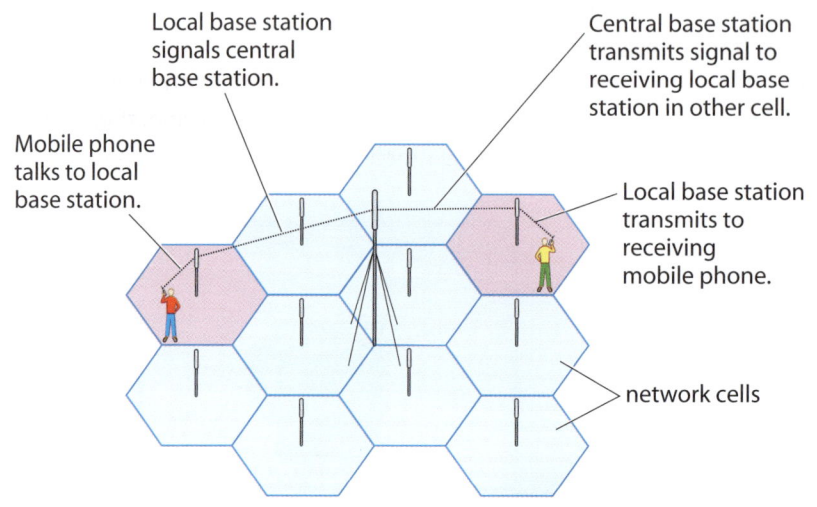

Figure 1 A mobile phone network.

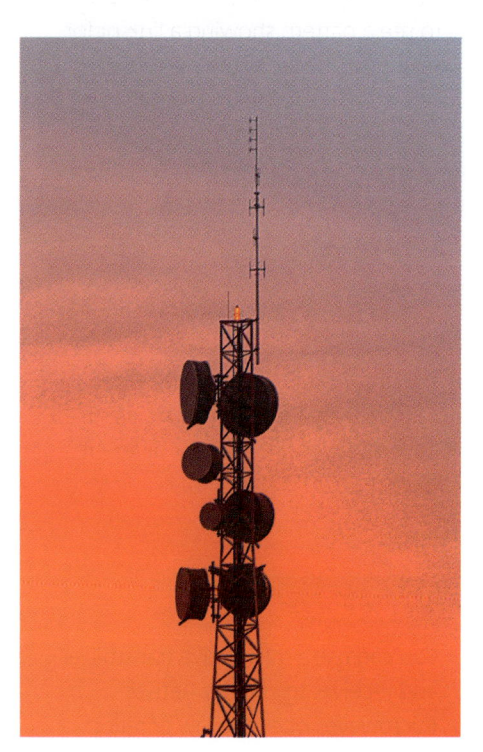

For longer distances, mobile phone microwave signals are sent via several masts because otherwise the curved shape of the Earth would block the signal. Microwaves need a line of sight, a straight line, between the masts as the wavelengths are too small to be diffracted around hills. For international calls, a satellite link is used.

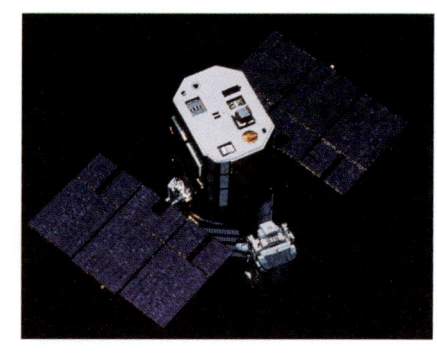

A microwave transmitter tower.

A communication satellite.

Bluetooth

Bluetooth is a low power (about one milliwatt) system that uses microwaves over a range of up to 10 m to connect up to eight items like televisions, mobile phones and PCs. Bluetooth uses a frequency of 2450 million Hz, the same as microwave ovens, but at a much lower power.

Are mobile phones safe?

The Health Protection Agency (HPA) is a government group, made up of independent scientists, that is looking at the evidence about the effects of radiation on health. This was the advice on their website in 2010:

'There are thousands of published scientific papers covering research about the effects of various types of radio waves on cells, tissues, animals and people. The scientific consensus is that, apart from the increased risk of a road accident due

Using a Bluetooth headset.

to mobile phone use when driving, there is no clear evidence of adverse health effects from the use of mobile phones or from phone masts. However, there is now widespread use of this relatively new technology and more research is needed in case there are long-term effects.'

They also said:

'Given the uncertainties in the science, some precaution is warranted particularly regarding the use of handsets held against the head. This is especially relevant to the use of handsets by children and the Agency recommends that excessive use by children should be discouraged.'

So the research so far indicates that phones are safe, but we can't be sure that there are no long-term effects until we have studied lots of people that have used phones throughout their lives – and that is going to take many years. The reason for taking extra care with children is that they are still growing, their skulls are thinner, and they are going to be using mobiles for many years to come.

Route to A*

You may be given some information about an investigation and asked questions about whether the study was well designed and if the conclusions are reliable. Sometimes the marks will be for the explanation you give. For example, if you are asked if a sample is big enough, sometimes it may be difficult to decide. In this case there may be marks for saying 'yes, because there is enough data to see a pattern showing a link' or for saying 'no, because the sample size is too small and a pattern could be just coincidence.' There is no mark for saying 'yes' or 'no' without an explanation.

Science skills

In 2006 a scientific paper was published reporting a Danish study of mobile phone use and cancer. 420 095 adults from all over Denmark who first used a mobile phone between 1982 and 1995 were monitored for up to 21 years. The number of people in the group who got cancer was compared with the number that would be expected to get cancer – the number of people in a similar sample who did not use phones but who got cancer.

	Number in study	Number with cancer	Number expected to get cancer
men	357 553	12 627	11 802
women	62 542	2374	2447
men and women	420 095	15 001	14 249

a Taking the whole group, did more or fewer people get cancer than expected?
b Why were the scientists more confident about the result for men than for women?
c The complete study looked at different types of cancer. Why do you think this might be important?

Questions

1 Why are satellites used for international phone calls?
2 A company wants to put a mobile phone mast next to a school. Give reasons for and against the positioning of the mast next to the school with your evaluation as to whether it is a suitable site.
3 Why has there been no study of the effects of mobile phones on the health of children who use them?
4 A mobile phone has a SAR value, which is a measure of the energy per second absorbed by the head while the phone is used. The SAR value must be less than 2.0 W/kg. Explain whether it is completely safe to use a phone with a SAR value of: (a) 0.25 W/kg (b) 1.8 W/kg (c) 2.1 W/kg.
5 The SAR values are checked by independent consumer organisations. Why is this important?
6 Two Bluetooth devices can communicate until one is placed inside a microwave oven with the door shut. The oven is not switched on. Explain why the devices can no longer detect each other.
7 Describe how you could use two mobile phones to find out if microwaves are absorbed by water.
8 Describe how scientists could research whether there is a link between mobile phone use and brain tumours.

P1 5.7 Making light work

Learning objectives
- describe the nature of the image produced by a plane mirror
- draw ray diagrams to show how images are formed by mirrors
- describe how light is used in photography.

Mirrors

Lots of objects reflect light but in a mirror you see an **image**. The properties of the image in a mirror can be explained by constructing a ray diagram – we draw rays rather than waves when investigating images. To keep ray diagrams simple we draw only a few rays. When light is reflected the angle of incidence is always equal to the angle of reflection, as shown in Figure 1.

If you look at an image of yourself in a plane mirror, the image is upright (the same way up as you are) and the same size as you, but laterally inverted (i.e. left and right are swapped over). The image also appears to be behind the mirror and it is the same distance behind the mirror as you are in front. The rays of light do not pass through the image but only appear to come from it. This kind of image is called a **virtual image**. In Figure 2, two rays from an object are drawn to show how the image in a mirror is formed. The rays are reflected from the mirror surface and the dotted lines show that they appear to come from the image.

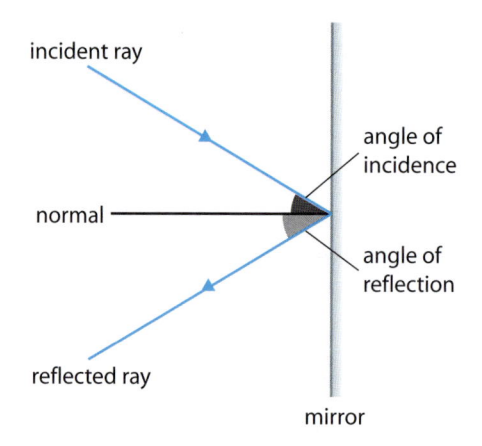

Figure 1 Reflection – the angles are equal.

For each ray, the angle of incidence = the angle of reflection

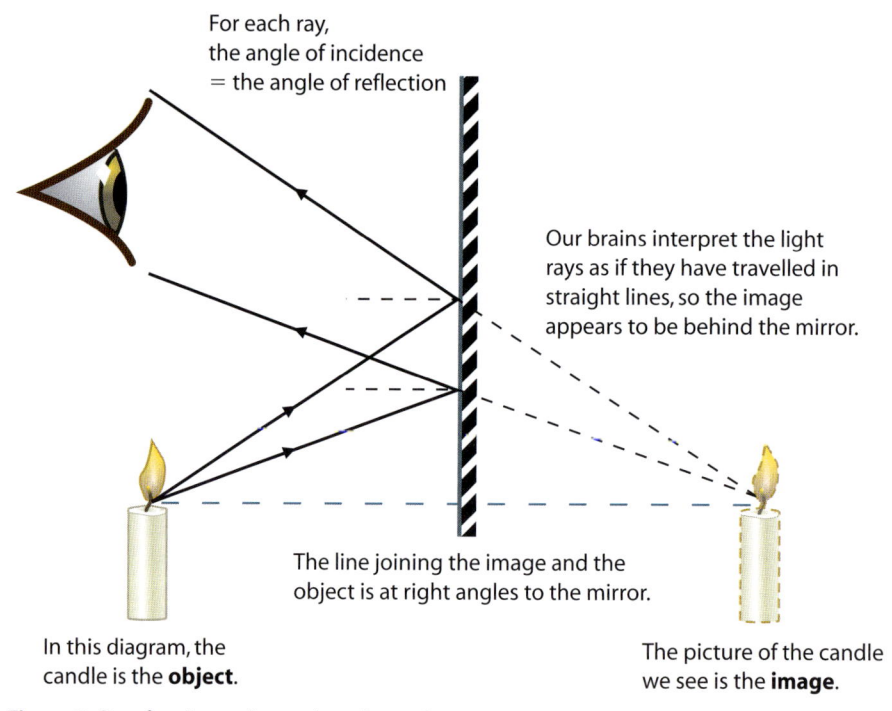

Our brains interpret the light rays as if they have travelled in straight lines, so the image appears to be behind the mirror.

In this diagram, the candle is the **object**.

The line joining the image and the object is at right angles to the mirror.

The picture of the candle we see is the **image**.

Figure 2 Rays forming an image in a plane mirror.

Examiner feedback
If you are drawing ray diagrams use a sharp pencil and a ruler. Rulers that you can see through make it easier to get the lines in the correct place. Angles are always measured between a light ray and the normal.

Photography

Unlike a mirror, a camera produces a **real image**. It is called a real image because the rays of light do pass through it. To record the image, it must be formed on a light-sensitive surface. This could be photographic film or sensors that produce an electronic signal. Figure 3 shows the simplest basic camera, one without a lens. The light rays enter through a very small pinhole and produce an upside-down image on the screen. Images from cameras like this are quite dim. However, if you make the pinhole bigger to let in more light the image will be blurred. Replacing the pinhole with a lens allows more light in and focuses the image to give a sharp picture. The image is upside down and smaller than the object.

The image is dim because not much light can get through the hole.

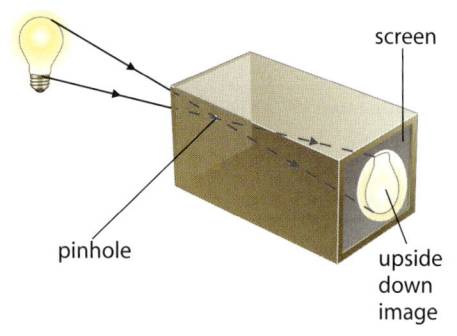

Figure 3 How a camera forms an image.

Questions

1. Which way up is the image in: **(a)** a plane mirror? **(b)** a camera?
2. Copy and complete Figure 4 to show how an object is reflected in a mirror.

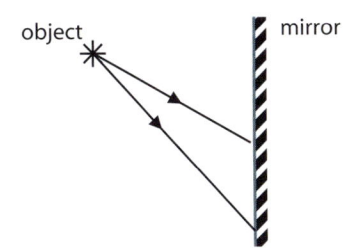

Figure 4

3. A mug is 8 cm tall, and you place it 10 cm from a mirror. **(a)** How tall does the mug appear to be in the mirror? **(b)** How far from the mirror does the image of the mug appear to be? **(c)** Is the image real or virtual?
4. Two mirrors are positioned so they are touching with an angle of 120° between them. Draw a ray of light incident on one mirror at an angle of 60° so that it reflects from both the mirrors.
5. Copy and complete Figure 5 to show how the periscope can be used to see over a high wall.

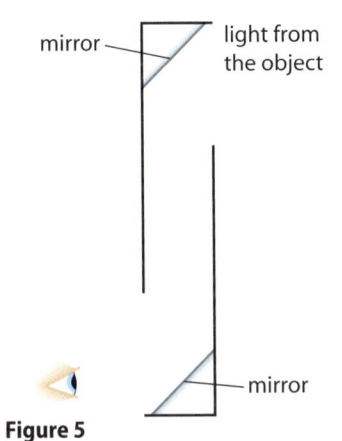

Figure 5

6. An optician's chart is on the wall 1 m behind the patient's head. The patient sees the chart in the mirror, which is 2.5 m away in front of the patient. How far away from: **(a)** the chart **(b)** the patient does the image of the chart appear to be?
7. The photograph shows a meter with a mirror behind the pointer. Explain how the mirror helps to read the meter accurately.

8. Write a Wiki page to describe how a digital camera produces an image of the object being photographed.

Science skills

Some students use a pinhole camera, as shown in Figure 3, to obtain images of objects. They keep the camera the same distance from the objects and measure the object height and the image height.

a Which is the independent variable?

b What type of variable is the object height?

c Plot a graph to show these results.

d Are any of the results anomalous? If so, which one(s)?

e Describe the relationship between image height and object height, and explain how the graph shows this.

Object height/cm	Image height/cm
12.0	0.9
20.0	1.4
24.0	1.5
30.0	2.1
36.0	2.6
40.0	2.9

Taking it further

When drawing ray diagrams for mirrors you might wonder why the angle of incidence and reflection are measured to the normal and not to the surface. The reason is clearer when the surface is not a plane. When light is reflected from rough surfaces, or from curved mirrors, convex and concave, the law of reflection is still true.

Waves **65**

P1 5.8 Light and infrared

Learning objectives
- explain that optical fibres are used to transmit light and infrared radiation
- list some uses of light and infrared radiation.

Science in action
In parts of the world where there is plenty of sunshine but not much fuel a solar cooker is very useful. This photograph shows one being used in the mountains of Nepal to boil water. The infrared radiation from the Sun is reflected from the metal onto the cooking pot.

Infrared radiation from the Sun boils water in this solar cooker.

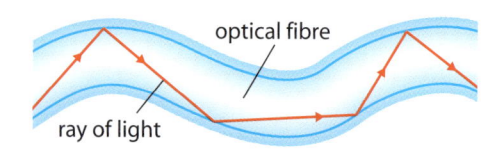

Figure 1 A ray travelling through an optical fibre.

Infrared signals
Remote controls for TVs and other electronic equipment use infrared radiation. If you look at the output of a remote control with a digital camera you can see the flashing code that is being transmitted. This is because digital cameras are sensitive to some of the infrared wavelengths that we cannot see.

Infrared reflections
Infrared radiation behaves in a similar way to light. It is reflected from surfaces, especially shiny surfaces. Infrared rays travel in straight lines and are reflected from walls and ceilings. A remote control will not operate a TV if it is pointed too far to one side. However, if you aim it at the wall behind you the beam will reflect off the wall and it sometimes operates the TV.

Optical fibres
Optical fibres are fibres made of glass. The composition of the glass varies across the fibre so that light or infrared radiation passing down the fibre is refracted and reflected to keep it travelling along the centre, as shown in Figure 1.

Science skills
A student wanted to investigate the absorption of infrared radiation. He used a 20 cm block of jelly to model an optical fibre. He placed an infrared LED at one end and a detector at the other.

He measured the length of the jelly fibre and recorded the voltage signal reaching the detector, then cut off a piece of the jelly, and repeated the measurements with the smaller length. These are the results

Length of jelly fibre/mm	Reading on detector/V
200	0.12
180	0.14
150	0.20
100	0.36
80	0.46
40	0.70

a Which was the:
i independent variable? **ii** dependent variable?

b What type of variable was:
i the length? **ii** the voltage?

c Plot a graph of the student's results.

d Describe the relationship between the length of the fibre and the reading on the detector.

e The student realises that he has measured the length of the jelly but the path of the beam was at an angle through the jelly and not parallel to the sides. What type of error will this cause in his results?

Signals, especially telecommunications signals, can be sent along optical fibres instead of copper cables or by microwave and radio links. Many copper cables have been replaced by optical fibres. Advantages are:

- Much more information can be carried by the waves because light and infrared have higher frequencies than microwaves and radio waves. This means that thick, heavy, expensive copper cables can be replaced by a thin bundle of glass fibres.
- The information is more secure because, unlike with copper cables, it is not possible to pick up radiation from outside the glass fibres.
- Signals in fibres do not pick up noise, or unwanted signals, from outside the cables. This can be a problem with copper cables.

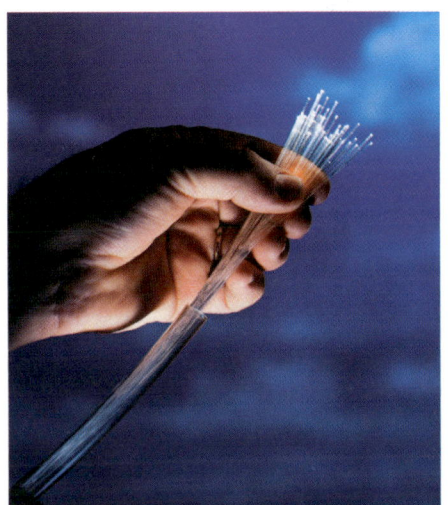

Compare these fibre optic cables…   …with these copper cables.

Science in action

These young people are only visible through an infrared or thermal camera, which picks up infrared radiation.

Objects emit radiation with a wavelength that depends on their temperature. Thermal cameras and night vision glasses allow us to see when there is no reflected light; see spread P1 1.1. They detect infrared radiation from warm objects like bodies and change the wavelengths to visible wavelengths that we can see. In the photograph, the faces are the objects with the highest surface temperature – higher than the clothes and surroundings.

Questions

1. What are the advantages of using fibre optic cables instead of copper cables for telephone wires?
2. Draw a diagram to show how an infrared remote control can switch off a TV by reflecting off the wall of a room.
3. Suggest why an infrared telescope would be placed in orbit around the Earth and not on the Earth?
4. A burglar alarm uses a beam of infrared radiation that falls on a sensor. If a burglar interrupts the beam an alarm sounds. Why is infrared radiation used and not light or ultraviolet radiation?
5. Infrared radiation is absorbed by gases like carbon dioxide and water vapour in the atmosphere. What effect does this have on the atmosphere?
6. An infrared remote control switches a TV on and off. Describe how you could use this in an experiment to see which materials transmit infrared radiation.

Route to A*

You may be asked a question about something you haven't studied, but which you can work out from what you *have* studied. It's important not to assume that you can't answer the question. For example, an infrared range finder works by sending out an infrared pulse and timing how long it takes for the reflection to return. You may not know this, but you know how infrared remote controls work, and how the echo of a sound wave can be used to measure a distance (see page 256), so you can apply this knowledge to explain how an infrared rangefinder works.

Waves   **67**

P1 5.9 Sound

Learning objectives
- describe sound waves
- explain that sound is caused by vibrations in a medium
- explain that the pitch of a sound is determined by its frequency
- investigate the speed of sound
- evaluate experiments to measure the speed of sound.

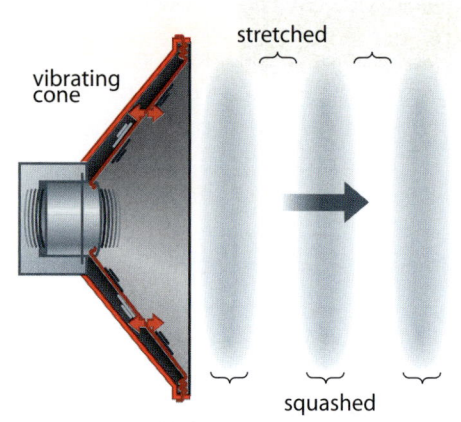

Sound
Vibrations send longitudinal waves travelling to our ears. Inside our ears the waves cause vibrations that are sensed and interpreted by the brain as sounds. In air sound travels at about 330 m/s. It is faster in liquids and fastest in solids like wood or metal because the oscillations can be passed on more easily in these materials. Using a microphone, you can display the *graph* of the amplitude of the sound wave against *time* on an **oscilloscope** or computer screen. Remember that sound waves are longitudinal and the screen shows a graph, not what the sound wave looks like.

The guitar strings vibrate and start the air oscillating.

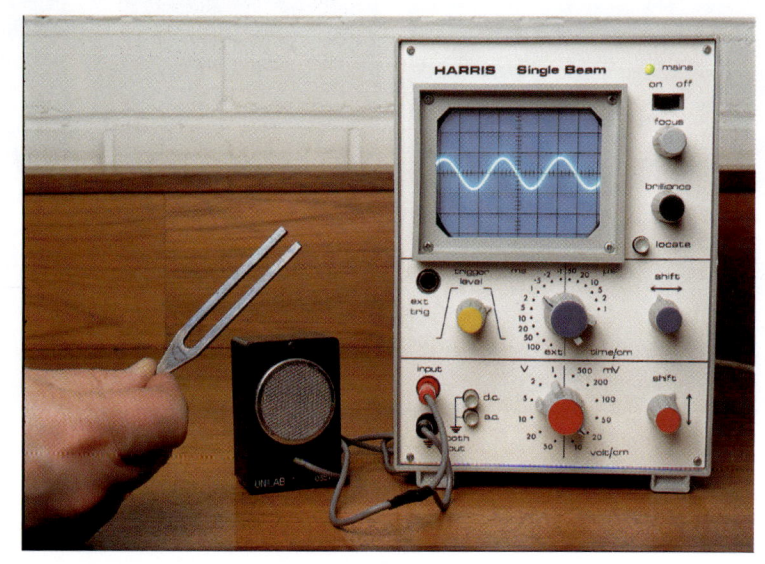

Figure 1 A loudspeaker vibrates, producing longitudinal sound waves in the air.

A graph of the vibrations of the tuning fork are shown on this oscilloscope.

Route to A*
To calculate the wavelength of a sound, if you are given the speed and the pitch, remember that the pitch is the frequency of the sound.

So, from the wave equation $v = f\lambda$:

Wave speed = pitch × wavelength.

So $\lambda = \dfrac{v}{f}$

wavelength = $\dfrac{\text{wave speed}}{\text{pitch}}$

Pitch and loudness
The **pitch** of a sound – how high or low it is – is determined by the frequency of the sound wave. The higher the pitch, the greater the frequency.
The loudness of a sound depends on the amplitude: the higher the amplitude, the louder the sound.

Human hearing
Humans hear sounds in the range from about 20 Hz to about 20 kHz. The highest frequency you can hear gets lower as you get older. Some animals, like whales, can hear lower frequencies, and some, like dogs, can hear higher frequencies.

Echoes
An **echo** is a reflection of sound from a hard surface. The further away the surface, the longer it takes for the sound to travel there and back. This delay can be used to work out the speed of sound, using speed = distance travelled ÷ time taken.

Examiner feedback
A common mistake is to think that we can't hear radio waves because the frequency is too high, but our ears only detect longitudinal waves; we can't hear any electromagnetic waves no matter what the frequency.

Refraction

Refraction occurs between layers of air at different temperatures. One example is when you hear a train in the distance only in certain weather conditions. When there is a cold layer of air next to the ground and a warmer layer above, the sound from a train can be refracted back down to Earth some distance away.

Diffraction

The photographer who took the photograph on the right would not have been able to see people on the other side of the doorway, but he would have been able to hear them. This is because sound has wavelengths of about 1 m so it is diffracted through gaps about the size of a doorway. Longer wavelengths are closer to the size of the door and are diffracted more, so the sound heard round a corner will have lost the higher frequencies.

Diffraction allows sound to travel round corners.

Science skills

Some students measure the speed of sound using a firework that ejects a flash with a loud bang. They are 500 m from the firework, measured with a tape measure. The observers use a stopwatch and start it when they see the flash. They stop it when they hear the bang. They repeat the experiment five times. Table 1 shows their results.

Table 1

Time taken for sound to arrive/s
1.31
0.94
1.45
1.67
1.52

a Why did they repeat the experiment five times?

b Are any of the results anomalous? If so, which ones?

c Calculate the mean value for the time.

d Calculate the speed of sound.

e Some students make the following statements about the experiment. Explain whether they are correct.

i The value will be much too big because the speed of light has not been taken into account.

ii The value would have been more accurate if a larger distance was used.

iii The value would have been more accurate if a more precise stopwatch, measuring to thousandths of a second, had been used.

iv We need to add the reaction time of the student starting the stopwatch.

f Explain whether the wind will affect the results.

Taking it further

Light has much smaller wavelengths than sound so the diffraction of light is much less.

Route to A*

The hum of a hummingbird is caused by the rapid beating of its wings setting the air vibrating. The wings of some hummingbirds beat 80 times per second. At this speed, the pitch of the hum is 80 Hz.

Questions

(Use speed of sound in air = 330 m/s)

1 The note middle C has a pitch of 256 Hz. What is the wavelength?

2 The speed of sound in water is 1500 m/s. What is the pitch of a sound with a wavelength in water of 0.03 m?

3 Draw a graph of a sound wave like Figure 2. On the same axes draw and label: **(a)** a sound wave that is louder; **(b)** a sound wave that has a higher pitch.

4 Describe how you would do an experiment to measure the speed of sound using the echo from a high brick wall at one side of a playing field.

Assess yourself questions

1. Many electromagnetic waves can be used in communication. Which wave types link with which communication uses? *(3 marks)*

Wave type	Communication use
radio waves	an endoscope – a glass fibre with a camera used by doctors to see inside the body
microwaves	a satellite TV signal linking the transmitter to the satellite
infrared	a fibre optic telecommunications link
visible light	a terrestrial TV broadcast

2. Choose the correct answer.
   (a) The shock waves from an earthquake are:
   - A all longitudinal
   - B all transverse
   - C both longitudinal and transverse *(1 mark)*

   (b) Longitudinal waves travel through:
   - A gases only
   - B liquids only
   - C liquids and gases
   - D solids only
   - E solids, liquids and gases *(1 mark)*

   (c) The wavelength of a longitudinal wave is the distance between:
   - A a compression and a rarefaction
   - B a crest and a trough
   - C two crests
   - D two rarefactions
   - E two troughs *(1 mark)*

3. (a) What is the difference between a transverse and a longitudinal wave? *(2 marks)*

   (b) Water waves are passing a breakwater. Each complete wave takes 2.0 s to pass. The distance between two crests is 3 m and the distance between the top of a crest and the bottom of a trough is 90 cm. What is:
   - (i)   the frequency of the waves? *(1 mark)*
   - (ii) the wavelength? *(1 mark)*
   - (iii) the amplitude? *(1 mark)*
   - (iv) the wave speed? *(1 mark)*

4. (a) When a train approaches, the noise of the rails vibrating can be heard before the train. Explain why this happens. *(2 marks)*

   (b) In many science fiction films, missiles and explosions in outer space make loud noises. Explain why this is unrealistic. *(2 marks)*

5. (a) Copy these diagrams and complete them to show the waves after they have passed through the gap. *(3 marks)*

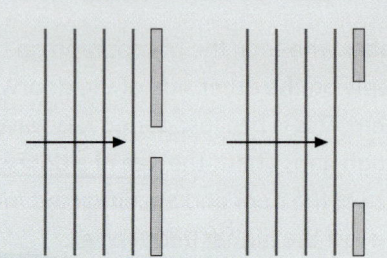

   Figure 1

   (b) What is the name of this effect? *(1 mark)*

   (c) A time signal for setting radio controlled clocks is broadcast at a frequency of 60 kHz from Cumbria and can be received throughout the UK.
   - (i) What is the wavelength of the signal? (Radio waves travel at a speed of 300 000 000 m/s.) *(2 marks)*
   - (ii) Explain how the signal can be received all over the UK.
     In this question you will be assessed on using good English, organising information clearly and using specialist terms where appropriate. *(6 marks)*

6. A company sells coatings for optical instruments. These graphs show the percentage of the incident radiation reflected at different wavelengths for three coatings: Premier, Choice and Luxcoat.

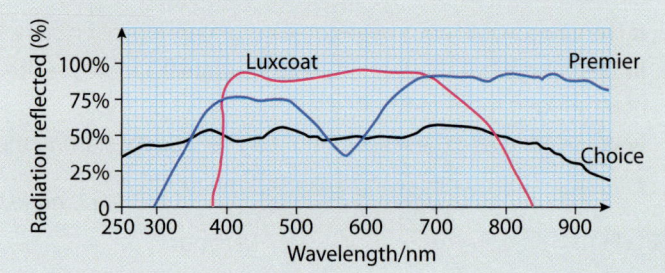

   Figure 2 Graph of optical coating performance.

   (a) Explain which coating(s) would be suitable for a beam splitter for visible light that transmits half of the beam and reflects the other half. *(3 marks)*

   (b) Explain which material would be suitable for a mirror to reflect all visible light. *(3 marks)*

   (c) Explain which material would be suitable as a mirror to reflect infrared radiation. *(3 marks)*

   (d) What percentage of the incident light does Choice transmit at 750 nm? *(1 mark)*

   (e) Explain whether the coating Luxcoat reflects ultraviolet light. *(2 marks)*

7 The data in Table 1 shows how heavy rainfall can affect the transmission of microwaves with a frequency 15 GHz (1 GHz = 10^9 Hz = 1 million kHz) and microwaves with a frequency of 39 GHz.

Table 1 How heavy rainfall affects microwave transmissions.

Rainfall rate mm/hour	Percentage energy loss per km travelled	
	Microwave frequency 15 GHz	Microwave frequency 39 GHz
0	60	64
10	82	78
20	80	96.8
30	88	98.5
40	97.5	100
50	99	100
60	100	100

(a) Explain which waves have the longest wavelength. *(1 mark)*

(b) Are there any anomalous results? If so, which ones? *(1 mark)*

(c) What percentage of the energy of the 15 GHz waves is left after 1 km when there is no rain? *(1 mark)*

(d) Which frequency is most affected by the rain? *(1 mark)*

(e) A student says that the absorption of the 39 GHz microwaves is proportional to the amount of rain. Explain whether you agree. *(1 mark)*

(f) A microwave signal has to travel 1 km. It can be recovered if 10% of the original energy gets through. Estimate the maximum rainfall rate before the signal is lost if:
  (i) 15 GHz waves or
  (ii) 39 GHz waves are used. *(2 marks)*

8 Figure 3 shows waves entering a harbour.

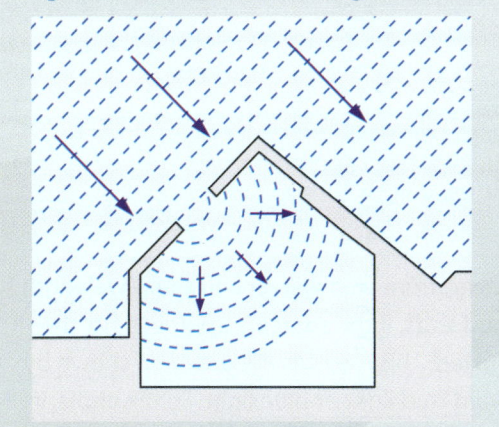

Figure 3 How waves change when they enter a harbour.

This effect is called:
A diffraction
B dispersion
C reflection
D refraction.

9 In 2010 the Cohort Study on Mobile Communications (COSMOS) was started. It is looking at the health and mobile phone use of people aged 18–69 in Britain, Finland, the Netherlands, Sweden and Denmark. It is one of the largest studies of this subject conducted. It will use data from volunteers' phone bills and health records as well as questionnaires.

Unlike previous studies, the study will look at long-term use, as people will be monitored for 10, 20 or 30 years. This will give time for diseases to develop. Findings will be reported during the study. Previous studies have depended on people remembering how much they used their phone in the past.

In Britain, COSMOS is inviting 2.4 million mobile phone users to take part, through the country's four top carriers: Vodafone, O2, T-Mobile and Orange. It hopes 90 000–100 000 will agree.

The study will examine all health developments and look for links to neurological diseases such as Alzheimer's and Parkinson's as well as cancer.

It will also take account of how users carry their phone, for example in a trouser or chest pocket or in a bag, and whether they use hands-free kits.

(a) Explain why the study uses such a large number of people. *(1 mark)*

(b) Why do you think phone bills and health records will be looked at, as well as questionnaires? *(1 mark)*

(c) Explain why the study will continue for such a long time. *(1 mark)*

(d) Explain an advantage of *this* study, which is looking at what happens over the next 30 years, rather than studies that look back over the last 30 years. Is there a disadvantage? If so, what is it? *(2 marks)*

(e) What do you think the organisers would do if they discovered a link between mobile phone use and a type of cancer after only eight years? *(1 mark)*

(f) Why is the study limited to:
  (i) people over 18?
  (ii) people under 69? *(2 marks)*

(g) Why do you think they will look at how users carry their phone? *(2 marks)*

10 Compare how a terrestrial TV signal from a transmitter reaches your TV set with how a satellite TV signal reaches it.

In this question you will be assessed on using good English, organising information clearly and using specialist terms where appropriate. *(6 marks)*

P1 6.1 The Doppler effect

Learning objectives
- explain what happens to the wavelength and frequency of waves when the source moves relative to an observer
- explain what is meant by 'red shift'
- describe how the light from distant stars and galaxies is red-shifted.

A moving source

Have you ever noticed that a vehicle, especially one with a siren like a police car or ambulance, sounds higher pitched (i.e. the frequency is higher) as it comes towards you and lower pitched as it moves away from you? This is called the **Doppler effect**. This happens to all waves, including electromagnetic waves.

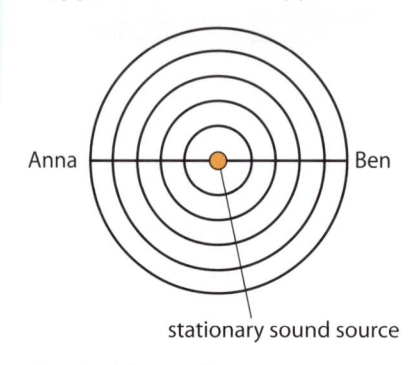

Figure 1(a) Waves from a stationary source.

Figure 1(b) Waves from a source moving towards Anna and away from Ben.

Figure 1(b) shows that the waves moving towards Anna are squashed together. The wavelength has decreased, and, as the speed of the waves has not changed, the frequency has increased. The waves moving towards Ben are stretched out, so he observes a longer wavelength and lower frequency. These small changes are called **Doppler shifts**.

Notice that it is not enough to say the source is moving. If the observer is moving at the same speed and in the same direction as the source there is no effect; the source must be moving *relative* to the observer. Some speed traffic cameras use the Doppler effect. A beam of microwaves is sent towards the car. The car reflects the beam back to the detector. Because the car is moving, the microwaves arriving at the detector will be Doppler shifted, and the faster the car is travelling the greater the Doppler shift. The Doppler shift is used to calculate the speed of the car.

Examiner feedback
Remember that as the source moves towards you, the waves will bunch up so the wavelength will decrease.

Electromagnetic waves

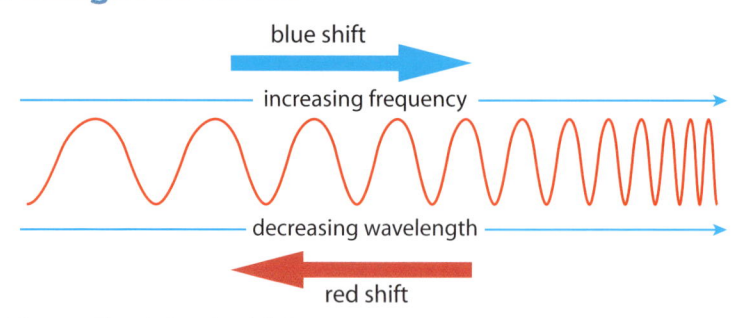

Figure 2 Blue shift and red shift.

When a visible light source moves away from an observer and the wavelength increases we say there has been a **red shift**. If the source is approaching, the wavelength decreases: it is **blue-shifted**. This refers to the direction shown by the arrows, which is not always towards red light or blue light. For example, if microwaves are red-shifted the new wavelength will be closer to radio waves.

A speed camera that uses the Doppler effect.

Starlight

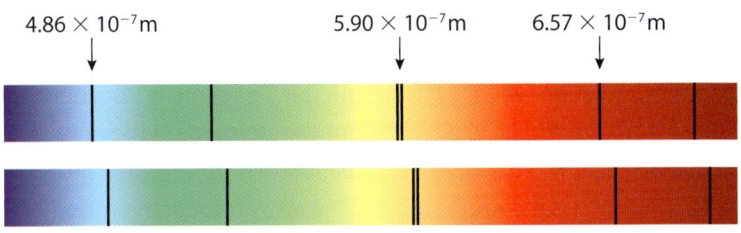

4.86×10^{-7} m 5.90×10^{-7} m 6.57×10^{-7} m

Figure 1(a) The spectrum of visible light from the Sun.
Figure 1(b) The spectrum of visible light from a distant star.

Safety note: do not look directly at the Sun with or without any optical instruments.

The spectrum of light formed by the Sun contains a number of dark lines. These are wavelengths of light that are missing because they have been absorbed by elements in the outer part of the Sun's atmosphere. Elements always absorb exactly the same wavelengths so when astronomers first looked at the spectra of other stars they expected to see the same black lines. They did see similar lines, but they found that the lines were often blue- or red-shifted. This indicated that the stars were moving relative to the Earth.

If a star is moving away from the Earth the lines seen are red-shifted; the pattern of black lines is closer to the red end of the spectrum. If the light is blue-shifted, the star is moving towards the Earth. The faster the star is moving the bigger the observed shift. Note that on a planet orbiting a distant star similar to our Sun, the spectrum of that star would look just like the Sun's spectrum. It is because of the relative movement of the distant star and Earth that we see the shift in the spectrum.

Taking it further

The red shift observed in starlight is not just due to the Doppler effect. Stars, including our Sun, are moving apart because the Universe itself is expanding – see lesson P1 6.2 for more details.

Questions

1. Describe the changes to the pitch of the sound heard by people on the platform as a train passes.

2. A light source is moving so that an observer sees the light 'red-shifted'. **(a)** What happens to the wavelength and the frequency of the observed light? **(b)** Draw a diagram to show how the light source is moving relative to the observer.

3. Two go-karts are being driven along a race track at the same speed. Explain whether the drivers notice any change in the sound of: **(a)** their own go-kart; **(b)** the other go-kart.

4. A satellite orbits the Earth transmitting a beam of microwaves. **(a)** Describe how the frequency of the microwaves received by a detector changes as the satellite passes overhead. **(b)** What is this effect called?

5. Explain how a driver of a moving car hears a siren but can **NOT** hear the pitch of the siren changing.

6. A laser beam is used to measure the speed of a car. The light is directed at the car and reflected back to a detector. **(a)** How does the wavelength change if the car is: **(i)** approaching the laser? **(ii)** travelling away from the laser? **(b)** The car is travelling towards the laser and it speeds up. What difference will this make to the wavelength of the light detected? **(c)** The laser and detector are now driven at the same speed behind the first car. Explain whether there are any changes to the wavelength of the light received.

7. Explain why the motion of a siren affects the pitch of the sound heard by a stationary observer. How can this effect be demonstrated in the science laboratory?

8. In Doppler ultrasound scans of the heart, computers use the Doppler effect to produce an image of the blood flow inside the heart. Ultrasound waves are sent towards the heart and are reflected back. Explain how the Doppler effect can be used to give information about the speed and direction of the moving blood flow in the heart.

Red shift

P1 6.2 The expanding Universe

Learning objectives
- explain that the red shift is evidence that all galaxies are moving apart
- explain that the red shift is evidence that the Universe is expanding.

What stars can tell us
All of the information we have about a star comes from analysing the electromagnetic radiation we detect from the star. The same is true for galaxies. The line spectrum from a galaxy tells us about the elements in the outer atmosphere of its stars. A red shift in the radiation tells us how fast the galaxy is moving and whether it is moving towards us or away from us. Astronomers also want to know how far away stars and galaxies are. They have several ways of working this out, for example, stars look dimmer the further away they are.

Distant galaxies
When astronomers look at the spectra from distant galaxies they find that almost all of them, in every direction, show a red shift. One explanation for this is that almost everything in the Universe is moving away from us in all directions. Astronomers also discovered that the further away a galaxy is, the more its spectrum is red-shifted, which means the faster it is moving away. To discover this they used a different method to measure the distance to some nearby galaxies. Once they had done this, scientists had a graph like Figure 2 that they could use to find out how far away other galaxies were.

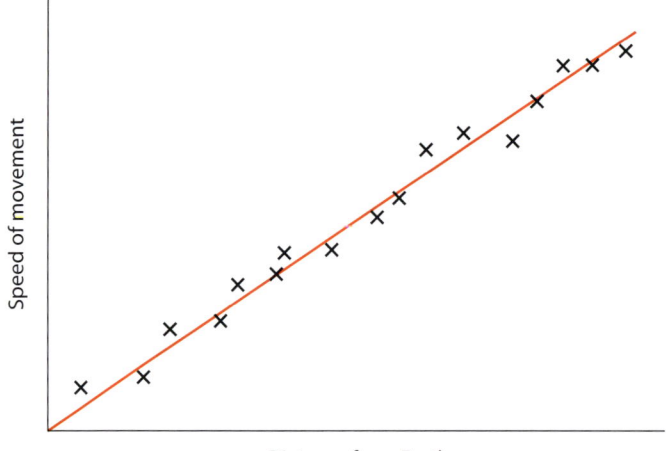

Red-shifted light from galaxies tells us they are moving away.

Figure 2 Astronomers' data showed that the further away a galaxy is the faster it is moving away from us.

Expansion
These observations led to the theory that the Universe is expanding. A balloon is a simple model of an expanding Universe. The rubber of the balloon expands when it is inflated, and everything on the surface expands. Galaxies A and C started off further apart than A and B, so when the balloon is inflated the distance between A and C increases more quickly than the distance between A and B. The balloon is just a simple model – the theory is that the Universe is expanding in three dimensions. Just as the rubber between the 'balloon galaxies' expanded, space is expanding in the Universe. It is difficult to understand that there is nothing outside the Universe for it to expand into; all the space is part of the existing Universe.

Figure 3 When the balloon expands, everything gets further apart.

Questions

1. If you see that light from a galaxy has a red shift, what does this tell you?

2. Two galaxies show different red shifts. How could you tell which one is moving away faster?

3. The Andromeda galaxy is unusual, as it has a blue shift. What does this tell us?

4. Distant galaxy A is further away than distant galaxy B. What can you predict about the electromagnetic radiation astronomers detect from these galaxies?

5. Spectrum X is part of the spectrum of the Sun. Spectrum Y is part of the spectrum from a distant galaxy.

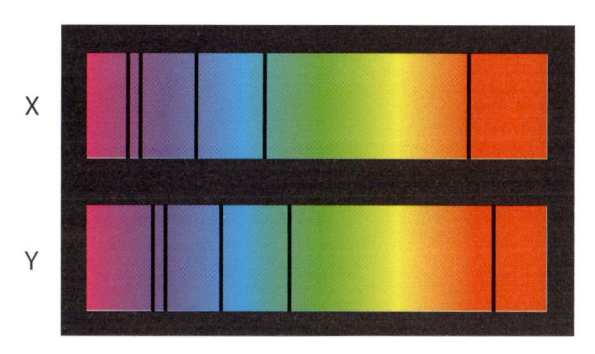

Figure 4 Spectrum X and spectrum Y.

Explain how the shift in position of the dark lines supports the idea that the Universe is expanding.

6. If the Universe is expanding at a constant rate, explain, with the aid of a diagram, why this means that a more distant galaxy is moving away faster than one that is not so far away.

7.

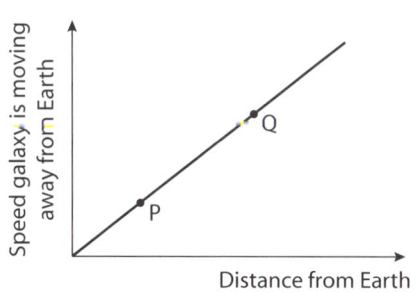

(a) What does this graph tell you about how the speed of a galaxy is related to its distance from Earth?

(b) Describe how the spectrum of galaxy P looks different from the spectrum of galaxy Q.

(c) A burst of radiation from a distant astronomical object was seen with the largest red shift ever recorded. What does this tell you about the object?

8. Explain what astronomers mean by red shift and how it provides evidence that the Universe is expanding.

Examiner feedback

Remember that red shift is not the same as 'getting redder'; the wavelengths get longer and the frequencies lower. For example, microwaves might become radio waves.

Taking it further

Scientists found that some stars vary in brightness with a frequency that depends on how bright the star really is. A star looks dimmer the further away it is, so by measuring the frequency they could work out the actual brightness of the star and compare it with how bright it looked from Earth. This allowed scientists to calculate the distance to the star, and so to the galaxy it was in.

Taking it further

The cosmological red shift is due to the whole 'fabric' of the Universe expanding. The space that the electromagnetic waves travel through is stretching, which causes the wavelength to increase and the frequency to decrease. Compare this to a Doppler shift, which is caused by the relative movement of the source and observer. The source and observer are moving away from the other through space, which is not stretching. The effect is the same, a red shift, but the reason for it is different.

P1 6.3 The Big Bang theory

Learning objectives
- explain that if the Universe is expanding this implies it must have started, from a small point, with an explosion called the 'Big Bang'
- describe cosmic microwave background radiation (CMBR)
- explain that red shifts in galaxies and the existence of CMBR are evidence for the Big Bang theory
- explain that the Big Bang theory is the only theory that explains the existence of CMBR in all directions
- consider the limitations of the Big Bang theory.

Going back in time

If the Universe is expanding, then last year it was smaller than it is now. When scientists realised this they suggested an explanation for how the Universe began. A suggested explanation is called a **hypothesis**. Their hypothesis was the idea that sometime in the past the Universe must have been very small and that it exploded and has been expanding ever since. If you were to make time go backwards, everything in the Universe would crunch back together into a single point about 13.7 billion years ago. Playing time forwards again from there, a tiny dot suddenly explodes and starts expanding to become the Universe we see today. The explosion is called 'the **Big Bang**'.

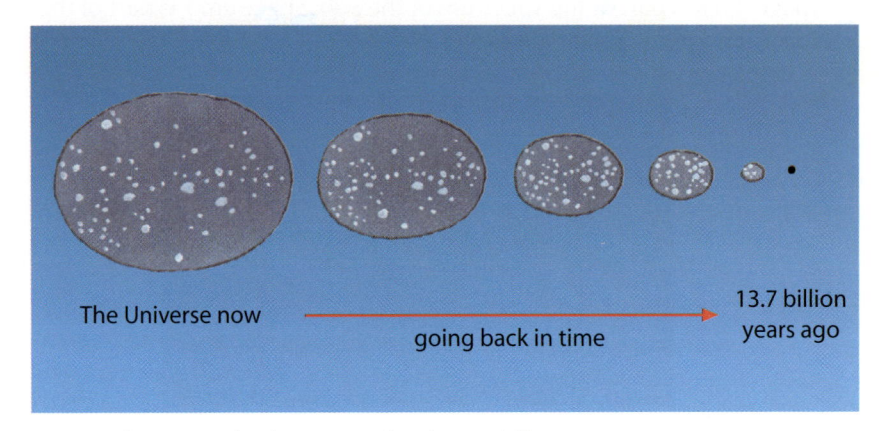

Figure 1 The Universe has been expanding for 13.7 billion years.

When the Big Bang hypothesis was first suggested some scientists disagreed with it. They already had a theory that the Universe had always existed. This theory is called the **Steady State theory**. It says that as the Universe expands new galaxies of stars are being formed in the spaces between the other galaxies. This would keep the density of the Universe constant; it would be a steady state.

Cosmic microwave background radiation (CMBR)

Scientists used the Big Bang hypothesis to make a prediction. They said that, if there had been a Big Bang, the small Universe would have been white hot. It has been expanding and cooling ever since, so they predicted that, by now, the radiation from the Big Bang would have been red-shifted as far as the microwave region of the electromagnetic spectrum. In 1964, at Princeton University in the USA, scientists started to search for this radiation.

At the same time, just 40 miles away, scientists Arno Penzias and Robert Wilson were experimenting with the horn-shaped radio wave detector shown in the photo. They wanted to get rid of all radio interference but, no matter how hard they tried, they could not get rid of a microwave radiation with wavelength 7.35 cm. They even cleared out some pigeons that had nested in the structure. The microwave radiation was evenly spread over the sky, 24 hours a day. They realised it came from outside our galaxy, but they could not explain it. When a friend told Arno Penzias about the work of the scientists at Princeton he contacted them and they all realised that the **cosmic microwave background radiation** (CMBR) had been found.

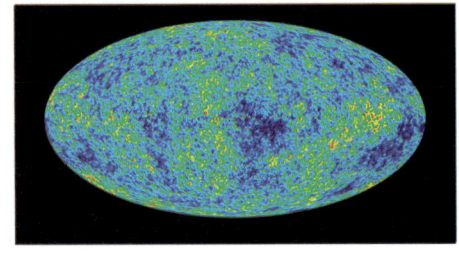

Penzias and Wilson with the horn-shaped receiver that detected CMBR.

Cosmic microwave background radiation.

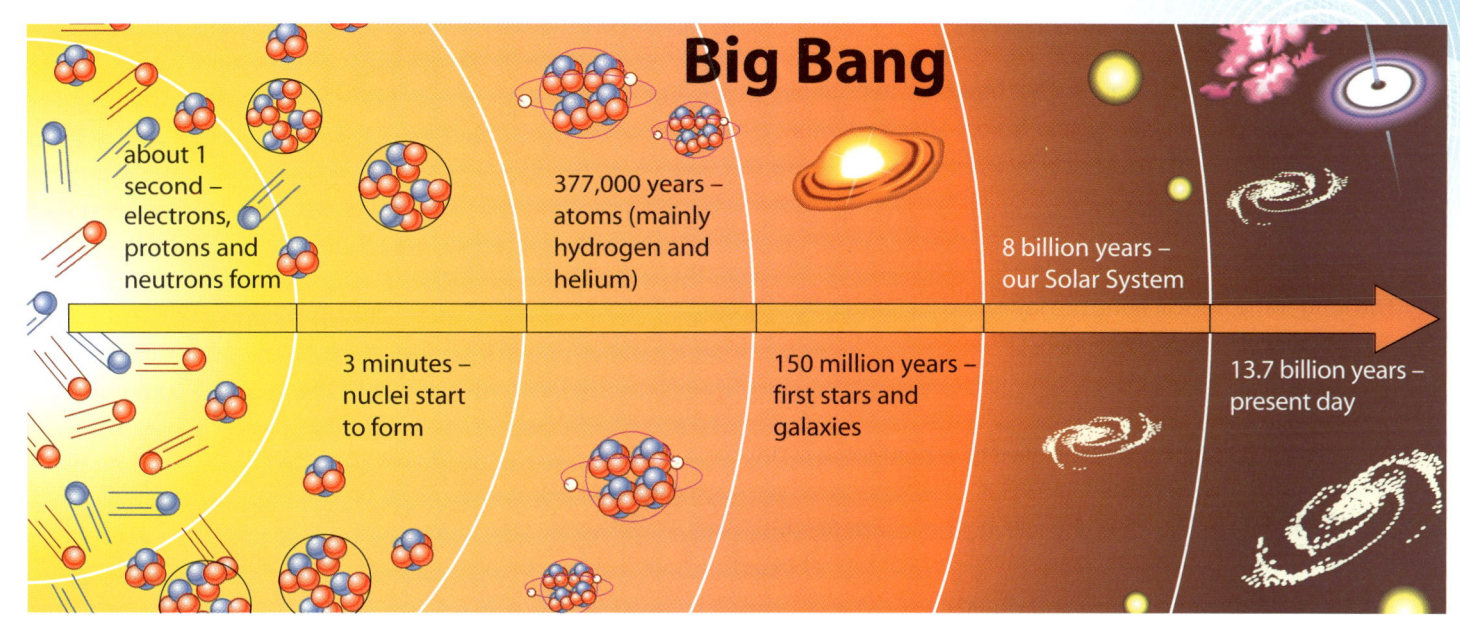

Figure 2 Timeline of the Universe.

Evidence for the Big Bang theory

The **Big Bang theory** is now widely accepted. The red shifts we see in the light from galaxies are strong evidence to support it. More importantly the CMBR is very strong evidence to support it, as there is no other explanation for CMBR arriving at Earth from all directions. Most cosmologists accept the Big Bang theory as the explanation for the origin of the Universe.

Why was there a Big Bang?

This is a question that science will probably never be able to answer. Time started, mass and space were all created at the moment of the Big Bang so there is no way to collect evidence of anything that happened before it, if anything did. The question is one that scientists will almost certainly never have enough reliable and valid evidence to answer.

Examiner feedback

You know that there are some questions that scientists cannot answer. 'Why was there a Big Bang?' is a good example to use. It is probably the most fundamental of these questions.

Questions

1. What does the Big Bang theory say?
2. Give two pieces of evidence for the Big Bang theory.
3. 'Why was the Universe created?' Suggest one reason why scientists cannot answer this question.
4. If new data were collected that did not support the Big Bang theory, what should scientists do?
5. Explain why the discovery of the CMBR was so important.
6. Some theories of the Universe suggest that there was a previous Universe that collapsed to a Big Crunch before the Big Bang. Explain whether scientists have any proof of this theory.
7. (a) Describe cosmic microwave background radiation (CMBR). (b) Explain why it is important in the Big Bang theory.
8. The Steady State theory of the Universe says that the Universe has always existed and as it expands new galaxies of stars are formed in the spaces between the other galaxies.

   Explain the main differences between the Steady State theory and the Big Bang theory, and why the Big Bang theory is the one accepted by most cosmologists today.

ISA practice: modelling optical fibres

You have been asked to investigate how the strength of a signal transmitted by an optical fibre is affected by the length of the fibre. The optical fibre will be modelled using a long rectangular block of jelly.

Hypothesis

The longer the optical fibre, the lower the light intensity reading will be in millivolts.

Section 1

1. In this investigation you will need to control some of the variables.
   (a) Name one variable you will need to control in this investigation. *(1 mark)*
   (b) Describe briefly how you would carry out a preliminary investigation to find a suitable value to use for this variable. Explain how the results will help you decide on the best value for this variable. *(2 marks)*

2. Describe how you would carry out the investigation. You should include:
   - the equipment that you would use
   - how you would use the equipment
   - the measurements that you would make
   - a risk assessment
   - how you would make it a fair test.

   You may include a labelled diagram to help you to explain your method.

   In this question you will be assessed on using good English, organising information clearly and using specialist terms where appropriate. *(9 marks)*

3. Design a table that will contain all the data that you would record during the investigation. *(2 marks)*

   Total for Section 1: 14 marks

Section 2

Two students, Study Group 1, carried out an investigation to test the hypothesis. They used a block of jelly to model an optical fibre. They measured the length of the jelly block. They sent light through different lengths of jelly fibre and used a detector in an electric circuit to convert the light intensity to a reading in millivolts.

Figure 1 shows their results.

```
20 cm jelly: 100 mV
16 cm jelly: 155 mV
12 cm jelly: 241 mV
8 cm jelly: 374 mV
4 cm jelly: 580 mV
2 cm jelly: 722 mV
```

Figure 1 The results of Study Group 1's investigation.

4. (a) (i) What is the independent variable in this investigation?
   (ii) What is the dependent variable in this investigation?
   (iii) Name one control variable in this investigation. *(3 marks)*
   (b) Plot a graph to show the link between the length of the jelly and the light intensity reading in millivolts. *(4 marks)*
   (c) Do the results support the hypothesis? Explain your answer. *(3 marks)*

The results of three other study groups are shown below. Figure 2 shows the results of another two students, Study Group 2.

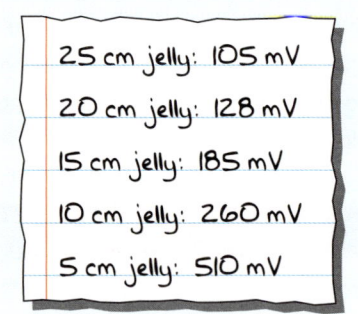

```
25 cm jelly: 105 mV
20 cm jelly: 128 mV
15 cm jelly: 185 mV
10 cm jelly: 260 mV
5 cm jelly: 510 mV
```

Figure 2 Results from Study Group 2.

Table 1 shows the results of Study Group 3, a group of students who used a brighter lamp with the same jelly.

Table 1 Results from Study Group 3.

Length of jelly/cm	Light intensity/mV			
	Test 1	Test 2	Test 3	Mean
3	764	771	769	768
6	378	380	385	381
9	270	268	356	298
12	182	187	186	185

Table 2 shows the results from Study Group 4, a company that produces fibres for transmitting infrared (IR) signals. It tested two fibre materials: one is a type of glass and one is a crystal. For this test, the company used an IR source with a wavelength of 0.002 mm and an IR detector in an electric circuit that converted the IR intensity to a reading in millivolts. It used different lengths of fibres and measured the voltage.

Table 2 Results from Study Group 4 testing two kinds of optical fibre.

Length of fibre/m	Percentage of signal transmitted (%)							
	HMF glass fibre				Crystal fibre			
	1	2	3	Mean	1	2	3	Mean
1.0	193	196	196	195	183	182	181	182
2.0	191	193	189	191	163	167	168	166
3.0	188	186	168	181	153	150	153	152
4.0	184	181	181	182	138	138	139	138

Study Group 4 then investigated how different wavelengths of IR radiation affected the transmission of the signal. Figure 3 shows their results as a graph.

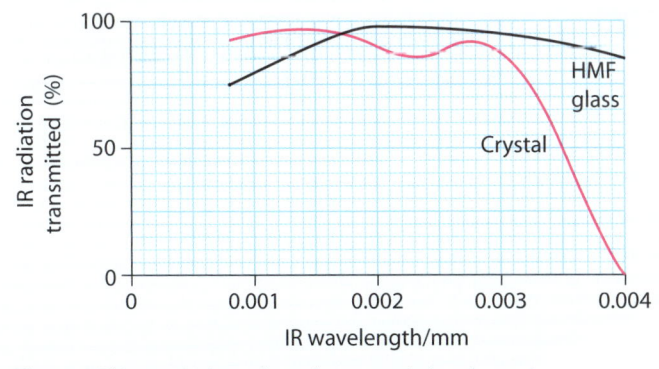

Figure 2 This graph shows how the transmission depends on the wavelength of the infrared radiation for a 1 m length of crystal and a 1 m length of glass fibre.

5 Describe one way in which the results of Study Group 2 are similar to or different from the results of Study Group 1, and give one reason why the results are similar or different *(3 marks)*

6 (a) Draw a sketch graph or chart of the results from Study Group 2. *(3 marks)*
   (b) Does the data support the hypothesis being investigated? To gain full marks you should use all of the relevant data from Study Groups 1, 2 and 3 to explain whether or not the data supports the hypothesis. *(3 marks)*
   (c) The data from the other groups only gives a limited amount of information. What other information or data would you need in order to be more certain as to whether or not the hypothesis is correct? Explain the reason for your answer. *(3 marks)*
   (d) Use Studies 2, 3 and 4 to answer this question. What is the relationship between the length of the fibre and the intensity of the light transmitted? How well does the data support your answer? *(3 marks)*

7 Look back at the investigation method of Study Group 1. If you could repeat the investigation, suggest one change that you would make to the method, and explain the reason for the change. *(3 marks)*

8 The fibre optic company is not convinced that the jelly is a suitable model for the fibre optic cable. Use the results of the investigation to help them decide whether or not the jelly is a suitable model for the cable. *(3 marks)*

Total for Section 2: 31 marks
Total for the ISA: 45 marks

Assess yourself questions

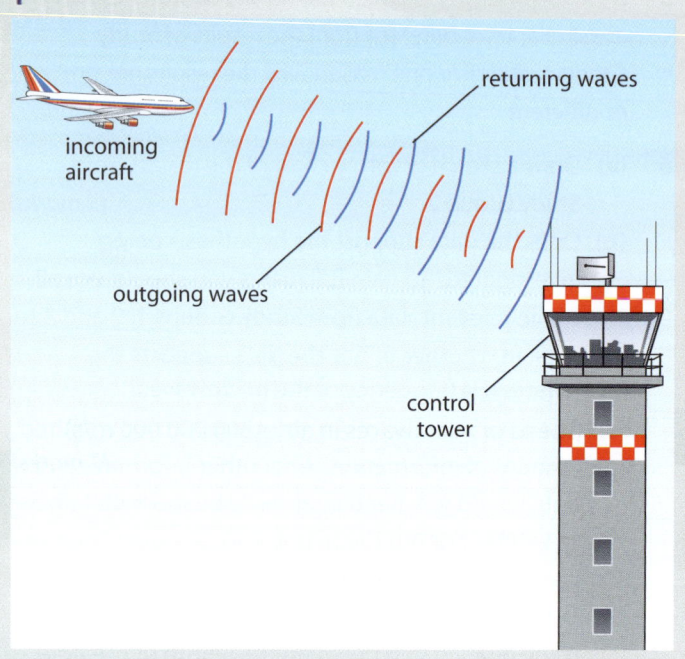

1

Figure 1 Aircraft being tracked by radar.

Figure 1 shows an aeroplane being tracked by radar.

(a) Which of these is used for radar?

gamma rays   infrared   visible light
microwaves   radio waves   *(1 mark)*

(b) The radar operators use the Doppler effect to tell whether the plane is flying towards or away from the tower.

Explain how the observers in the tower can tell if the aeroplane is flying towards the tower. *(2 marks)*

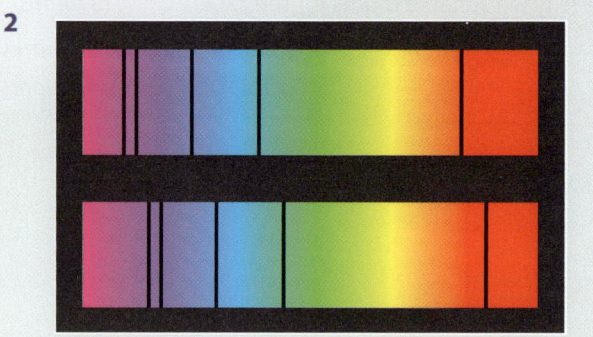

2

Figure 2 Spectra from two distant galaxies.

Figure 2 shows the spectrum of light from two distant galaxies. Decide whether each of these statements is **TRUE** or **FALSE**.

(a) The red end of the spectrum is the higher energy end of the spectrum.

(b) The dark lines are missing wavelengths of light.

(c) The red end of the spectrum is the longer wavelength end of the spectrum.

(d) The top spectrum is for the galaxy that is furthest away.

(e) The bottom spectrum is for the galaxy that is moving fastest. *(5 marks)*

3 Table 1 shows the distance from Earth of different galaxies and the speed at which the galaxies are moving away from Earth.

Table 1 Distance to galaxies A to E.

Galaxy	Distance (light years)	Speed/km/s
A	77 000 000	1100
B	1 000 000 000	15 000
C	1 500 000 000	23 000
D	2 500 000 000	4000
E	4 000 000 000	60 000

(a) Are there any anomalous values in this table? If so, which value(s)? *(1 mark)*

(b) What does the data tell you about the distance to a galaxy and the speed it is moving away from Earth? *(1 mark)*

(c) Explain what data scientists collected and what they measured to produce this table. *(2 marks)*

4 The cosmic microwave background radiation (CMBR) is important evidence for the Big Bang theory. Explain what it is and why it is important.

In this question you will be assessed on using good English, organising information clearly and using specialist terms where appropriate. *(6 marks)*

5 Some students investigate the Doppler effect. They use a loudspeaker emitting a sound with a frequency of 256 Hz and put this in a car that is driven along a straight racetrack at speeds of 10 mph, 20 mph and up to 70 mph. The frequency is picked up by a microphone and a computer displays the frequency received. The students record the results in a table, and work out the speed in m/s and the increase in frequency. They plot a graph of frequency increase against the speed of the car.

Figure 3 shows their graph.

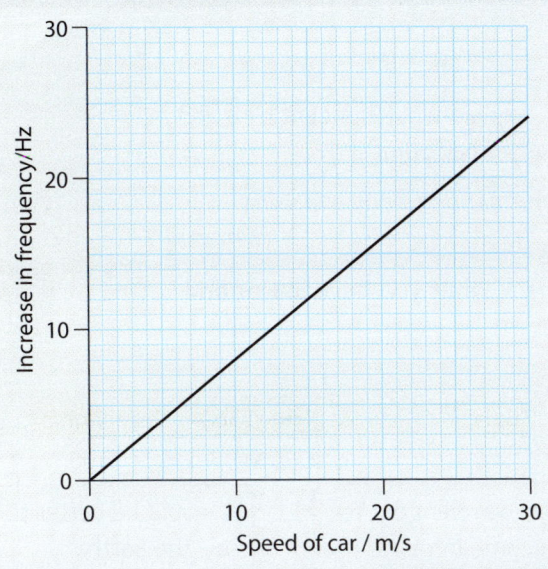

Figure 3 Graph of increase of frequency against speed of car.

(a) How can you tell that the car was driven towards the students and not away from them? *(1 mark)*

(b) Which is the independent variable in this investigation? *(1 mark)*

(c) Describe the relationship between the frequency increase and the speed of the car. *(2 marks)*

(d) Explain how the graph tells you this. *(1 mark)*

(e) Use the graph to find the frequency increase at 29 m/s. *(1 mark)*

(f) From your answer to (e) work out the frequency heard by the observers when the car was travelling at 28 m/s and explain whether the observers could hear the sound. *(2 marks)*

6 The Steady State theory is an alternative to the Big Bang theory. In the Steady State theory, the Universe expands and has always existed. As it expands, matter is created in parts of the Universe to keep the density of matter, like stars and galaxies, looking the same.

(a) What is the difference in the way that the Steady State theory and the Big Bang theory consider the origin of the Universe? *(2 marks)*

Radiation detected from distant galaxies has a red shift.

(b) Explain what is meant by 'red shift'. *(2 marks)*

(c) Explain whether the red shift evidence:
  (i) supports the Big Bang theory' *(2 marks)*
  (ii) supports the Steady State theory. *(2 marks)*

(d) Suggest a reason why scientists cannot answer the question, 'Why was the Universe created?' *(1 mark)*

7

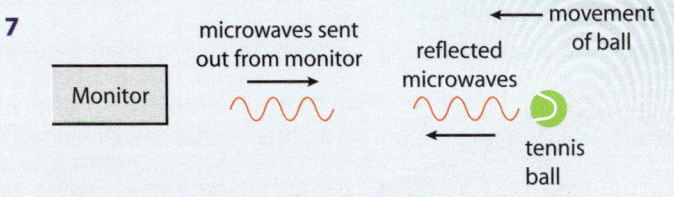

Figure 4 Equipment for measuring speed.

A monitor to measure the performance of a tennis player's serve sends out microwaves towards the ball, and displays the speed of the ball. The microwaves have a wavelength of 12.5 cm.

(a) What is the frequency of the microwaves?
  (speed of microwaves in air = 300 000 000 m/s) *(2 marks)*

Some microwaves are reflected from the ball, and detected by the monitor.

(b) Describe how this can be used to calculate the speed of the ball. *(3 marks)*

GradeStudio Route to A*

Here are three students' answers to the following question:

Dark lines in the spectra from most distant galaxies shows a 'red shift'. Explain what is meant by a 'red shift' and how this supports the theory that the Universe began as a very small point.

In this question you will be assessed on using good English, organising information clearly and using specialist terms where appropriate. (6 marks)

Read the answers together with the examiner comments. Then check what you have learnt and try putting it into practice in any further questions you answer.

B Grade answer

Student 1

> A red shift is when the dark lines move into the red part of the spectrum. When there is a red shift it is because galaxies are moving away from us. This means the Universe is expanding. So a long time ago it must have all started from a small point.

- This is incorrect – a red shift is a shift towards longer wavelengths, for example, blue might become green, or red might become infrared.
- It would be better to say 'the Earth'.
- This sentence is not needed, the fact that they are moving away suggests they started from a point.

Examiner comment

This candidate has understood that red shift shows the galaxies are moving away from the Earth, and that this implies that at some time in the past they were all at the same point. The explanation of red shift is incorrect and they have not mentioned the change in the frequency or wavelength.

A Grade answer

Student 2

> The dark lines are missing wavelengths in the spectrum. They are shifted towards the red end of the spectrum when the galaxies are moving away from Earth because the galaxies and the Earth are getting further apart. If most are red shifted, most galaxies are moving away, so 14 billion years ago they were all at the same point, implying the Universe started from a very small point.

- The important point to note is that we know what the wavelengths should be (so we know they are red shifted).
- This is true, but is not needed. If they had, by mistake, written 14 *million* years it would have lost a mark. It would be best left out.

Examiner comment

Like student 1, this candidate has explained how the red shift leads to the idea that the Universe started from a point. They did not point out that the dark lines were known wavelengths, or the effect of red shift on the size of the wavelength, or of the frequency.

AIM HIGH
FOR THE TOP GRADES

A* Grade answer

Student 3

> The dark lines are where certain, known wavelengths are missing from the spectra. When these are compared with our Sun, the lines from distant galaxies are all at longer wavelengths; this is called a red shift. This shift in wavelength happens because the source is moving away. This tells us that the galaxies are all moving away from Earth, and if all the galaxies in the Universe are moving away then some time in the past they must all have started from the same small point.

- Refers to 'known' wavelengths
- Clear explanation of red shift, and reference to change in wavelength.
- Use of correct terminology.

Examiner comment

This candidate has covered all the main points in the process:
- Dark lines occur at particular wavelengths.
- In the spectra from the distant galaxies the lines are shifted towards the longer wavelength, or red, end of the spectrum.
- The wavelength appears to have increased (or frequency decreased).
- This occurs because the galaxies are all moving away from the Earth.
- This suggests that a long time in the past they all started from the same point.

MOVING UP THE GRADES
- Read the question carefully.
- These questions carry a maximum of either five or six marks.
- Plan your answer by noting at least five/six relevant points you are going to make.
- Put these points into a logical sequence.

Examination-style questions

1 The following is an extract from an advertisement.

> **Experience a new level of comfort with warm-water under-floor heating**
>
> Central heating radiators warm a room by moving cold air across our feet, warming the air and convecting it round the room. Most of the heat from under-floor heating is transferred by radiation. We are most comfortable when the heat we feel is radiated, making our heads slightly cooler than our feet.

(a) Explain why the air heated by a central heating radiator moves round the room. *(4 marks)*

(b) The diagram shows a section of the floor of a room. The room is heated by under-floor heating.

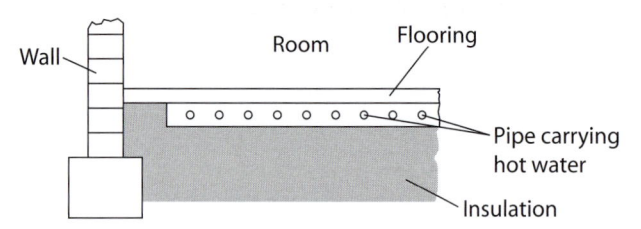

(b) (i) How is energy transferred by heating from the hot water pipes through the flooring into the room? *(1 mark)*

(ii) The table gives information about different flooring materials.

Flooring material	U value in arbitrary units	Nature of the flooring surface
Ceramic tiles	23.0	Dark-coloured, matt
Concrete	12.5	Light-coloured, matt
Vinyl	20.0	Light-coloured, shiny
Wood	1.5	Dark-coloured, shiny

Which flooring material would be most suitable for use with under-floor heating? Give reasons for your answer. *(4 marks)*

(c) A room has a concrete floor of mass 480 kg.

The specific heat capacity of concrete is 2400 J/kg/°C.

The under-floor heating system during one day transfers 9 MJ of energy.

(i) Calculate the maximum temperature rise of the concrete floor.

Write down the equation you use. Show clearly how you work out your answer. *(3 marks)*

(ii) Give a reason why the temperature rise of the floor is likely to be less than the value you have calculated. *(1 mark)*

2 (a) The diagram shows two syringes, **A** and **B**.

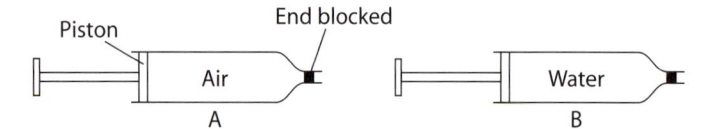

Syringe **A** contains air. Syringe **B** contains water.

One end of each syringe is blocked.

A force is applied to the piston of one of the syringes as shown in the diagram.

Force ⟶

Does the syringe above contain air or water? Give a reason for your answer. *(1 mark)*

(b) A woman spills some liquid nail varnish remover on her hand. She notices that the liquid soon disappears and that her hand feels cold. Explain why her hand feels cold. *(2 marks)*

(c) When someone runs water for a bath, they notice that one of the taps becomes coated in a film of moisture.

Is it the hot-water tap or the cold-water tap that becomes coated in moisture? Explain your answer. *(2 marks)*

(d) Use the kinetic theory to explain why a liquid cools down when it evaporates.

In this question you will be assessed on using good English, organising information clearly and using specialist terms where appropriate. *(6 marks)*

3 The bar chart gives the cost of generating electricity in the UK using different types of power stations.

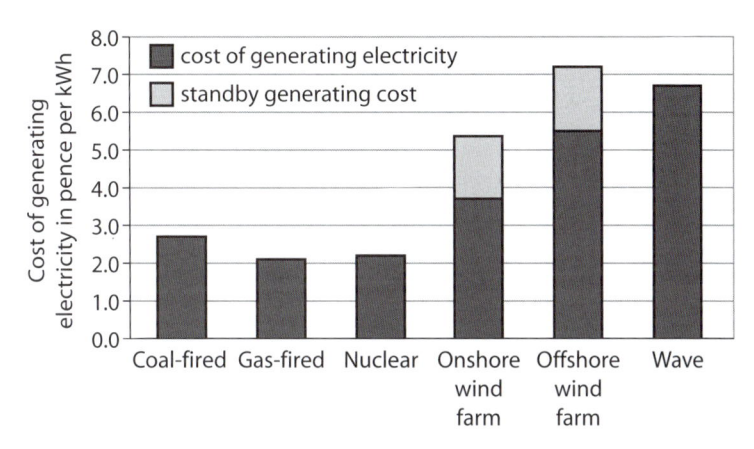

(a) Choose the correct ending **A**, **B**, **C** or **D** to complete the sentence.

The information is displayed as a bar chart because …

A both variables are categoric.

B one variable is categoric, the other variable is controlled.

C one variable is categoric, the other variable is continuous.

D both variables are continuous. *(1 mark)*

(b) The cost of generating electricity at a wind farm has a *standby generation cost* added. This is to cover the cost of generating electricity when the wind farm is not working.

(i) When is a wind farm not likely to be working? *(2 marks)*

(ii) Why do the other types of power station on the bar chart not have a standby generation cost added? *(2 marks)*

(iii) Why is a gas-fired power station most likely to be used for standby generation? *(1 mark)*

(c) The costs of generating electricity given in the bar chart include:
- the capital cost of building and equipping the power station
- the cost of the fuel burned (where applicable)
- the cost of operating and maintaining the power station
- the cost of decommissioning the power station.

The costs do not include the cost of removing carbon dioxide emissions.

   (i) Why do nuclear power stations have high decommissioning costs? *(2 marks)*

   (ii) All new fossil-fuel power stations will, by law, have to remove carbon dioxide emissions. Explain why. *(2 marks)*

   (iii) If the cost of removing carbon dioxide emissions is added to the values given on the bar chart, which type of power station will produce the cheapest electricity? *(1 mark)*

4 Describe, as fully as you can, the similarities and differences between the ways that sound and light travel from one place to another.

In this question you will be assessed on using good English, organising information clearly and using specialist terms where appropriate. *(6 marks)*

5 The diagram compares the spectrum of light from the Sun with the spectra of light from three galaxies, **L**, **M** and **N**.

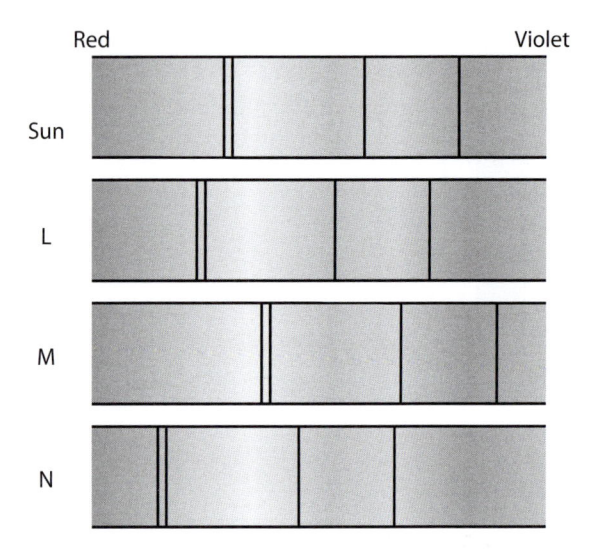

(a) Describe the differences between the spectra and use these differences to deduce what you can about the galaxies **L**, **M** and **N**.

In this question you will be assessed on using good English, organising information clearly and using specialist terms where appropriate. *(6 marks)*

(b) The spectra of light from distant galaxies provide evidence that the Universe is expanding and support the 'Big Bang' theory for the origin of the Universe.

What is the 'Big Bang' theory? *(2 marks)*

(c) In 1948, George Gamow predicted that there should be microwave radiation left over from the 'Big Bang'. This radiation was discovered in the 1960s and was confirmed by the Cosmic Background Explorer (COBE) satellite in the early 1990s.

Which of the following statements best describes the discovery?

A It disproves the involvement of a god in the origin of the Universe.

B It gives information that helps us know what happened before the 'Big Bang'.

C It provides evidence that eliminates all other theories of the origin of the Universe.

D It provides evidence in support of the 'Big Bang' theory. *(1 mark)*

6 (a) Some students investigated the diffraction of microwaves using the apparatus below.

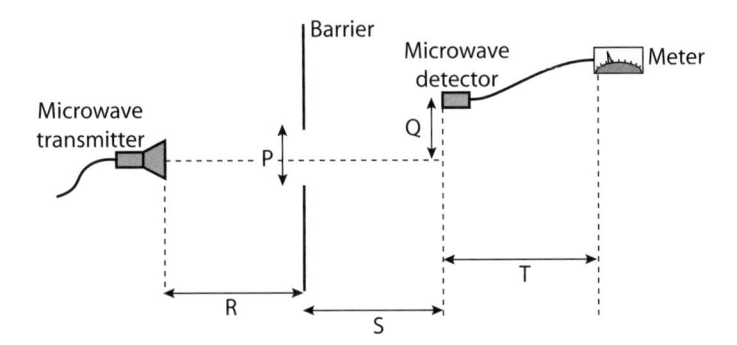

The students wanted to find out how the reading on the meter changed with the distance **Q**.

(i) Which was the dependent variable and which was the independent variable? *(2 marks)*

(ii) To make it a fair test, which distances had to be controlled?

A P, Q and R

B R, S and T

C P, R and S

D P, Q and T *(2 marks)*

(b) The teacher told the students to make the gap width, **P**, the same value as the wavelength of the microwaves.

The frequency of the microwaves was 1×10^{10} Hz.

The speed of microwaves is 3×10^8 m/s.

What should the gap width be, in centimetres? Write down the equation you use. Show clearly how you work out your answer. *(3 marks)*

(c) Television and radio programmes are often transmitted from the same transmitting mast. The carrier wave for television programmes has a higher frequency than the frequency of the carrier wave for radio programmes.

There is a high hill between one particular house and the transmitting mast. The householder receives signals from the mast by diffraction round the hill. He finds that he can receive radio programmes but not television programmes.

What can be deduced about the diffraction of waves round an obstacle and the wavelength of the waves?

Explain your answer. *(3 marks)*

Course Structure

	Print	Digital	Both
Biology	Student Book 978 1 408253 74 8 *Spring 2011*	ActiveTeach 978 1 408262 25 2 *Spring 2011*	Teacher and Technician Planning Pack with CD-ROM, also online and via your VLE 978 1 408253 76 2 *Spring 2011*
	Teacher Book 978 1 408253 75 5 *Spring 2011*	ActiveLearn Online Student Package *Autumn 2011* Single user 978 1 408280 20 1 10 user pack 978 1 408280 28 7 50 user pack 978 1 408280 27 0	Activity Pack with CD-ROM, also online and via your VLE 978 1 408253 73 1 *Spring 2011*
Chemisty	Student Book 978 1 408253 79 3 *Spring 2011*	ActiveTeach 978 1 408262 26 9 *Spring 2011*	Teacher and Technician Planning Pack with CD-ROM, also online and via your VLE 978 1 408253 78 6 *Spring 2011*
	Teacher Book 978 1 408253 80 9 *Spring 2011*	ActiveLearn Online Student Package *Autumn 2011* Single user 978 1 408280 26 3 10 user pack 978 1 408280 25 6 50 user pack 978 1 408280 24 9	Activity Pack with CD-ROM, also online and via your VLE 978 1 408253 77 9 *Spring 2011*
Physics	Student Book 978 1 408253 83 0 *Spring 2011*	ActiveTeach 978 1 408262 27 6 *Spring 2011*	Teacher and Technician Planning Pack with CD-ROM, also online and via your VLE 978 1 408253 82 3 *Spring 2011*
	Teacher Book 978 1 408253 84 7 *Summer 2011*	ActiveLearn Online Student Package *Autumn 2011* Single user 978 1 408280 30 0 10 user pack 978 1 408280 31 7 50 user pack 978 1 408280 29 4	Activity Pack with CD-ROM, also online and via your VLE 978 1 408253 81 6 *Spring 2011*
Science	Student Book 978 1 408253 85 4 *Spring 2011*		
	Teacher Book 978 1 408253 86 1 *Spring 2011*		
Additional Science	Student Book 978 1 408253 71 7 *Spring 2011*		
	Teacher Book 978 1 408253 72 4 *Spring 2011*		

Visit
www.pearsonschools.co.uk/aqagcsescience
to download sample material

Only three-and-a-half minutes from the heart of the city to the 26 hectare Botanic Garden with panorama views of Wellington and beyond.

Above: Similar to other cable car cities in the world, the view from the top is as breath taking as from the Hill in Hong Kong or from Nob Hill in San Francisco. On a clear day in winter, snow capped mountain ranges can be seen in the distance.

Left: The halfway point in the journey is between the second and third tunnels at Talavera Terrace Station where the cable cars pass.

Right: The city terminus of the cable car is off the main city shopping street of Lambton Quay diagonally across the Quay from Grey Street, at the end of Cable Car Lane. The Cable Car Lane Shopping Arcade is adjacent to the Cable Car Shopping Centre.

Above: An early 20th century view of Lambton Quay. Cable Car Lane, then Kelburn Avenue, is on the right. Lloyd's are advertising Christmas and New Year gifts. The electric tram is bound for Oriental Bay. On the right is the same scene today.

Above: Lambton Quay by Cable Car Lane in 1961. Many of the city commercial buildings were about to be replaced with towering modern structures. The electric trams were nearing the end of their service

The same view of Lambton Quay today. Gone are the electric trams and the majority of the old buildings. A yellow City Circle bus cruises by, a convenient way of travelling between the many city attractions. After a trip on the cable car, a yellow bus can take you to the Museum of Wellington City and Sea in the Bond Store on Queens Wharf.

2

*Spanning 100 years...
we take a Cable Car ride
to the skyline of
Wellington
city...*

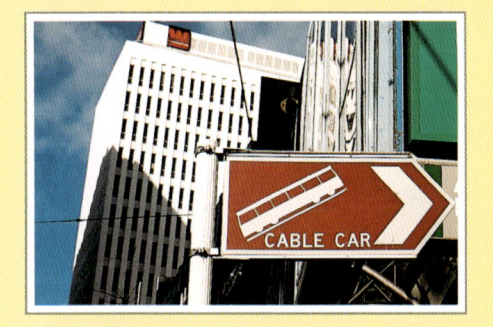

Above: The entrance to the Lambton Quay cable car terminus at the end of Cable car Lane c1950 *Evening Post,* and (*right*), the same entrance today.

Cable Car Lane was given the name in February 1966. It was originally Kelburn Avenue.

Far right: The high steps of the first generation cable cars were a challenge for all ages.

The city terminal (*below*) is underneath a downtown building and at the entrance to the first tunnel. A 1970s view (*right*).

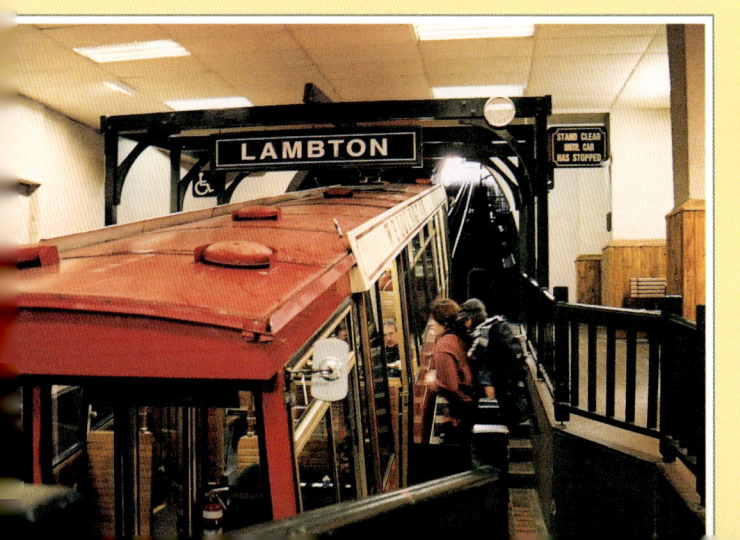

Today commuters have level access to the cable-cars.

First Stop...

The building of the Wellington motorway in the 1970s and the disappearance of the pioneer residential wooden homes on The Terrace, replaced by towering office buildings, changed forever the face of the Clifton Terrace Station. A cable car emerges from the first tunnel under The Terrace.

A 1971 view before the motorcar came to town in big numbers.

Clifton Terrace Station before and after the motorway. Now buried under concrete pillars supporting the passage of thousands of motorcars each day.

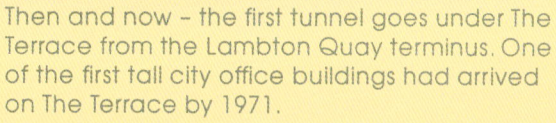

Then and now – the first tunnel goes under The Terrace from the Lambton Quay terminus. One of the first tall city office buildings had arrived on The Terrace by 1971.

Clifton Terrace was named after one of the ships the New Zealand Company used to bring early settlers to the region. The *Clifton* first arrived at the Port of Wellington on 18 February 1842.

A city bound cable car and trailer glides past the old Clifton Terrace Station in the early 1970s where the Clifton Terrace Carpark now stands.

Tramway Avenue was a victim of the motorway and new building developments.

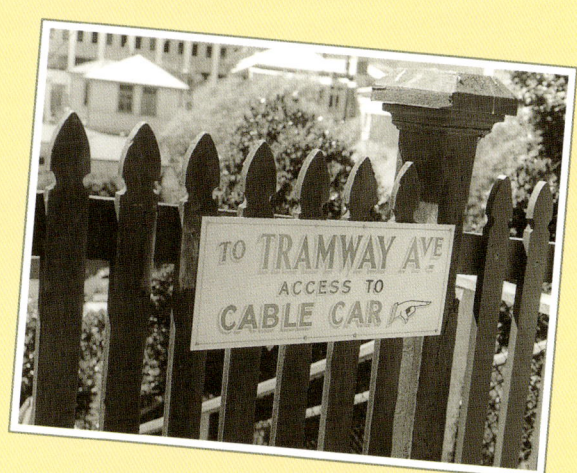

Looking down on the Talavera Station c1950.

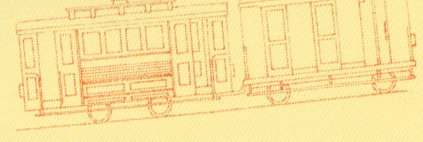

Second Stop…

Talavera is a city in Spain about 100 km south-west of Madrid.

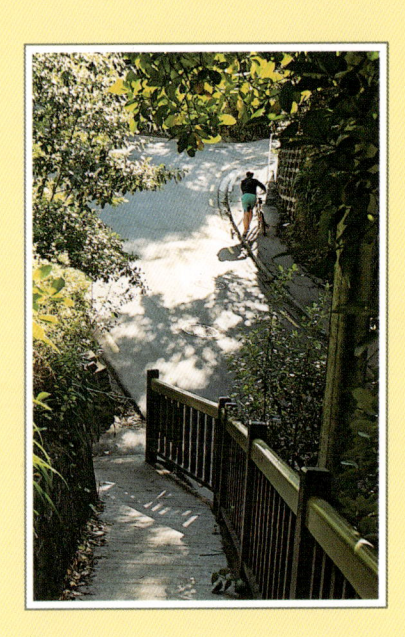

Today at Talavera an overhead footbridge carries pedestrians across the cable tramway tracks.

4WD Country – Everton Terrace viaduct viewed from the pathway to the Talavera Station.

The Victoria University of Wellington hall of residence Weir House built in 1932 stands proud on Kelburn heights high above the Talavera Station.
Timber merchant William Weir bequeathed money for the building when he died in 1926. 1902 vintage cable cars pass during the final week of service of the original system in September 1978.

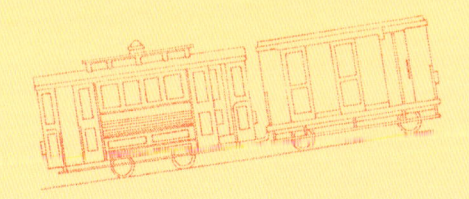

The final week of the 1902-1978 system. Cable cars numbers two and one pass at Talavera.

Left: Looking toward the city from the third tunnel in 1971. Commuters were allowed to cross the tracks at Talavera Station in those days.

7

The early 20th century cable-cars passing at the Talavera Station during the final days of the 1902 system in September 1978. *Evening Post*

The Southern most Cable Car in the World

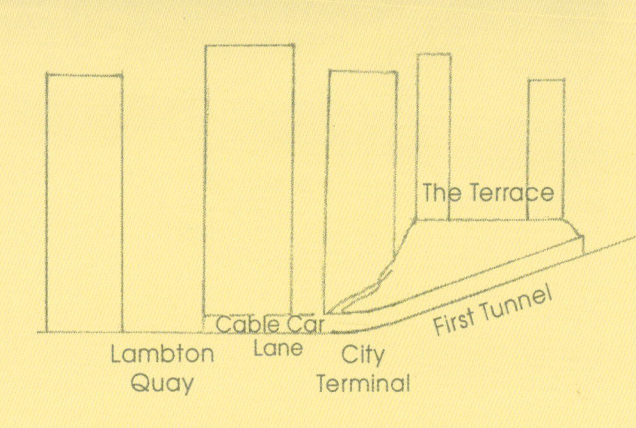

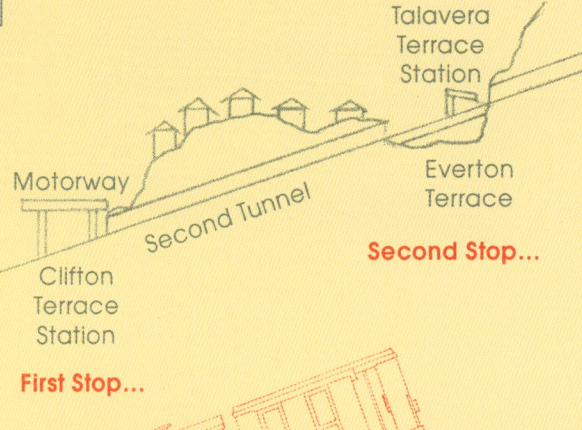

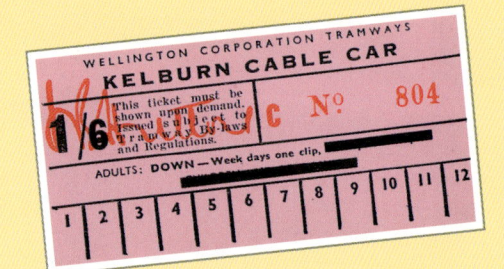

"Suprema A Situ the motto goes
The steel wire string still tows
You breathless to the view
Seen every day anew"

Denis Glover

A postcard published by A.H. & A.W. Reed in the early 1970s shows a trailer and cable car arrving at the old Salamanca Road Station. *postcard photograph by Norman Forrest*

8

Talavera Terrace Station — Third Tunnel — Everton Terrace — Weir House — Salamanca Road Station — Salamanca Road — Rawhiti Terrace — Kelburn Summit — Skyline Restaurant — Cable Car Museum

Third Stop...

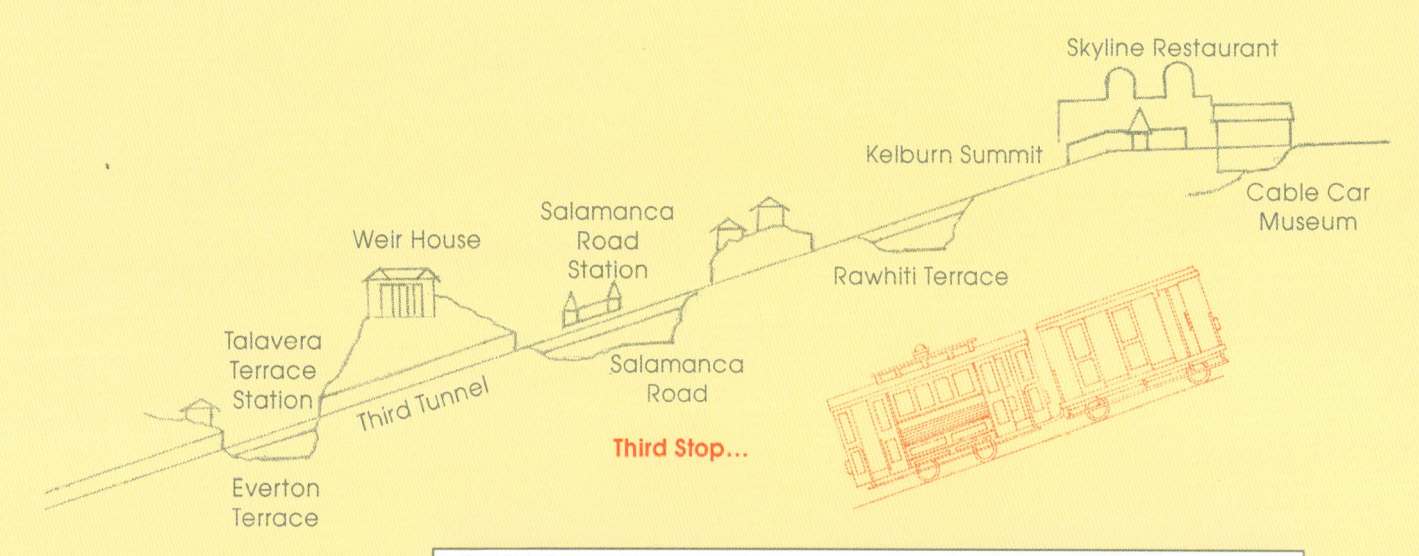

'Kelburn Park, a verdant expanse of "the greenest grass that ever grew," with scare a trace of having been made to order by cutting off a hilltop and tipping it holusbolus into the adjacent gully.' – *The Streets of My City by F.L. Irvine-Smith*

Today the cable cars still pass at the Talavera Station, the halfway point between the city and Kelburn.

The original Salamanca Road Station waiting shed in the early years. Kelburn Park is in the background. *F.T. Series No. 1107, John Bettle collection*

9

Right: A penny postcard showing the first Salamanca Road Station on the right by the entrance to the third and last tunnel on the journey from the city. Printed on the back of the postcard was a message telling people they could use the blank space "for communications in N.Z. or the British Empire."

Left: Nearing the top of the climb shortly after the service opened in 1902. The waiting shed at Salamanca Station had not been built. The last tunnel brought passengers the sight of paddocks and farmlands, a welcome change from the busy streets in the city below.

Third Stop...

Salamanca Road – a name very fitting for the University stop. Salamanca is a university city in Spain about 200 km west of Madrid.

Left: In private company days of the last century. On the horizon can be seen the kiosk and to the right the tall smokestack of the Cable Tramway powerhouse.

Above: A view from the first Salamanca Road Station shelter, looking over Kelburn Park c1910 to where the Victoria University campus now stands in Kelburn Parade.

University Stop: The final leg to the summit at Kelburn in 1971. Today the Salamanca Road Station is on the Salamanca viaduct (*right*). When the system was rebuilt in 1979, the station was repositioned further up the gradient. This made it possible for the down car to stop at the Clifton Station when the up car stopped at the Salamanca Road Station.

Below: The suburb of Kelburn today with the Victoria University campus on the left – the cable cars still climb right up to the stars.

The second Salamnca Road Station was built on the southern side of the line. Trailer number five shown in the foreground, now sits in retirement in the children's playground in Kelburn Park.

The Salamanca Road Station today on the overhead viaduct showing former cable trailer number five in the foreground.

Below: Trailer number five and two others started service as horse-drawn tramcars going from the city to the suburb of Newtown. These vehicles served the city from the 1880s until withdrawn from the cable car service in 1974. This photograph was taken in Lambton Quay looking towards the Willis Street intersection. Hunter Street is on the left.

Arriving at the Salamanca Road Station on the downward journey.

Cable trailer number five with the mock-up 'steam tram' in the Kelburn children's playground. They represent the first form of railed public transport that started service in Wellington in August 1878.

12

The Salamanca Road viaduct 1950c.

Below: The same bridge today with more cars parked in the busy suburban streets of Kelburn.

A pen drawing by Wilhelmina G. Irving of the Salamnca Road viaduct used on a greeting card in c1970.

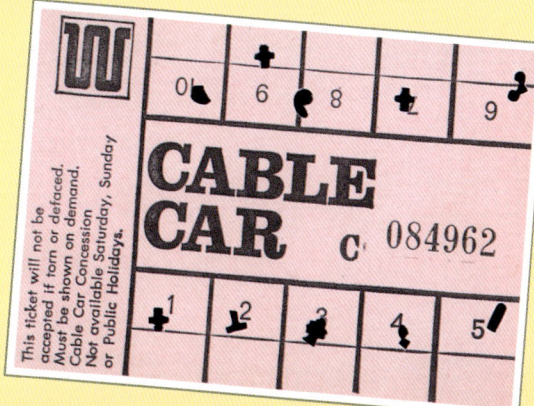

13

Wellington at twilight – a view of the city from the top of the Kelburn cable tramway.

Kelburn – named after Viscount Kelburn, the eldest son of the Earl of Glasgow, Governor of New Zealand 1892-1987.

40 years separates these two views of the final viaduct over Rawhiti Terrace before the cable car reaches the summit at Kelburn.

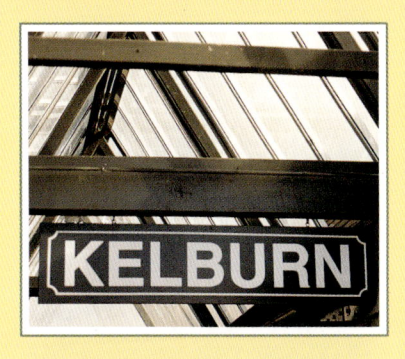

KELBURN

CABLE CAR TO LAMBTON QUAY

Visitors get a magic view as the cable car rolls to the summit at Kelburn.

An early 20th century postcard from the top of the cable car incline. *Grabham Ltd., Wellington*

Cable car driver Chelsea Taylor keeps up the tradition started in October 1977 when Mrs Elizabeth Parrant became the first woman to qualify to drive a cable car in New Zealand. That was back in the days of the original cable car system when she was known as a gripman. The title 'gripman' was used for drivers of the cable car as the braking had to be done by heaving on large levers in the centre of the cable-car.

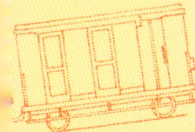

15

Above: The famous Welington icon of the 20th century, the Tea Kiosk that stood on the Kelburn horizon for 78 years, was severely damaged by fire in April 1982, and replaced with a new building known as the Skyline Restaurant. A glimpse of the new building can be seen behind the terminal of the cable car.

Left: The Tea Kiosk built in 1904 featured on many postcards. *Gold Medal Series, W28*

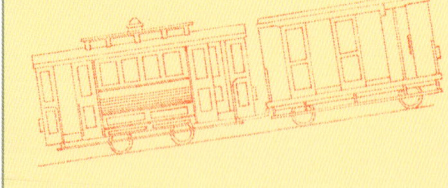

Gold Medal Series. Tea Kiosk Kelburne and Cable Tram, Wellington, N.Z.

Today the view of Wellington at twilight from Kelburn is far more exciting with all the high rise buildings – the author had the cable car and trailer specially stopped for this time exposure photograph in the winter of 1958.

DO NOT WALK ON TRACKS

The Kelburn cable car station at twilight.

The view from the top – only a short ride from the city and you are transformed into another world – to visit the quaint village of Kelburn, the Carter Observatory, the planetarium or take a stroll through the Wellington Botanic Garden.

Below: Faithful servant for 76 years – a c1900 cable car and trailer wait in the evening for departure time at the Kelburn terminus.

Left: Friday, 22 September 1978 – the last day of service for the original system. Cable car Number one is city bound.

17

The Story of the Kelburn Cable Tramway

The creation of a new suburb – The building of the Kelburn cable tramway and the road formation and cuttings along Upland Road, Kelburn. In the foreground is the power house, winding equipment house and a maintenance depot for the cable cars. The section of the building on the left now houses the Cable Car Museum.

A windmill was purchased by the company to pump water from a spring near Salamanca Road to the thirsty coal-driven steam engine boilers. *Alexander Turnbull Library, Rowe collection 3768 1/1*

Valuable suburban land waiting to be exploited was the primary motive in the building of a cable tramway from the heart of Wellington to Kelburn at the turn of the 20th century. The conquering slopes which rose over 150 metres above the embryo city's Lambton Quay were slowly tamed by men wielding picks and shovels and removing spoil in wheelbarrows. Tunnelling through ridges and spanning gullies with bridges was gruelling work for engineers and labourers alike on this mountain face. Even teams of prisoners from the old Terrace Gaol were put to work, slogging to build the incline. The Kelburne (as it was then spelt) and Karori Tramway Company was formed, with shareholding held by the Upland Estate Company, to develop the open farmlands and scrub areas of the Pharazyn and Copland estates. Cutting through back gardens and bush, the double track right-of-way was 785 metres in length, with a ruling and steady grade of more than 1 in 5.

On a Saturday morning, 22 February 1902, the slap of cable over well-oiled pulleys was heard for the first time. From the skyline terminus at the top, horse-coaches owned by the company and a Mr Spiers met the cable cars to convey settlers to the then remote village of Karori. The cableway was a brilliant success, new homes spreading like an infectious rash as real-estate sharks flourished. So great was the demand that three 'Palace' horse-trams were bought from the Wellington City Council for use as trailers to cope with the traffic. These cars were dragged by a team of horses up Glenmore Street and through Kelburn to Upland Road, where they were shortened and converted for their hill-climbing role.

Kelburne Tea Kiosk and Cable Tram. Wellington

On the reverse side of this early postcard of the Kelburn tea kiosk and cable car is a square for the postage stamp with the words 'One Penny'. This card is credited to having been printed in Berlin. *G & G Series No. 107*

A familiar landmark until the engine-house was electrified in 1933 was the smokestack towering above the steam-driven winding machinery at the top of the incline. The drift of smoke from this chimney became a convenient weather vane for the town. To cater for the upsurge in commuting from the hilltop suburbs, the company later formed a subsidiary, the Kelburn-Karori Motor Bus Company, which used a fleet of motor-buses for feeder services. To the delight of shareholders, traffic grew from 425,000 passengers in 1902 to 2,000,000 in 1926. In December 1946 the Wellington City Council exercised its right of purchase and the cable line became an integral part of the city's transport system. With the scrapping of the street cable lines in Dunedin after the Second World War – in spite of a large section of the community strongly voicing claims for their retention – the Kelburn cable cars became the last remaining link with the tramway age until the Christchurch tourist electric tramway was opened in February 1995. Wellington had grown fond and proud of these novel wooden trams with their garden-type seats, coupled to diminutive little trailers harking back to the days before the horseless carriage. Through dark tunnels and out into daylight the cars were carrying over 1½ million passengers each year.

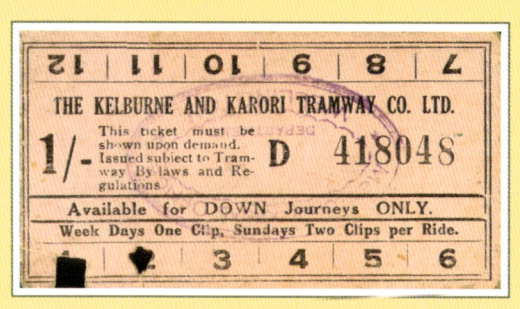

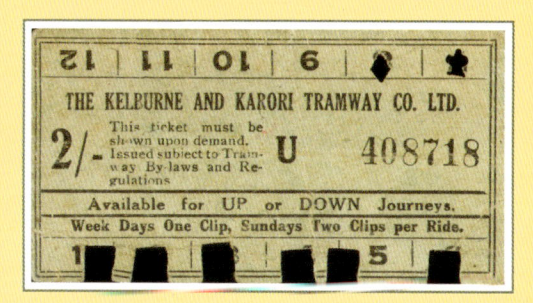

The original steam engine in the power house at Kelburn.

19

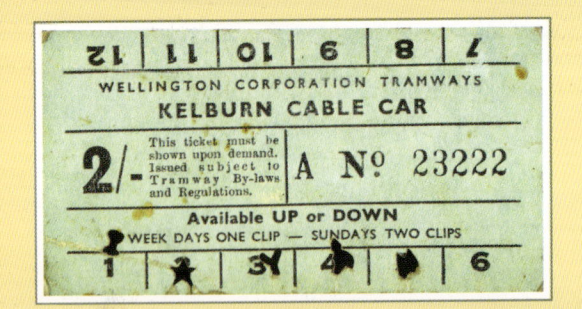

In July 1974, Wellingtonians' sentimental attachment for their cable cars came to the fore. Following an accident, the then Ministry of Works suddenly ordered the removal of the brakeless trailer cars, halving the cable cars' capacity, as they did not conform with modern safety standards.

A battle between the council, citizens and the ministry followed, with a report by a panel of engineers recommending that, even if the present system were given a stay of execution for two years while the system was upgraded, the lifespan would be only another eight years. Since 1902 the cable cars had carried 100 million people and there had only been one fatality. Seventy-two years of almost accident-free running had suddenly become a safety hazard.

A scene from 1958 of the cable tramway taken from the summit terminus. Trailer number four, now an exhibit in the Wellington Cable Car Musuem, is pictured being pushed to the top.

The Mayor of Wellington at the time, Michael (later Sir Michael) Fowler, fought hard for the original system to be retained. When the council finally conceded to a new Swiss system, Michael Fowler expressed dismay when discussing the replacement of the old cable cars with 'modern Swiss tin cans'. The new cable cars would, he said, spell the end for one of his favourite pastimes – kicking the tunnel walls, while sitting on the outside seats. He and his family had been doing it for years, as had many other people. The contract for the new cable car system went to Habegger AG of Switzerland. The line would be a single-track of metre gauge, with a crossing loop at the mid-point, Talavera station.

On Friday 22 September 1978 the original cable cars made their last trips. "Thousands thronged Cable Car Lane and the Kelburn terminal to farewell Wellington's most-photographed asset," reported the *Dominion*.

Throughout the afternoon every trip was packed with people taking their last ride on the 76-year-old tramway. Just after 11pm, cable car No. 2, loaded with invited guests (including the author), made the last historic journey from Lambton Quay. At Talavera, about 20 young people sang 'Auld Lang Syne'; then, as the tram passed Salamanca station, students from Weir House marked the last trip by throwing eggs and water bombs at the tram. Hundreds of people surrounded the cable car as it reached the upper terminal where a pipe band played a last tribute.

The open side seats on the 1902 cable-cars were popular with commuters.

From the summit in the early 1950s – not a high-rise building in sight in the CBD area.

Just over a year later, on 20 October 1979, the Swiss system, with new chalet style stations, opened. Thanks to Michael Fowler, a noted architect, who insisted the new trams have incorporated in their design some 'old world' atmosphere, the interiors were furnished in varnished hardwood and synthetic woodgrain panelling – a decision that must have helped the new Kelburn tram to retain the former system's rating as a front-line New Zealand tourist attraction. Workers, residents and university students still mingle with visitors from around the world, who make a trip on the tramway to experience a unique mode of travel in this part of the world and to view the magnificent panorama of Wellington.

Tourist itineraries make a ride on a San Francisco cable car a 'must'; perhaps these hill-climbers and a similar topography give Wellington some claim to the title of the San Franciso of the Southern Hemisphere. San Franciso has its Market and Powell Streets, Hong Kong has 'The Hill' and Wellington has Kelburn.

From the book *The End of the Penny Section* by Graham Stewart

Fifty years later – a modern cable car nears the summit with a backdrop of big buildings.

Cable car number one with trailer attached waits at the Kelburn summit in c1950.

The old Winding House now houses the Cable Car Museum

Right: A view of the Winding House built in 1902 taken before the service opened.

Below: The Winding House partly hidden by trailer cars which were withdrawn from service in July 1974.

The morning after the original cable tramway system closed, one of the cable cars is loaded on to a road transporter for cartage into storage.

The Wellington Cable Car Museum

After many years of indecisions, it was the tireless efforts of the volunteers of the Cable Car Heritage Society who lobbied the city fathers, that brought to fruition the Wellington Cable Car Museum which was opened in December 2000. Cable car number one and trailer number four were restored by the Society to 1974 condition, the year the trailers were taken out of service.

The old Winding House now contains not only an original cable grip car and trailer from the early 20th century system, but visual and moving pictorial displays of the history of this now southern most cable car line in the world.

Downstairs visitors can view the original winding equipment that served Wellington city for 76 years. The Museum is managed by the Wellington Museums Trust with funding from the Wellington City Council.

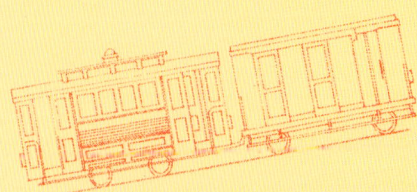

For more information, contact the Wellington Cable Car Museum on their Website: www.cablecarmuseum.co.nz

Fathers of Cable Cars...

Andrew Smith Hallidie
SAN FRANCISCO

George Smith Duncan
DUNEDIN

James Edward Fulton
WELLINGTON

Andrew Smith Hallidie, English born, built the world's first street cable car line in San Francsico in 1873. He had witnessed an overloaded four-horse team, hauling a horse-tram, roll backwards, the brake snapped, and the horses were dragged down to the bottom of the hill. The horses had to be destroyed. Horrified by the accident as a young man of 33 years of age, Hallidie, a wire rope manufacture, went on to invent the wire rope system of hauling passenger carriages up steep grades.

George Smith Duncan, Dunedin born, first suggested a cable tramway for Dunedin in 1879. Duncan, only 29 years of age, engineered the first street cable tramway to operate outside the United States. This was the Roslyn line that served Dunedin from 1881 to 1951. Duncan designed the 'pull curve' which enabled cable cars to travel up-hill and around curves while still gripping the steel cable. He went on to design the Melbourne cable tramway system.

James Edward Fulton, also Dunedin born, was already a noted and experienced New Zealand engineer of railways and major bridges when appointed to design a tramway from the horse congested streets of Wellington to the farmlands of Kelburn. His survey and recommendation of the route with three tunnels and four viaducts will forever be a lasting tribute to his professional skills. Fulton died in 1928 at the age of 73.